OUTLAW BALLADS

SONNY HAYNES STORIES

BY

BRIAN TOWNSLEY

Starlite Pulp

Many of these stories were first published both in the pages and on the websites of *Black Mask*, *Mystery Tribune*, and *Danse Macabre*. Wicked, Wicked Rain made the Distinguished Stories list in *Best American Mystery Stories, 2019.* Many thanks for that.

For information, contact : editor@starlitepulp.com

www.starlitepulp.com

Instagram : @starlite_pulp

Book and Cover design by Tristan Townsley and BT

ISBN: 979-8-218-10290-6

First Edition: December 2022

This book is dedicated to my mom. For her bravery, for the move, and for all of the rest of it.

"You only have so many fucks to give in your body, so don't give a fuck about what's not fuckworthy."

John Mellencamp

"I needed a drink, I needed a lot of life insurance, I needed a vacation, I needed a home in the country. What I had was a coat, a hat, and a gun. I put them on and went out of the room."

Raymond Chandler

OUTLAW
BALLADS

LET YOUR SAD ANGELS SING

Lake Arrowhead, January, 1951

Sonny Haynes slid the Merc along the two-lane road of highway 30 up the mountain. He hoped that the engine could handle the stress of the climb after the nearly two hours it had taken him from Los Angeles to get here. He hoped the same for the cargo in the trunk. Truth was, he hoped lots of things, and considered the process to be bereft of possibility—but he smoked the cigarette to his fingers and tossed the thing out the window like there was no such thing as wildfire. The road was pitchblack despite the ghostlike stutter of the white line separating one side from the other, the depth of night outside the headlights not worth pondering without angst and poetry. The cold was palpable in the cab of the car and the moon was hung this night above a dearth of clouds so ominous the earth seemed to set itself in silence. The turns on the mountain road were severe along the more than 5000 foot climb to Lake Arrowhead. He slipped the sled around cars in front of him like every lane a free agent. Everyone knew there were no cops up here. Sheriff's Department handled this area, a very large area sprinkled with a sparse population, thus the slightly higher independence level among these folks of the mountain and its resort towns.

He had come here once with his wife, Betty. To the mountain resorts and lakes that dotted the San Bernardino mountains like stars amid the bowl of sky. They had stayed at the Lake Arrowhead Resort shortly after moving to Los Angeles. Had walked the western rim of the lake under the moon and neglected boundaries of sexual restraint in the assigned bedroom. This, of course, was before her death by gunshot in bed with a jazz musician, before the investigation claiming Sonny as the main suspect, before his exile to Mexico. Before *that.*

But this was a classless job, a favor, nothing more. A delivery of goods. So despite the fact that he could, on certain nights, still smell the perfume his wife wore like a necklace he could not be rid of, this trip held for him all the allure of a closed casket. A deposit for which no receipt is required.

He had gotten the job the way so many had come. A guy who knew a guy, a favor for an old friend, money rarely mentioned but delivered like the mail. Sonny had built a reputation by this time, and everybody seemed aware of the consequences of being unprofessional. It was presumed that he had killed Sanchez down in the flatlands of Mexico, though nobody knew for sure. It was a fact that he had killed one of Mickey Cohen's bodyguards at a Hollywood Stars baseball game—in a restroom, no less—but the details were equally sketchy. Anybody with a story about Sonny Haynes knew that it included a violence for which few men were comfortable, despite their talk. He did what other men boasted of. And then, of course, there was his wife. Nobody quite knew the story on that one, but the LAPD still wanted a conversation, and they had yet to have their tea party—and being that the mountain had few uniformed officers of the law, this area offered conditions more favorable than the surrounding counties for his continued lack of cooperation.

The guy who knew a guy in this case was George Sizemore, born with the kind of handle few men dreamed of. He was a man pushed from the womb in a blue suit and slicked back hair, who had graduated from 25 to 50 in a blink and so seemed forever middleaged and ageless. Sizemore was a linguist who worked with police agencies across the West, but common knowledge claimed that his familiarity with the Russian mob and the Italian mob grew to more than translation. George's daughter, Natalia, was currently otherwise engaged to the knots and twists of twine that tied one piece to another in the Merc's trunk. Sonny had considered the tape over the mouth; he had seen too many errors with the consequences of such a thing, but as he was checking the knots after laying her down next to the spare tire, she had, in fact, tried to bite him. Succeeded, even. She held on firmly to his tattooed forearm briefly before he introduced the gunbutt of his revolver to her forehead. Once she fell back in, he taped her mouth. He felt the cratered impressions from her teeth along his forearm like some predatorial Braille as he drove.

"The Wild Side of Life" by Hank Thompson came on the radio and Sonny turned the volume up, muffling the bass overtures in a staccato rhythm coming from the trunk. The song vacillated between clarity and static on the turns like anything of worth is wont to do.

Sonny took the Running Springs turnoff and pulled in to the parking lot of a lighted liquor store. There was but one other car, and this Sonny assumed was the property of the owner. He exited the Merc, ran his hands through his pomaded hair once and walked the store down, the windows illuminated with neon like so much subtlety.

A man stood smoking near the door in blue jeans and cowboy boots. He was holding the wall up and nodded in Sonny's direction as he approached. Sonny nodded back, once, figuring that it was too cold to not be cordial, and entered the store. He walked to the counter and there a man seated behind it attending a radio.

"Damn reception," the man said out loud. It was unclear whether he knew he had an audience.

Sonny stood in front of the register. Cleared his throat.

The man looked up then. He wore glasses an inch thick and appeared allergic to a razor, his chin and jowls and neck covered in a salt and pepper stubble too long to be a mistake and too short to constitute anything called a beard. His eyes were bulging from the bastardized magnificence of his spectacles.

"You know anything about radios, man?"

Sonny thought about not answering, then didn't: "No I don't. But they piss me off when they don't work."

"Ain't that the truth," the man said, and shook his head at the truth of it.

"This your joint?" Sonny asked.

The man peered back at Sonny and looked him over once as if he had not noticed him before. Seemingly satisfied with some unknown expectation, the man answered: "Yup. My place. My dang radio. Antenna done broke off, right here, near the tip." He showed Sonny the lack of a tip in case he did not understand. "Now I cain't get nothing but static." He shook his head again at the impossibility of it all.

"Put a hanger in the tip," Sonny said.

"A what?"

"A clothes hanger."

"A hanger?" The man responded, as if hangers were a thing yet to be brought up from the flatlands.

"Yeah. A hanger, a wire hanger. Stick it in the tip and you'll probably get reception."

"Huh. A hanger." This time there was no question attached to it, just possibility. "Maybe I'll try that. Now, what is it you came in here for?"

Sonny looked at the multicolored bottles behind the man stacked orderly and without a gap as if none had ever been sold. Vodka, Rum, Gin, Whiskey—all manner of checkmate and desire. He saw his brand, Four Roses Bourbon, and wanted nothing more than to say the name. As if saying it out loud would be enough to banish everything that he had done while under its tutelage. Momentarily, he had an urge to beat the man into submission, put back half the bottle of Four Roses right there, and drink himself unconscious as the night wore on. Shoot anybody who came in the store and play with a broken radio while the whiskey blossomed his liver into utopian toxicity. That is what he *wanted* to say.

"A coupla packs of Chesterfields, please."

"Matches?"

"Sure."

The man grabbed two packs from a mostly empty carton and put a box of matches on top. "That it?"

Sonny sighed, and looked at the bottles once more in spite of himself. The pull of an undertow. Then: "Yeah. That's it."

They exchanged goods for cash and Sonny exited the store. He stood on the cement and pulled a cigarette from the pack he had previously and returned it to the reliquary of his pocket. He struck a match and lighted the cigarette and inhaled and exhaled into the night. The man in the cowboy boots was still leaning against the wall, still smoking. He pulled his jacket tighter as Sonny neared and nodded again.

"You from up here?" The man asked, his mouth emitting clouds of breath or smoke, it was impossible to tell in the cold. He pulled the cigarette from his mouth and picked a piece of tobacco from his tongue and flicked it outward.

Sonny stretched his arms out in contemplation and puffed his smoke. Finally: "Nope. Got friends up here though. Visit some. You?"

"Just 'bout a year or two. Originally from Montana, by way of Utah." He didn't explain the curious geography, and Sonny didn't ask him to.

Each of them stood there smoking into the night.

"You got something in your trunk, by the by. Something that might not be too happy to be in the trunk, maybe. But maybe you knew that," the man said, looking away and both of them watching his breath dissipate in the darkness.

"Must be that coyote I hit on the road," Sonny said.

"Sounds like one *big* coyote," the man commented. "Sure it ain't a bear? Or didn't you hit one of those?"

Sonny smiled then. He flicked his cigarette end over end like a warning flare until it bounced on the blacktop. "You want to take a ride in the trunk too? I hear it's comfortable. That's what all these dead animals keep telling me." He turned and looked the man in the eye then, still smiling.

The man did not respond to that. Truth is, he had no idea what to say. He had the feeling like he had suddenly found himself in deeper water than he was used to and was unsure of how to get back to shore. "Look, man," he finally said. Then nothing.

"Anyway, you keep that request in mind, Montana by way of Utah. Always more room back there. No better way to take these winding mountain roads, you ask me." Sonny winked then at the man and walked from under the awning and out to his car. He felt something altogether weightless but not without import land on him. And again. He looked up and saw that the night had filled with ten thousand wings, snowflakes softly jerking on sightless hooks.

"Well shit," Sonny exclaimed, and put his hand out to catch a palmful of mystery. He knew he needed to get to George Sizemore's place, and quickly. He had maybe an hour before the snow began accumulating enough to provide any interference on the roads. Arrowhead was only twenty minutes away, but he didn't know the roads well. All of these things went through his head until he thought of Natalia. He grabbed an Indian blanket in the backseat of the car and walked to the rear of the sled. There, he popped the trunk open and placed the blanket on top of the girl while she kicked and bucked and poked her head above the sightline twice. Sonny slammed the trunk back down, and, seeing that Cowboy Boots had taken in the scene with mouth agape, he smiled widely at the man and started the car with a thick chortle, its exhaust exploding into the night like the breath of a beast awakened.

Sonny drove Highway 18 towards Lake Arrowhead. He had visited George Sizemore's place twice prior, one for the business he currently found himself driving in the snow for, and the first visit was one of leisure. The snow was falling like confetti, fast, and all-encompassing and seemingly aimed entirely at his windshield, making the icy roads of the slope-shouldered mountains more difficult than usual to navigate.

Upon seeing the same landmarks that had marked his way in the past, albeit now covered in an impossibly white disguise, he turned left onto a road that led to a small outcropping of buildings all belonging to one man. It was a left where he saw Kuffel Canyon go to the right, which in actuality is Skyforest but everybody refers to it as a part of Lake Arrowhead, George had explained. He had also explained that Skyforest was next to Cedar Glen and that Skyforest and Rimforest were oftentimes confused with one another, even to the point where there were Rimforest signs on Skyforest businesses. So here Sonny had taken the Skyforest turn that was really just another part of Lake Arrowhead and driven the long private drive in the snow until he came upon four buildings, three of them set close together.

The house stood at attention at the end of the circular drive. It was a house quite unlike many of the ski lodge and A-frame cabins that dotted the hillside. This was an old craftsman house with large, wide windows lit from within like an invitation. The porch ran the width of the house and stone made up the foundation and base of the structure and its pillars, which faded to angular woodwork. The house was, in many ways, not unlike a face with a square jaw and wide cheekbones. Beside it sat a miniature guest house on one side and a three-car garage on the other. Off to the left some fifty yards sat a barn, painted red and peeling.

The snow fell softly as Sonny exited the car and walked to the front door, stamping his brogues free of detritus on the porch. Before he could knock, a man opened the door and stood in its width. He nearly fit the frame itself. This was Sammy, a giant Hawaiian, Sonny knew from past visits, who was not known for his friendliness, but more for his excitable and untamed hair, which, even when in its pony tail, seemingly had a mind of its own.

"Mr. Sizemore thought you'd be up earlier," Sammy said.

"I see. Nice to see you again as well. I'm here now. It's snowing." Sonny said these things as if they were completely obvious and entirely unconnected.

"*Mr. Haynes*," a voice said from somewhere behind the man taking up the doorframe. The Hawaiian moved aside and George Sizemore, who appeared to be only half the man who opened the door, stepped forward onto the deck. He was dressed in a pinstripe suit and his hair was slicked straight back, and when he smiled, as he did when he reached out and shook Sonny's hand, his eyes danced with mischief.

"You have my Natalia?" He asked, lowering his head and looking up at Sonny as he did so.

"She's in the trunk. I offered her the seat, but that didn't work out," Sonny said.

"The trunk was necessary?"

"She bit me."

"Was Natalia *uncooperative*?" He asked, the last word seeming to take twice the syllables it was composed of. George Sizemore smiled as he asked the question he very well knew the answer to.

"She was a real peach until I found her. After that it was all downhill," Sonny said. He felt along his forearm and then added, for emphasis: "She bit me."

"Hmmmmm," George retorted. "Perhaps my little bundle of sweetness didn't want to come home," he said, absentmindedly. He motioned with his hand that they should walk to the car, and they all followed that directive.

Sonny popped the trunk and Natalia immediately sat up and began using imaginative names for each of them though they had to use their creativity as the duct tape over her mouth made everything sound the same. Sammy the Hawaiian stepped forward and threw the girl over his shoulder like he was practicing for the part of a caveman in a play. Seeing her so small atop the mammoth's shoulder, Sonny wondered at how she could have caused any harm at all. She looked like a baby ready for a burping. Except that the baby was a petulant nineteen-year old, currently tied up and her mouth taped.

Inside the warm parlor, Natalia was now tied to a chair. Her mouth was still taped though that was to be removed soon enough. Sammy sat behind her slightly. George stood at the bar and poured himself a drink with tonic water and a slice of lime. Sonny sat on the leather couch, his feet on the coffee table, watching the scene unfold its corners in front of him. Thinking he should leave, knowing it was snowing, waiting for a circumstance more palatable.

George sipped at his gin and tonic and walked to the girl. His daughter. He ripped the tape off of her mouth in a single motion.

"AAHHHHH!" The girl gasped. She breathed in deeply once, eyes trained on Sonny all the while with a singular focus of hatred. "You fucking *ANIMALS.* Apes! Fucking Apes!" She shouted. She writhed in her bindings like any animal, anywhere. She began to lose the balance of the chair and saw better of it.

"Natalia, *my dear,*" George said. "I needed this man to bring you back. You must be able to see that—"

"What I see, *dad,* is you hiring a goon to bring me back up to this fucking mountain! I left for a *reason*, George."

George sipped his drink. If calling her father by his given name was a new decision, he did not show it.

Sonny lit a cigarette.

Sammy sat like a stone idol on the shores of an unreachable land.

Natalia sat in her chair as if she had a choice. She didn't, of course, but perception is reality. It appeared, rather quickly, that she had committed to the baptismal waters of captivity and embraced it with aplomb. She shook her head from side to side to remove a tuft of thin black hair that hung in front of her eyes and cleared her throat. For a moment, she looked less a feral animal and more an openhearted, sensual girl—the kind the world opens its arms for.

"I'm sorry. I just...I don't think it needed to be handled like that. I'm sorry. Now, *please* daddy, let me out of this chair. I'm asking nicely. You've got to let me out of here. You don't understand—"

George, who had been rimming the lime in a circular motion on his glass, put his hand out for her to stop. She did. That was a first.

"Natalia, you need to comprehend what has *happened* here, he said. You don't get the benefit of the doubt this time. You've broken a trust that is not going to be forgiven because you ask nicely. You've got to earn it back—*do you understand that?*"

The girl had tears flooding the rims of her eyes. "Yes, daddy, I understand, she acquiesced. I understand. And I'll try to make it up to you, but you've *got* to let me go now. They're going to—"

George slapped her then, once, from right to left. It left a sound not unlike a butcher throwing down a slab of pork onto the chopping block, and it hung in the air for much longer than seemed necessary. As if it was the turning point upon which things would change. Sonny thought something similar and lit a cigarette to confirm his brilliance.

Natalia hung her head in silence. The clock ticked, its voice suddenly audible though it carried on exactly as it had. The snow fell silently outside. Sonny looked at Sammy and they shrugged at one another. When Natalia raised her head, she did so in the throes of a scream that seemed to shake the bearings of the house itself. It was if something wild and terrible had been loosed upon the world. George, after a momentary loss of sanity, nodded once to Sammy, who unsheathed a syringe he had been hiding in his hand—his hand was so big he could have hidden small woodland animals in there as well—and he seamlessly stuck the girl in the neck whereupon she flopped sideways in her ropes as if her bones themselves had been removed.

George and Sonny carried the girl to her bedroom. Sonny had his hands on her shoulders and wondered why George had chosen to share this task when he could have very easily had Sonny or Sammy do it by themselves. It was when they placed Natalia on her bed that the light attached itself in such a way that Sonny saw the needle tracks along the inside of her elbow. He was surprised he hadn't noticed them earlier, but then, lots of things surprised him.

George leaned down to her face gently and whispered: "Do you remember when we used to hum *Let Your Sad Angels Sing* before bedtime? How I miss those days, little girl." He took her hand in his and squeezed it once. Then he walked out humming a plaintive song, straightening the frontside of his suit jacket while Sonny looked down at the girl like something broken into so many pieces that not all of them can ever be found enough to reassemble things that were.

Sonny sat on the porch in a rocking chair smoking Chesterfields and watching the snow drift noiselessly, collecting on the roof of his car. Solving the unsolvable problem. He tucked the blanket he wore over him tighter as George walked out to join him. He carried with him an envelope and he handed it to Sonny wordlessly.

"Guess I'll be spending the night, then," Sonny said, looking out at the snow in the driveway covering any hope of getting off the mountain.

"I've included a little extra to take that into account," George said. He paused. "It's possible that someone may come for her. You should know that."

Sonny looked up at the man. "Well," he said. "I hope that's not tonight. This favor is already more than I bargained for."

"You've been *paid*, Mr. Haynes, don't get licentious."

"No no, I don't mean that. Yes, I've been paid, and I'm sure you've been generous. But I don't like being a part of your drama. This was supposed to be was a dropoff." He paused, exhaled into the night. "It's become a lot more than that."

"Yes. My and Natalia's relationship is complicated, ever since her mother died. I'm not sure that I've done as good a job as I would have hoped raising her. But it is surely not your drama, sir."

"Your girl up there is a hophead, Mr. Sizemore. She's trouble a mile wide, and you can't see it because she's yours. Which I get. You know where I had to find her, Mr. Sizemore? She was high as a kite in a mobster's apartment. Lucky for you, he wasn't there—or else that envelope wouldn't be nearly enough. But what she's messed up in don't get cleaned."

George Sizemore did not respond immediately. In fact, Sonny wondered if he would respond at all. He stood next to Sonny looking out at the snow with a look on his face that Sonny had seen before. There was hurt that impacted your day, your mood, and there was hurt that was bottomless and could never be fixed, only soothed with whatever addiction currently captured your affections. This was the latter, and Sonny wanted none of it. It was a world he had already inhabited and found it not without its own undertow.

"I am sorry for the difficulties of the job, Mr. Haynes. But the reason I hired you to begin with was I did not know where I could find her, even with my contacts—which meant, of course, that she was involved with the same people in the families I know. This came as quite a shock to me. I have always tried to keep her as far away from that as possible." He paused, upon some reflection Sonny had no eye for. Then: "We used to vacation here, when she was a child. I watched her make snow angels where your car now sits." It seemed like he had more to say, but nothing came. He stood there looking out at the snow like there were answers writ among the accumulation. Sonny stood then, put his hand on the man's shoulder, and walked into the house.

He slept that night in a spare bedroom. He jammed the desk chair against the handle and slept with his .45 under the pillow and dreamt of long ago times with a wife he would never hold again. Dreams carry with them the possibility of loss and gain, reality and its opposite. Thus the hopelessness of impossibility is merely a perspective in an argument won by a lack of reason. His wife did not really look like his wife, not altogether, but there was no doubt of her position.

And the boat that they were on, though neither of them had ever taken lessons a day in their lives, was beholden to their desires and navigation exactly.

The first shot was a single pop, like a backfire. Sonny woke and sat up and felt for his gun. He had slept in his undershirt and pants and his brogues were immediately on his feet. He slapped his own face and ran his hand through his hair. And waited. Then another three shots, quickly, and a large crash, like a sandbag dropped from a distance. *That must be Sammy*, he found himself thinking.

He removed the chair as quietly as he could and cracked the door open. The hallway light had been left on and he saw nothing between where he was and the hallway opening. He stepped out, feeling exposed in a house he didn't know well against adversaries he knew nothing about, and made his way to the doorless opening. This led to the living room, the room where Sizemore had his chat with Natalia, and he peered out quickly. At the far end of the room, he heard whispers, and saw, in slight delineations amidst the darkness, two figures, one kneeling and one crouching, over something he assumed was Sammy. Sonny fired once and blew the brainpan wide open of the one who was crouched. There was a moment that followed that seemed not to be held in the same manner of time. The spray from the man's head struck the wall behind him thickly and his body fell forward as if drunk. The other man seemed to do nothing for a time. Sonny crossed the doorway quickly to get a better angle for the second shot.

Then the lights came on. The room was illuminated by a chandelier made of antlers, and Natalia and George, gun in his hand, entered the room.

The man who had been kneeling, stood, gun outward, and posed there. He was a short man, dressed in a black jacket and pants, black hair slicked straight back. His nose was hooked and clearly Italian. He smiled warmly. The exposed brain against the wall was next to him and in it patches of brown hair.

Natalia ripped free her hand from her father's grip and ran towards the man. "Tony!," she cried. "Natalia," he called back, not taking his eyes off of the man with the gun outstretched towards him. Sonny recalled thinking that it was all very Romeo and Juliet, except that this wasn't going to have a happy ending. Then he recalled that that had been a tragedy as well. Fuckin *love*, he thought. He stayed where he was. With all the commotion, nobody had seen him hiding in the hallway entrance, despite the fact that the brains on the wall were his responsibility.

Natalia reached Tony and they embraced, him holding the gun with his right hand the whole time. She buried her head in his chest, talking something inaudible given Sonny's distance.

George spoke: "I needed my daughter back. I will not allow you to turn her into a Mafioso widow. And those needle marks!" He shouted that last bit, waving the gun slightly as he did so.

Tony held Natalia with one arm and the gun with the other. "Look, Old Man, I don't want no more trouble than I already got here. You didn't have no right to just show up and take Natalia. She's nineteen now. Her choice." And then, as if just realizing that he wasn't done: "She's not yours no more."

George stood there in his buttonup pajamas and looked back and forth at the two of them. Finally, he settled on Natalia, and spoke: "Sweetie, I always tried so hard to keep you *away* from this life." His voice cracked when he spoke.

"It's too late, daddy. We're gonna get married. I love Tony. We got plans." She looked at Tony as she said this and rubbed her hand along his chest. It was too much for George to bear. He fired once, striking Tony in the chest as he was giving his attention to Natalia's affections. Tony stepped backwards once and tripped over the two bodies already on the floor. His gun clattered on the hardwood and Natalia picked it up. George had not moved since he had fired. He seemed trancelike, and Sonny knew this action better than he cared to admit and had seen men react the same. It never ended well. Despite his better judgment, he stepped from the entranceway.

"Okay," he said, announcing his entrance. "Now everybody just relax. George, I want you to drop your gun. That's enough from you. And Natalia, you do the same, and tend to your boyfriend over there. *Toss the gun down.*" He said the last four words slowly, as if very few people understood the concept.

George looked over at Sonny blindly, as if he had never seen him before, wearing an expression like he wanted to take back everything he had ever done.

"SHUT UP!!!!," shouted Natalia. "Shut up! You don't make the rules!" She swung the gun wildly from her father to Sonny and back again, her hands fluttering like a hummingbird's.

"Look at your boyfriend, Natalia," Sonny said. "Look at *Tony.* Is he breathing—because if he is, you've got to get him to a hospital, and I can help you get that wound tended to. Is he?"

Natalia looked back briefly, once, and looked again at her father. "I can't tell!!" She shrieked, her voice full of a panic Sonny hoped that he never felt. "You did this!!," she said to her father, both hands on the gun and shaking badly.

George stared back and said nothing. He looked like he may never speak again.

"Natalia, do you want your Tony to die? Because he's going to, if you don't help him. Don't worry about your father. Look at Tony, and—"

She fired then at her father, the gun jerking wildly with each of the three shots as she pulled the trigger. Sonny fired as well, more out of reaction than desire, and hit the girl in the throat immediately. She fell backwards near the fireplace, her fingers continuing to click the revolver onto empty chambers as a tide of blood advanced down her shirt unimpeded and seemingly without end.

Sonny ran quickly to George, who had been hit with the first two rounds and lay dead as his own ex-wife on the floor of his living room. Looking up at the chandelier as if the deceased owners of those antlers were showing him a way to the afterworld. "*Shit*," Sonny said, under his breath. He stood and walked over to the small battlefield of death near the fireplace. Natalia sat against the metal screen roughly, one leg twisted unnaturally behind her, blood pooling around her thighs. Tony lay on top of Sammy. Tommy was still breathing, if barely were a thing entire. The headless guy was still bent at the knees as if looking for something under the couch. Maybe the rest of his head, Sonny thought. He moved Tony to his own place on the wood floor, and, with some effort, flipped Sammy over, the man's massive hair forever tending its own laws. He had hoped the big man's girth would have provided some protection, but he had been shot three times, twice close to the heart. Sonny grabbed the man through the shoulders, looping his own hands around the armpits, and dragged him with some effort over to a chair facing the fireplace. He then put him in the chair as best he could. When he was done, he felt like he needed five cigarettes, and the big Hawaiian looked like a slumped drunk.

Sammy had obviously been sleeping when the two men came upon him, because his gun was right next to where he had been, at the ready and on the table. Sonny took this and shot the wall twice. Then he shot Natalia again, in the chest. She shuddered once and slumped to the left, still dead. He took stock of the room. Sammy had been in a firefight. They would find George dead from the gun his daughter held, so they would chalk that up to family issues. That same gun had also shot Sammy three times. The bullet that had taken the man's head off could not be found, he hoped, and that left Tony. Sonny walked over to Tony and picked him up by the ankles and dragged him to the spot Sammy had vacated. That would make more sense. Sonny liked to think of himself as a kindhearted, misunderstood man who did what he needed to do. Actually, that's not true. He didn't think that. But he hoped others did, sometimes. Regardless, however much sympathy he might have had in other circumstances, his level of pity for greaseball mafia junkie runners had been exhausted. He looked down at Tony, who looked back at him, wheezing, eyes rheumy and half-lidded. Sonny raised Sammy's gun and shot him once in the heart, then once in the head. He took the gun and walked to the kitchen and wiped it clean with a rag. Then he walked back and placed it in Sammy's right hand, making sure to impress the fingers as necessary.

Sonny stood at the entranceway and took in the scene. Besides the fact that there were two bullets unaccounted for, the scene made a lot of sense. And a dead bodyguard, two dead Mafioso, and a dead translator with ties to said Mafia and his junkie daughter weren't going to make the department work overtime looking for answers. Plus, he figured, it'd be days, perhaps more, before this was found what with the snow and how isolated the place was. He went back to his room and put on his coat over his wifebeater. Lit a cigarette. Then he walked the house down looking for any evidence that he had ever been there. He put cigarette butts into his jacket pocket, wiped down door handles and decided to take the blanket he had used on the deck. He finally found George's room, and while he knew nothing would be indicative of his presence there, he wandered in anyways.

The blanket had been tossed to the side as he had gotten up that night, and everything else looked in order. He had turned to go when he saw a framed photo on the nightstand. Sonny picked it up and looked at it. The picture contained George, perhaps ten years prior, wearing a camp shirt with his arms around a woman Sonny guessed to be his wife on the right, and a pretty little girl with freckles and eyes of mischief resting her hand on her father's stomach to the left. Sonny understood how George must have looked at that photo every night before bed and how badly he had wished to have some semblance of that moment back. He felt for the man then, more than he had felt for anything in some time. He knew what it was like to lose something without hope of getting it back. He wiped the frame off on the blanket, and placed it softly back on the nightstand.

Sonny stood on the deck and made preparations. They were mental preparations, to be sure, because he couldn't leave with this much snow, and he didn't look forward to the amount of shoveling that awaited him as the hours passed. He would be on his way to Vegas by the afternoon. Back to the work that required his attention there. He lit a Chesterfield and exhaled into the morning, the dawn light having just broken the seal of darkness to the east, as nights turn to days with a reliable madness Sonny recognized as his own.

WICKED, WICKED RAIN

February, 1951

1.

Sonny Haynes sat in the Wagon Wheel Diner in February of 1951 and stared out the window at the night as the endless rain carried on, vandalistic and angry. He sipped his coffee. Lefty Frizzell sang "If You've Got the Money, Honey" on the juke, and could barely be heard above the biblical downpour flooding the desert outside.

Sonny was waiting here on a man—well, of course, there would be more than one man, but the only one of import was a Mr. Saul Bernstein, who also happened to be a relatively successful Hollywood director. Mr. Bernstein was 'missing,' and certain people in Los Angeles needed him returned sooner than later. And, he was told, the situation was *delicate*. And while Sonny Haynes was generally not someone who would spring to mind when the word *delicate* was brought up, he was beginning to build a bit of a reputation for handling the types of situations people associated with that word.

His hat lay crown down on the table, drops of rainwater circling the brim and dripping onto the plastic tabletop. It was designed to look like wood, the tabletop, with grains running lengthwise and adorned with red and yellow ketchup and mustard dispensers, salt and pepper shakers, and napkins. His waitress was like a girl you grew up next to and believed to be pretty and then you grew older and left town and gained experience in all things mundane and eccentric and returned home to realize she was quite mundane herself. And there is both wisdom and sadness in that. Sonny smiled to her and raised his cup an inch as a gesture for a refill.

"Everything here okay, sir?", she asked, as she poured the steaming coffee into his mug. Her name tag said Josie. Sonny placed her at maybe 25.

"Everything is just fine here, Ms. Josie. Glad to be out of the rain," Sonny answered, and raised his glass again at her, this time as a salute.

"Okay then. You let me know if you'll be wanting any dinner," she said, and glanced out the window at the darkness and rainfall. "My mama woulda called this here rain a reckoning, somethin' brought down by God hisself to cleanse those things that need cleansin." She paused. "But then, mama was always findin' biblical meanin' in things that just seemed like things, to me, you know?" She scrunched her nose and raised her shoulders together at once as if a question had been asked to which she did not know the answer and looked at Sonny as if perhaps he had meanings for things, too.

"Well. Folks are going to find meaning when they need meaning in things," he answered, and winked, sipping his coffee.

"'Course, my mama was crazy as an outhouse rat sometimes too, so who knows?" she said, and laughed quickly afterwards, collecting herself at once. "Well, lookit me, carryin' on."

"It's just fine, Josie. Bring me some French fries. I think the meaning in the rain for me is that I need some French fries," Sonny said.

She placed the coffee onto the table and wrote something on her menu ticket and said, "French fries, comin' up." With that she picked the coffee carafe back up and gave Sonny one more glance, and he saw her look at his neck and the inkwork there, then embarrassedly back into his face and hurry off.

The diner had a western motif, as most things did out here, with a horseshoe above the door and a wallpaper of spurs and horse profiles. Faux-wood tables. Faux-wood vinyl stools at the counter. There were only three other people in the place at the moment, an elderly couple near the door in a booth and a gentleman sitting at the counter, finishing a chicken-fried steak covered in gravy and drinking a soda. He was perhaps a tribal Indian, though Sonny couldn't be sure. He was pretty sure though. The couple were white-haired and the man wore a gray western shirt, slacks, and boots. The lady had her hair cut short and wore a navy blue dress trimmed in white. Sonny sipped his coffee. The jukebox began "I'm Movin' On" by Hank Snow, and the rain continued its onslaught outside.

The fries were overcooked with burnt nubs and ends but truth be told Sonny liked that type more than any other so he dipped them in the mustard pooled on the plate and tried not to look at the door any more than necessary. He motioned again to Josie to fill his cup and knew now that regardless of what happened throughout the rest of the evening he may never sleep again, such was the amount of caffeine he had consumed.

The diner had gone silent and Sonny wasn't sure how long it had been that way. He stood and hatted himself and walked to the juke. He dropped a dime for two plays and chose *Moanin' the Blues* by Hank Williams, and then searched the titles for something he hadn't heard. He settled on *Mercury Blues* by K. C. Johnson for the second song and walked to his seat in expectation. His coffee mug had been filled again and was steaming. He removed his hat and placed it on the table. Hank began crooning the tune and Sonny stared for a moment at the congealed yellow grease on the plate and the lack of French fries. Such things undone. He looked at the clock on the wall, felt unconsciously for the .45 he carried in a shoulder holster. It was still there. His imaginary friend hadn't taken it, yet. He sipped the steaming coffee and realized that he had to piss something fierce. It was no wonder, he figured. Four cups of coffee and 40+ years will do that to a man. He didn't want to leave, either. Find his mark, Bernstein, out here sitting with whatever model of greaseball Chicago had come up with for the New Year. But still. He stared at the coffee, unhappy with it now.

The record finished and was replaced with all manner of efficiency and the stacking of vinyl. *Mercury Blues* began on the juke and the tune was a traditional blues song that featured a Mercury, as Sonny had hoped that it would. He sipped his coffee and smiled as the bell rung above the front door, and three men entered the diner. The first and last were large men, both in black suits and fedoras and arrived in the diner ducking and dodging as if the rain were ignorant to the pugilistic arts. The man between them was a good six inches shorter than either, and more narrow by half; if they were 250 lbs, he was

150, soaking wet. Which he was. He had not been given a hat to wear and wiped his bald head and face vigorously as he entered. Sonny looked away in recognition.

The men hung their dripping coats on the rack near the door and left their hats on. They ushered the man before them like a child, and laid stakes at a booth near the front entrance and stuck Saul Bernstein on the window side as the two sat across from one another. Sonny still had to pee, badly now, but tried to focus. Josie came over to the men and they ordered coffee. They didn't allow Saul to order, Sonny observed. *Mercury Blues* finished and Sonny noted with a small sadness that he had missed the end of the song. He would have to remedy that in time. He liked that song, he decided.

A few minutes later Sonny saw with an immense amount of relief that one of the lugs had stood and started towards the restroom. Sonny counted to twenty and followed. He approached the door with his hand under his coat, only to push the door open and find an unused urinal. The greaseball had taken the stall, and if his feet were any indication, he wasn't draining the weasel. Sonny took to the porcelain and unzipped and released a torrent of rented coffee that seemed to continue longer than there was liquid consumed. Finally he zipped up and walked to the sink, looking in the mirror at the stall. The lug was still in there, grunting away. He took note of his escape route. There was a small window in the wall, but it would be a piece of work to get through that. He smiled quickly at the thought of shooting a man in the stall and then getting stuck in the window, his bottom half scissoring in impotence as the authorities arrived.

He pulled the switchblade from his pocket and released the blade there as he coughed and turned quickly and slammed open the stall door with his left palm and drove the knife into the man's chest until it went no further. The man grunted once and shuddered and fumbled awkwardly at Sonny's arms. Sonny pulled the knife out then and drove it upward into the man's chin, the blade exiting through the cheek. Sonny grabbed the man by the hair and looked at him. He was perhaps 35, black hair, slicked back. Chubby but not fat. Dead, now. And nary a sound. Sonny pulled loose the weapon and saw it exit the man's cheek obscenely and wiped the blade on some toilet paper he wadded and pocketed the knife. He then ran his hands down the man's sides and first keys with a Cadillac keychain, which he pocketed. Then lower still and there a piece, a .38, removed and placed in the backside of Sonny's waistband. No taped up drop, serial removed, to be found at the ankle. Sonny shrugged. They weren't worried, apparently. The man was bleeding mostly downward into the toilet water, so that worked well. Sonny flushed once and turned in the tight stall, two elephants in a phone booth, and tried to lock the latch but he had busted it. So much for secrecy. He wadded some toilet paper near the top of the stall doorjamb to keep it in place after he had exited and walked out of the bathroom. He realized with no small amount of irony the regularity with which he seemed to be killing people in bathrooms. Life and death in the shitter—not exactly the stuff of Chandler, he thought.

Sonny guessed that he had probably five minutes, to be safe. There were very few folks in the place, the old couple had since left, so there was really only the guy at the counter or one of the cooks that would enter the men's bathroom anytime soon, but he also realized the guy wasn't just going to sit on the pot and bleed into the toilet all night either. The next man that entered, whether in 30 seconds or 15 minutes, was going to find himself a mess. So, he figured, he had better get to work.

He grabbed his hat off of his table and slid into the booth opposite the huge meatball and the small Jew.

"Alright, big boy, this is how this is gonna work," he said, before either of them could react. The mobster's facial expressions morphed quickly from surprise to confusion to anger, none of them making him look any smarter. Saul Bernstein, on the other hand, just looked terrified. He had sparse and wiry grayblack hair popping out on his scalp and his eyebrows were made of the same stuff and were bushy and wild. His eyes were small and kind; his nose was wide with large nostrils. Sonny noted that the jukebox had gone quiet again.

"You've got a gun pointed this instant at your twig and berries," he said to the man across from him. "As far as I see it, you've got two options—1. You can do exactly as I say, and you'll live. I promise that. Although you will end up in the trunk of your car in the rain. But you'll live. 2. You can either try to take out myself or Mr. Bernstein there, most likely with the pistol from your shoulder holster on your left there-," he motioned with his left hand to that shoulder in case he didn't yet have a handle on left and right, "-and never be able to piss normally again."

"Wha—," the man began, more grunt than speech, before pausing, as if the situation were simply moving too quickly for comprehension.

"Yeeeeeesss," Sonny answered, in mock condescension, "gun. Your dick. Go bye-bye." He paused then, winked at Saul, and continued: "Your partner is taking a huge dump in there," he motioned to the bathroom, "so we're not going to wait for him."

The greaseball seemed to have composed himself, finally. "Look here, circus freak, I ain't giving you nothing. You—,"

"Circus freak?" Sonny interrupted. "Because of the tattoos? That's very clever. I knew you were using that big brain up there for something during all of this. You're supposed to be professionals, right?" Sonny waited briefly for an answer.

Receiving none, he continued: "Your boy in there is bleeding from multiple holes into the toilet. If anybody in this room, *right here*," and he lowered his voice to a whisper, though no less audible, and all three of the men briefly looked around the diner, taking stock of the numbers, "*any* of them, finds him while we are sitting here, you are dead. *I will paint the walls here.* So really, we're playing a game of truth or dare—with a clock. You do as I say, right now, or we bullshit here, and somebody eventually walks into that bathroom. And then all hell breaks loose—and I'm the devil."

The man across from Sonny looked like he needed directions for his next move. The guy on the shitter must have been the brains of the operation, Sonny hoped. Saul had broken out in small beads of sweat on his forehead, and his eyes moved quickly from one man to the other. Josie appeared suddenly at the edge of the table.

"Anything I can get you all here?" She asked, before looking at the greaseball and adding "Your food should be out in just a sec."

"You know what, Josie?" Sonny said, keeping his eyes leveled on the men across from him, "These guys are old friends of mine—we haven't caught up in years. Do me a favor and pack that food up to go." Sonny looked up and her and smiled, for just an instant.

"Mmmkay," she said, sounding confused.

"And you know what?" He continued. "This gentleman here has offered to pay my bill, as well. So he'll just go ahead and clear both bills up now."

"Well," she remarked, "that's awful nice of you." She patted the man on the shoulder to show how nice it was.

"I know," Sonny answered. "I mean, it's not like I had to put a gun to him or anything. He just offered—for old time's sake." Sonny slapped the tabletop with his left hand in a show of appreciation, and both men across from him flinched.

Josie took out both tickets and placed them on the table. "I'll go back and bag up your meals."

"K, hon. When you come back we'll have the bills set," Sonny answered as she walked off.

The man glowered at Sonny, although there was more than a small sense of shame and fear in there as well. Something unrecognizable. He began to reach into his left coat pocket.

"Anything comes out of that coat besides your wallet and you have no penis," Sonny said.

The man removed his wallet and removed a twenty from the billfold.

"Put it on top of the checks," Sonny said. "Leave all of it for Josie. She's a nice kid."

The man did as he was told, and Josie returned with a brown paper bag folded once horizontally along the top. "Here you go, guys." She left the bag on the table and swept up the cash and checks.

"Keep the change," Sonny said. "And you have a nice night, Josie."

"Well, thank you kindly, boys. You try to stay dry now," she answered, and paused, looking puzzled. "Did the other gentleman who was here leave?"

Sonny smiled at her. "Oh, that was Eugene. He's a little crazy in the head sometimes. I'm not sure where he's gone off to. He always did like the rain though."

Sonny orchestrated the lug leaving, to Saul leaving, to him following out of the restaurant and the ropes of rain in wait. They walked until Sonny told them to stop. Their shoes were all near ankledeep in puddle and it was difficult to hear. They stood there in the parking lot, the three of them, like the first family.

"Take off your hat, and place it on Mr. Bernstein's head there," Sonny shouted, and motioned with the gun in his hand.

The lug looked at him as if he had not heard, then nodded. The diner shone like a lighthouse in the allover darkness that the rain and night had colluded to.

The restaurant windows were only some 50 feet away but looked like another world entire given the weather and the night and the large man lifted the soaking hat off of his head and plopped it softly onto the dome of the small man beside him.

"Good man," Sonny said. "Now, where's your car?"' He asked, loudly.

Each of their shoes were stuck in the muddy deluge at this point. The lug looked around for a second, then pointed at a Caddy not 30 feet distant.

"Okay", Sonny said, "now reach in your jacket and pull out the gun. S*lowly.* Then drop it in the mud. Mr. Bernstein, when he does that, I want you to pick it up and hand it to me. Can you do that?"

"I can do that," Saul answered, and his voice sounded more assured than Sonny would have given him credit for.

The big man in the suit sighed and reached into his jacket and pulled on the butt of his pistol and removed it with two fingers, dangled it once in the air to show it, and dropped it into the mud. It made a palpable splat upon landing. Saul bent carefully near the man, picked up the gun with an amount of caution you might give a feral animal, and walked it to Sonny. If he had any sense of what he should do with the gun, it did not show. He handed it over and Sonny placed it into his overcoat pocket.

They walked to the Caddy and Sonny had the man unlock the trunk and get in. He felt for a drop near the ankle, and, upon finding none, stood back and looked at the large man prostrate in the trunk.

"You shouldn't be doing this," the man said, above the din of rain. "It'll come back."

"Yeah," Sonny answered. "I know. It always does. Everybody pays."

He looked up then at the rain for a moment and sighed, then sideways at Saul, who looked back at him without expression. The light from the diner showed one side of his face and most everything else in darkness.

"What's your name, soldier?" Sonny asked.

"Frank," the lug answered without hesitation.

"Alright, Frank. You were cooperative tonight. Thanks for that. So you get to live, like I said." He snapped his wrist down quickly then, slapping the gunbutt hard against the man's face. The sound spoke of viscera and bone amidst the rainfall and the man grunted twice and exhaled.

"Sorry about that. That was a favor, though. If your boys found you, and without even a scratch? Like you just gave it up? So hey, you're welcome," Sonny said, shrugged, and slammed the trunk down, leaving the man in darkness as the rain beat incessantly as on a tin roof in the Tennessee home Sonny believed himself rid of. He smiled at this, and walked with Saul to the Merc that would ferry them westward toward the City of Angels.

2.

They drove west on the 10 in the rain. Neither man spoke. Sonny rolled his window down and threw the Cadillac keys into the night at one point.

They stopped in a town called Banning and looked for a motel there. On a frontage road they ran across the Hi-Line Motel in neon, VACANCY rimmed in red across the bottom. Sonny stopped the car a block away and killed the lights. The windshield wipers continued their monotonous uniformity, carrying hopelessly on.

"Okay," he started, "here's the deal. I am not the bad guy here. I am taking you back to Los Angeles for a friend—he is, I think, someone you know well. In return for bringing you back, I am getting something very important *from* him." Sonny looked at Saul then, the shadows and bars of light horizontal. "I'm telling you this because I want you to know that this is a job for me, and an important one. If I were in your shoes, I'd wonder what the fuck is going on." Sonny paused then, unsure of what to say next.

"S-so you're taking me back to LA?" Saul asked, with a brief stutter. Disbelief spread across his features in the halflight.

"Yes."

Saul exhaled then, loudly, and put his head into his hands. He raised his face and looked at Sonny, at once pleading and incredulous.

"YES," Sonny said, again, and nodded.

"Thank you," Saul said. It was dark and the rain was loud but Sonny was pretty sure he saw tears that rimmed the man's eyes.

"Don't thank me yet. Thank me when I drop you off. Thank me when I'm driving away. Right now, we're going to crash in a motel room. Tomorrow morning, we're going to LA. By tomorrow afternoon, you'll be seeing your family again. But that's only if you do *exactly* as I say. Got it?" Sonny asked. The man nodded.

The Hi-Line office was empty as the two men entered, but contained a universe of pamphlets and postcards in a metal case that held them all. Sonny and Saul dripped onto the carpet and removed their hats. Sonny secretly wished that he could shake himself dry like a dog. He pulled some pamphlets from the assortment and spread them on the counter to read as they waited, his hands dripping water onto the colored paper, distorting and reshaping the message. They advertised tours of western movie sets, movie star's escapes in the Palm Springs area!, and hiking and trails in the Joshua Tree National Forest. He finally rang the bell loudly when no one arrived.

"I'ma comin'", came from a back room, in a high voice, at once old and strong. A lady arrived around a corner with blue curlers in her hair and a cigarette dangling from her lips. Sonny placed her at 70, but she may have been 90. She was five feet tall at best. She shuffled behind the counter and looked up at the two of them with creased eyes.

"So, you want a room at the Hi-Line, do ya? Want to get out of this rain?" She looked at the two of them then, and ashed her cigarette into the glass tray on the counter. "And I suppose you realize that it's damn late out, and you're gettin' an old lady up from her bed?" She was throwing questions at them pell-mell, but neither of them expected that they were required to answer. They were right.

"I know men like you," she continued. "and they're called *men.*" She laughed at her own joke and inhaled her cigarette anew. "Selfish and hopeless, like the rest," she said, as she exhaled. Then she looked at them as if seeing them for the first time. "One room, or two?"

The room contained two double beds and a nightstand, adorned with an attendant lamp, between them. The carpet was brown, and the artwork contained desert scenes. The two men sat across from one another, each to each, on his own bed.

Sonny had removed his jacket and collared shirt and sat in his A-shirt and trousers with a Lucky Strike behind his ear. Saul, after some time in the bathroom, had emerged with a towel around his shoulders and his pants still on. His socks, shirt, and jacket hung on the shower curtain rod.

"Be straight with me," Saul said, as he sat. His face had lost much of its stress, and Sonny saw in it a mirth and boyish impishness that had been vacant earlier in the evening. "What is this whole deal? Is this what you do?" Sonny saw Saul looking over his tattooed neck and shoulders, the inkwork loosed upon his arms, hands, fingers.

Sonny caught eyes with him then and did not answer for several seconds. Saul dropped his eyes and shook his head, as if realizing he had perhaps overstepped his bounds. Whatever decision Sonny had been making in his silence, he finally made it and put out an arm to show the small man that everything was fine.

"I do jobs for people. I protect them. I pick them up. Sometimes, I do more than that. But this job is different," Sonny said.

"How is this different? And that guy, back there, the one in the car, what's gonna happen to him? And, I mean, the other guy...", he said, and didn't finish.

"The guy in the car will be fine. He'll get found tonight, or more likely tomorrow morning. He'll be cold and wet and in more trouble with the spaghettiheads that hired him than anything I did." Sonny smiled at this. "The other guy was found last night. I stuck a knife through his face. Look, the situation was this: Dealing with one greaseball is pretty easy, most of the time. They don't get paid for thinking much. But dealing with two—that changes the odds quite a bit. Plus, I had to piss. So I took one out of the equation. After that, you saw how easy that was. Anyone could do it," Sonny said. He grabbed a toothpick from his wallet and began to pick at his teeth.

Saul took this in and it was quite clear from the look on his face that he did not believe that 'anyone could have done it' though he did not reply.

"Oh, I forgot," Sonny started, pulling the toothpick from between two of his bottom teeth, "you asked why. No, I don't go around rescuing guys just 'cause somebody needs rescuing. I got bills too. But I got a call from an old partner in Vegas a week ago. Me and my daughter, she's a bit of a poker shark, and so we had to get outta town anyways, and I get this call with a deal. See..." He stopped here, thinking he had already told far too much of the evolution of the thing but knew also there was no chance he was stopping now. Plus, Sonny had to admit, as he looked at the man across from him, he liked the little guy.

So, cards on the table and all that, he figured. If it didn't work out, maybe the guy helps him out down the road. Or it all goes to shit. C'est la vie, what will be, and all that nonsense.

"I used to be a guy on the force. LA. I'm investigating Cohen, my wife gets killed, and I'm the suspect. It was all a mess. So," he paused here, flipped the Lucky Strike into his mouth and lit it with a match he struck on the nightstand, "I'm not exactly welcome company in the City of Angels with my old peers, if you get my drift."

"You're a wanted man," Saul said quickly, showing he had been following along quite nicely.

"That's one way of putting it," Sonny said.

Saul smiled at this. "Is there another way?" He asked.

"Look, little Jewish director..." Sonny said, and wagged his finger at him. He smiled then, and realized that yes, there was something in this guy he liked. He exhaled a lungful of smoke at the popcorn ceiling.

"So, what's the deal you got?" Saul said. "And," he looked at the door quickly, "what's to keep 3 more guys from busting down the door tonight?"

Sonny took a drag from his smoke, exhaled, and waited for the cloud to dissipate before answering: "The deal is I give you back to the studio head, untouched and ready to go into your next picture, and DA Simpson gets off my back." He mashed the remainder of the cigarette into the glass ashtray on the nightstand.

"Ahhhh," Saul said. "You get LA back."

"Yup."

"You want your old job back?" Saul asked.

Sonny spit out a laugh then, a staccato burst of something he barely recognized. Then: "No. No, I don't want it back, I don't expect they'd ask, and I wouldn't take it if they did. Very, very done with that group." He paused a moment. "Plus, I like what I do. A lot more freedom."

"As for more goons," he continued, "they had no idea I'd be there. No idea where we are. Probably haven't even found Frank yet, and whether they've gotten the word on the other lug, I doubt that as well. In a day or two, somebody associated with Cohen is gonna lose their shit. But for now, we're good." Sonny smiled, not so much at Saul but for the admission itself, and lay back on his bed. "And," he continued, "if they do, I've got something for them," and he motioned to his .45, and the two .38's that lay on the bed next to him. He lit another cigarette and exhaled toward the ceiling.

"Ever had any thought of acting?" Saul asked.

"Noooo," Sonny said, quickly. He didn't look at Saul when he said it, as he was still staring at the ceiling and the smoke negotiating the nooks and crannies of the ceiling. "I make fun of actors. I don't act."

"My next film," Saul barreled forward while getting underneath the covers of his bed, "is being filmed out this way, mostly in 29 Palms. It's a western. If you ever want to get on the set, let me know."

Sonny said nothing to this, and turned out the lamp. Saul wasn't sure if he had even heard him, but lay back and watched as the embertip of Sonny's cigarette sat suspended in the darkness atop his lips.

***

The rain was a light mist in the morning as Sonny stood next to the Merc. Saul emerged from the room and walked to the office with the room key. When he returned, he looked at Sonny over the hood.

"Ready?" Sonny asked.

Saul looked himself over once, at his dirty clothes he had worn for a week straight and put his hands out once, then ran them over his wiry and unruly hair. "I guess," he said.

The 10 west was littered with puddles from the night before and the windshield wipers continued working on the dusting that remained as they moved towards Los Angeles. The radio was tuned to a jazz station and neither man talked much. At one point, Sonny turned the volume down and asked: "What did the wops want from you anyways?"

"I dunno. Some guy, close to Cohen I guess, some Capo, he wanted his daughter in the picture. He sends her to me. Girl couldn't act sick if she had a cold. I said no way. They said, think again. I said, I got sick just from thinking of it. Next thing I know, I'm getting picked up in a car I don't recognize." The two men looked at each other and Saul shrugged his shoulders. Sonny laughed out loud.

"You regret it now?" He asked, when he had finished.

"Not if it means she's not gonna be in my film," Saul answered, and looked out the window. Sonny laughed again and turned the radio back up. Saul Bernstein was one stubborn bastard.

PRIZE FIGHT

Spring, Palm Springs, 1951

Sonny Haynes tried desperately to focus on the passing landscape from the backseat of the cab in which he found himself. At least it was a cab, he reasoned. Of the three kinds of cars in which one suddenly finds himself in the backseat, the cab is clearly the best of the lot. There was no iron grate, no siren, and no goons on either side of him, so that was something.

He remembered sitting at the bar of the hotel where he was staying. He remembered the job going to shit. He remembered that it was 1951, already. He remembered his nine months of sobriety, before tonight. He remembered ordering rye with a beer back. More than once, he remembered that. There may have been more. Many more, even. Who knew? What he knew now, however, was that the Cathedral City nightlife was passing him quickly enough that he could hardly focus. He knocked on the window as a means of getting the driver's attention. He wanted out—*needed* out, in fact. He rapped his knuckles on the window and said what he was pretty sure was 'stop here.' The particulars were fuzzy, and his voice was difficult to discern, even to him, but he got his point across. The driver, a French gentleman who sang and hummed in his home language as he drove, stopped the vehicle and looked back at his sole customer, concern etched on the not inconsiderable features on his face. Sonny thought the concern ridiculous, of course, and asked 'how much' that sounded a bit more like 'dowmusssh' than he intended, but details were really not the point here. He tossed the bills at the man and exited the cab and found the level concrete a challenge.

Upon sitting on the curb, his reason for desiring fresh air was revealed as he projectile vomited heavily between his brogues in the gutter. It was mostly pink and thick and voluminous, filled with rye and chunks of bread and cheese snacks from the bar and it was hot and shot onto the concrete with verve. He heard women gasp behind him on the sidewalk and young men laugh out loud and without looking he knew other men were guarding the frail eyes of their dates as they passed. He laughed at this, which evolved into a cough and when he did this his head bobbed slightly as if a puppet, his pomaded hair nodding towards the pavement. He said something to them, these passing model civilians, but it was without handle and sounded a bit like a slurred blasphemy. But man, did he feel better. He reached into his pocket and removed his handkerchief and wiped clean his mouth and then the wingtips he had sullied with the contents of his stomach, which lay now steaming and given character on the pavement. He tossed the white cotton square into the gutter. No use in keeping *that*, he knew even without the gift of sobriety. He fumbled awkwardly at a pack of cigarettes until a single soldier was unearthed, at which point he stuck it in his mouth, unlit, and took in the evening.

He knew without looking at the signage that he was in the part of town in which he could not swing a dead cat without hitting a whorehouse or nightclub or saloon that did not have roots, or books, with the mob. The job may have fallen apart, but the night was still young. He spit once then, a thick gob that turned over upon itself and raised majestically above the street before catching the window of a passing car and was ferried away into the night. He stood, removed the fedora from his head and raked his slicked black hair with his fingers before rehatting, took note of his increased balance and the possibilities therein, and peered skyward at the bowl of stars presented. Then he lit his cigarette, inhaled deeply, and exhaled the remains into the desert night. A beginning, again.

***

Cathedral City is so named because of the southern canyon which rims its borders and reminded travelers long before of a cathedral; the fact that the city was now well known for those actions one would not partake of in a cathedral was, of course, a paradox that the honorable founder Colonel Henry Washington could not have foreseen. For while the neighboring city of Palm Springs held the sobriquet of being the vacation home for the rich and beautiful on location from Hollywood, Cathedral City was surely the slutty younger sister, bereft of elegance, manners, and the money that often accompanies such things, but no less full of the lascivious desires therein. In short, Cat City was the place to go after dark. The mob had its hands in prostitution and nightclubs, after hours gambling and the habits that went with it.

Unlike the city which housed it, The Hotsy Totsy Club was appropriately titled. As Sonny took his bearings, the neon sign, which formed an X on the repeated O in the words, called to him like a lighthouse to the wayward stranger adrift. He checked for the brass knuckles in his jacket pocket and felt the weight of them before his hand had even found purchase. By the same measure, he knew without checking his shoulder holster that he had left the .45 in his room before he had gone down to the bar. Which had apparently led to too much rye, which had somehow led to him hailing a cab, which had led to his date with the curb, which led directly to the Hotsy Totsy. Quite the straight line, if you thought about it. So he was without his piece tonight. No better reason to avoid the need for one, he reasoned optimistically. Feeling an idiot, nonetheless.

What he knew about the Hotsy Totsy was this: there was plenty to drink and eat, women of domestic repute if one was so obliged, card games on certain nights, numbers games most nights, and dog fights on a given night. Problem was, he couldn't quite remember what night it was at present, and reconciling that knowledge with the given night for said entertainment was downright hopeless.

The joint was set up thusly—it was a two-story establishment, the lower of which was mainly for drinking and the mentioned card game at the back on said given nights. He, however, did not have Katie with him and certainly would have to cheat at solitaire to pull anything nearing a victory from the 52 this fine evening. The upstairs was generally where guests frequented in couples. Even this thought briefly reminded Sonny of his deceased wife and with it brought no desire for cheap Cathedral City whores. Or even the moderately-priced ones. The back, which, truth be told, only the invited were able to frequent, featured other forms of entertainment. He sat at the bar with a crash and raised his finger while ashing his cigarette with his other hand. He had to really focus on this daring show of double-handed dexterity, and realized that was probably the extent of his coordination at present.

He looked around briefly, which he knew any good detective should do to 'take in the scene', he had read Chandler and Hammett and Doyle and was aware of the fact that he should be able to discern slight mannerisms and throw barbs upon those who would engage him, but he found his vision blurry and even his thoughts still slightly slurred. There were, he noticed, many people here tonight. Most moving more quickly than he. So, no Sherlock tonight. More along the lines of a violent W. C. Fields, perhaps. He looked for the bathroom, primarily because of the rather morbid reality that he kept killing men in that particular room. The benefit was that there was indeed a sink to wash after said episodes, not that he had taken advantage of that particular, but it would certainly be a benefit at some point. The negatives, well, there were really almost too many to count if he were to be honest. Regardless, he couldn't find the thing, so it followed that perhaps everyone in here was safe tonight.

The bartender appeared before him, placed both hands on the bar, and smiled the smile of a man not really smiling.

"I'll have a beer and a shot of rye," Sonny approximated.

The barman nodded, then flicked his forefinger at his own chin. As if to send a message. Sonny immediately believed that he was referring to one of his many tattoos, not that he had one on his chin, but the teardrop at the eye or perhaps the inkwork blasted about his hands as he smoked.

Sonny saw the gesture and stared back at the man.

The barman said, "You've got pieces of vomit on your chin, sir. This is a respectable establishment. Please...," and he trailed off, as if the words were in hiding.

"*Fuck.* Seriously? Hand me your fucking towel," Sonny said, and, when the man did not move, Sonny leaned forward and grabbed the towel on the barman's shoulder and brought it to his own mouth and chin and wiped vigorously. Sonny's eyes never left the other man's. When he had finished, he put the towel into the back pocket of his own trousers and said, "As for this being a respectable establishment, if it was, I wouldn't be here." He winked. It took some motor control, but he believed that he may have pulled it off. "Now, be a good little boy. Get me a beer and a shot."

The man turned reluctantly, as if thinking that perhaps he had a choice in the matter, and returned soon after with the order. Sonny drank from the beer thirstily. He took the room in again. The lights were red and yellow and there were lots of them and most of the people seemed to be couples. He saw two obvious greaseballs, outside of the random spaghettihead out on a date, the first a short one at the end of the bar with his hands folded over his nuts, an old tough guy pose, probably the bar manager, and a much larger one standing near an emergency exit. Because those need guarding.

Sonny sipped his beer, then shot the chaser, and the night started to gain focus.

2.

Things had been going well earlier in the day. Sonny was still sober and following his mark around Palm Springs as if they were both on a date. Which, in retrospect, perhaps the mark may have enjoyed. The man was a young actor making his way about town, minding the Hollywood 90-mile rule and partying with the entertainment set at the pools and resorts. Sonny had been following him for two days for a director to whom the young man owed a not insignificant amount of money. Was Sonny proud of the work? He would have preferred multiple root canals without the aid of anesthesia. But the director was a friend he had helped out in the past, and this was cake work. This wasn't exactly dealing with goons or wiseguys or button men. The guy was an actor, for chrissakes. Little girls are more dangerous. But then his mark had gotten into a tiff, no other word for it considering, with another actor at a pool party who just happened to be the squeeze for Rock Hudson, who, while not at all gay, was clearly concerned for his friend. Said friend had been pushed into the pool, no major crime there, but had hit his head on the concrete during the fall and cleared out the pool (of which a number of the Hollywood elite and near elite and not elite found themselves) as he bled. And bled more. He was going to be fine, to the happiness of Mr. Hudson, but the man Sonny was following, a young mister Charley Hutton, was currently in a Palm Springs cell, with nobody to bail him out and nobody waiting for him when he was to be arraigned for assault. Therefore, the job had gone to shit, and Sonny called Saul Bernstein to tell him the news. Then he checked up on Katie, seeing that she was fine. She was. She was playing a house game of poker. And having dinner with a young man Sonny needed to meet, and let the young man know that there were rules involved, here. He needed to do that. But, she was fine, as fine goes.

And then, for whatever reason, Sonny went down to the bar without his piece, and started drinking after nine months. Again. There was no analysis needed, of course—there were battles, and sometimes you lost. And here he was, at the Hotsy Totsy, with not enough middle fingers to raise at the world. There never are.

3.

Sonny's way of dealing with a closed door was generally to knock it over and with a closed window it was generally to break it, but instead he passed the large Italian man at the door a $50. Each party involved was as surprised as the next and so rather than requiring his brass knuckles, which sat at the ready, he slipped them from his fingers and found himself in the rear of the establishment, outdoors, near a manicured garden (a strange accessory, he realized even in his current state), and following a cement path. There were flowers and bushes of which he had no idea the name but it was clear someone had spent significant care on the area. There was, at one point, a man in a suit urinating on a large bush, but that did not seem irregular. The man even looked at Sonny and smirked, as if they shared a joke.

They walked further. It may have been the beer, or it may have been simply the distance, but the night had elongated with the walk. Then, without introduction, came a guttural hymn of the crowd, and a brief whine of the participants. Sonny, despite his state, recognized the evening for what it was. Dog Fight night. Now, he was not a fan of these events, but he had seen plenty of them in his time in Mexico, years before. They were mostly grisly and predictable affairs where men placed their dogs where they wished their dicks to be, and, paradoxically, generally the shorter, stouter dog came out on top. Many of these were pit bulls, or, as the Mexicans referred to them 'chamuco's', who were bred for fighting their own. Unlike a terrier bred to hunt rats on ships or multiple breeds bred to herd sheep or cows or lions, these were dogs meant to fight other dogs. Which, in Sonny's condition, seemed both alien and, somehow, to make perfect sense.

The din became louder as he came upon the small amphitheater and two dogs were at work below. There were men of every race and color standing on the benches looking down upon the fenced pit, and the trainers of the dogs stood just outside. The descending standing levels allowed the fans access to the fights with clear viewpoints. Two bulls were in the ring at present, though it was clear to Sonny from the first view that the fight was done. He wished for an official, somebody to waive the fight off. The mostly white bull had the face and jaw of the brindle-colored bull firmly attached and the rear legs of the prey already on the floor. Two puddles of blood, nearly joining, lay beneath. It was a sad sight. Sonny didn't understand why the losing prizefighter of the dog match faced death while the human boxers went home to their wives and kids. It's all fighting. Live, or die.

As he was drunk and fixated on the bull fight in the ring, Sonny failed to see the two wop's until they lifted him by the armpits and carried him up the stairs of the amphitheater. It would be kind to say that there was something noble in it, but there really wasn't. They carried him as he impotently wacked his forearms about until they reached a plot of grass near the garden and dropped him. He got to his knees. Each of the meatballs stood next to him as he took it all in. He recognized the man in front of him then: Sally Campinella. He was still short, still ugly, Sonny noted. He was in a suit with a red flower at the top pocket. He couldn't remember what that was called. Sally said: "You can't just come down here, you motherfucker. What the fuck you think you're doing? Take in the sights? Some of the guys in LA still make you for the Big Vinnie hit!? And you're just gonna walk in here, like a swinging dick, and take in a dog fight?"

That was a lot of questions, right there, Sonny thought.

Campinella paused then, ran his thumb across his lips. Then he said, "If I had one iota, you tattooed freak: I'd plug your ass right here. Drunk, like you should be. I can smell you from here." He shrugged. "But I'm a nice guy. The old days is the old days." He smiled at Sonny, with teeth too large for his face. Then he hit him once, twice about the head, and Sonny felt his right ear bleed as the warmth of it ran down his neck. Then Sally turned, quickly, back towards the fights, and said, as he walked away: "do your shit." Now, Sonny had been drunk, as anybody near him would attest; and he had been distracted, as he had been carried off like a misfit child; but this newest insult, as if middle fingers had not been invented, woke him anew. One of the lugs stepped on his ankle and twisted his boot on it with his full weight. Sonny grunted and put his left hand out to the two lugs as if asking for time, just another second, while he reached for the brass knuckles in his coat pocket with his right hand and affixed them. He sprang upon the men then from his knees, breaking the tibia of the first man immediately (upon which he would never walk with a normal step again), and collapsing the face on the left side of the second as he sprung upward and towards him. It was a brutal three seconds. The first man, his leg bent slightly at an angle wholly unnatural, began sobbing quietly. The second man twitched slightly, face down. Sonny limped towards the small amphitheater again, feeling much less drunk, now. His ankle throbbed and he could already feel the swelling and his heartbeat down there.

There were two dogs beginning another dance anew: this time an undersized bull and a German shepherd, not a pup but barely into manhood. They barked, snapped, and growled at each other as they were held back. Sonny spotted Sally Campinella at about 0300. Sally was not looking at him, as the frenzy towards the alpha spectacle drew him as well. Sonny started walking that way upon the top row as the fight began. Both dogs were game, but it was clear within 30 seconds that the bull was taking the fight from the shepherd as he latched upon the neck and blood dripped, then ran onto the dirt below. The shepherd, however, was a savage as well. Despite realizing the game was up, he gripped the ear of the bull with his long snout, pulling blood, bossing the ring as he could. Sonny continued around the uppermost row, then descended the benches gingerly with his gimpy ankle until he stood directly behind Sally C. Sally was enraptured with the fight, and he put his own hand up as if to protect him from the bull; Sonny grabbed his greasy, pomaded hair by the top of the head and pulled him backward and pummeled him once, twice in the face; he felt teeth and bone give; no words were needed. He drew his hand back again and looked at the fractured visage below. Some partial person, now. The brass knuckles were slicked crimson and Sonny wiped those on the man's shirt collar. Then he stepped downward in the rows amid the crowd and climbed the fence into the ring. He kicked the bull with his right foot twice and when it did not give he punched it brutally in the ribs with his brass knuckles. The blow emitted an immediate howl and the bull released and retreated. The crowd had quieted, unsure of how to react. Sonny picked the bloodied shepherd up and put it over his two shoulders and walked through the fence from which both trainer and dog entered. Neither man approached him.

4.

It was a strange sight, this thick and bloodied man limping about the streets with an even bloodier dog about his shoulders. The dog was licking the man's right ear and it made his fedora lean forward to the left, hanging about his head by gravity and angle alone. The man held his left hand out as if to hitch a ride, as if those about were so foolish as to take such a pair.

A cab did stop, however. It was the same French driver from before, Sonny realized, and of course it was. If he could handle Sonny nearly puking in his cab and now carrying a dying dog on his shoulders it must indeed be a part of some larger mythic quest which, truth be told, may not have been the case. But fault the cabdriver none for the thought. Sonny leaned down into the backseat and (very awkwardly) placed the wounded dog on the red plastic bench seat and said 'animal hospital' in a much more sober manner than before and watched the night pass as the cab drove west.

Sonny had fallen asleep in a plastic chair in the lobby of the hospital as the medical personnel did what they could do for the wounded shepherd. He woke to a man in a lab coat standing above him. He had no idea the time. He grunted a sort of greeting and snorted and removed his hat. He cupped his eyes in his palms and raked his hands through his hair and looked back up again. The man in the lab coat was still there.

"Sir? Sorry to wake you...but I have news on the dog that you brought in," the man said.

"Yeah. Okay. Right, dog."

"The animal sustained a good deal of blood loss and some significant puncture wounds, but will otherwise be fine. You got him here in time." The man paused, and, seeing that Sonny was not responding, added: "He's shaved in some areas and bandaged in others, but...he'll be okay."

Sonny smiled at that. A grin nearing a grimace that made his face ache anew from the pounding he had taken earlier in the evening. He was sure, now that he thought of it, that he still had the caked blood on his face and neck. The man in the lab coat sat down in a plastic chair across from him and looked severe. Or whatever other expression passed for serious. He half-grinned, and began: "Sir, you look as if maybe you need some care as well. And..." he paused here, clearly searching for words he was uncomfortable finding, "well...about your dog. How *did* the animal get those type of wounds?" Sonny was tired and his head was aching and ringing and he felt as if he might come out on the right side of tonight regardless of the sobriety slip and it suddenly sprang to mind that honesty sometimes is the best policy. Sometimes.

He looked down at the fedora on the chair next to him and rubbed his stubbled cheek and flakes of dried blood fell to the floor. He nodded to the man, fumbled for a cigarette and lit it. Inhaled, exhaled towards the neon above. "Okay," he said.

"So here's the thing: I don't know this dog from Adam. He's a shepherd, I liked his spirit. He was going down, he knew it. But that fucker," he accentuated this by pointing with his cigarette towards where he imagined the dog to be, in the innards of the animal ER, "well, he just wouldn't give an inch. Here's the thing, doc. Are you a doc?"

The man nodded, once. He was young with curly hair and round spectacles and sat attendant. Sonny dragged the smoke, and continued: "I was at a dog fight tonight, and took a bit of a beating myself. Drunk myself into a stupor first. And this Dago goes by the name of Sally Campinella slaps me up a bit with his muscle and claims I had something to do with a murder of this shitbag Vinnie in LA, who was close with Mickey Cohen, and so he figures I deserve what I got coming. It's all shit. I kill people with some regularity these days, doc." He said this last bit with a clarity that surprised even him. As if he had confused the early morning lobby of an animal hospital for the confessional. "But dogs, now..." he continued, "dogs, well, they ain't got a choice. That's bullshit in my book." He dragged his smoke, exhaled. "And it's only my book we're talking here, right, compadre?" The doctor looked at Sonny as if there was a script for the scene and he had not been given it. He was surprised and embarrassed and interested all at once.

"I'm glad the dog is gonna make it. He'll come home with me. My daughter will like that." He smiled briefly at the thought. "As for me? Nothing that some iodine and an ankle brace won't cure." He looked the doc in the eyes then, and dragged his cigarette.

"Well," the doctor said, "I...uh, I'm glad that you brought the animal in when you did. The events that you describe make it difficult to quite understand...but, he couldn't have sustained that blood loss for much longer." He began to reach for Sonny's knee for sincerity, then thought better of it and rested it on his own, and continued: "This was a good thing you did. I...don't understand the rest of what you spoke of, but this was good."

Sonny smirked around the cigarette between his lips. "Yeah, maybe you should stick to animals, doc," he said, and stood, his ankle flaring immediately upon taking weight. He stretched his arms and shoulders, and looked down at the man still seated. "Hey, by the by, you wouldn't happen to have any leashes, would you?"

The hospital ended up only being a few blocks from Sonny's hotel so he decided to walk the way home. What better way to get used to one another, he reasoned. He spoke to the dog the whole way home, telling the shepherd about his resolve in the ring and of Katie who would be another part of the new family and of his drinking slip which he hoped to keep between the two of them.

Regret is best held for the loser, or the fallen, and thus each of them stumbled home in his way, leashed and limping, unable at times to tell one from another, but entirely together, a union at once primal and whole.

HOUSE DICK

Palm Springs, Summer, 1951

Sonny Haynes stared at the ashtray on his desk. When the morning began it had been full. He had done his job, then. Emptied it. A dynamic start to the day. Now the numerous butts stood upright again like some poor facsimile of stalagmites in a middle school science fair. When Saul Bernstein had told him about this job, being a house dick at the Starlite Hotel & Resort in Palm Springs, he had talked on and on about the Hollywood starlets and side action coming through the place, well, Sonny had envisioned something besides staring at his brogues while they sat propped on his desk, and filling his ashtray with dead soldiers. But then, most things don't work out, do they?

As afternoon set in, he sat forward in his chair and buried the newest butt in the ashtray and snapped his fingers. The dog in the corner, a shepherd recently healed from a dogfight Sonny had extracted him from, stood attentively and looked on—both of them at attention. Then the man ran a comb through his pomaded hair and hatted himself with the gray fedora from the hatrack, placing it low on his brow. The dog was not allowed in the hotel, of course, but, Sonny reasoned, neither was *he*, really, for any number of reasons. A voucher from Saul Bernstein went a long way, apparently, and so Sonny was thusly vouching for the dog. Whatever.

The shepherd followed at his heel as the man walked through the lobby towards the front door. The large windowed room was mostly empty now, for while Palm Springs and its felonious cousin Cathedral City provided a refuge for the Canadian 'snowbirds' in winter and a destination come fall and spring, even the most hardy of vacationers were hesitant to test their mettle in August, when the mercury rose to between 110 and 120 degrees on a regular basis. The hotel, of course, was air conditioned.

"*Mr. Haynes*" a sharp voice called from behind him, from, in fact, behind the front desk, he presumed. He turned.

"You know that we do not allow pets on the premises. My understanding is that you have been apprised of this, and yet you continue to bring along your...that *dog* of yours," the voice continued. The voice belonged to a lady in a maroon suit jacket whose nametag claimed *Wanda, Supervisor*. She was a handsome woman, with sky blue eyes and a nose relatively attractive when not being flared, although those times seemed in limited supply. In short, a lady who was comely only in the most unguarded of moments. Her hair was cinched back into a severe blonde ponytail and it was clear to every guest who entered that she was one of those who had never once been young, even in her youth.

Sonny walked to the desk, slowly, not answering. The dog followed at his heels, and sat and looked up in expectation, panting, when Sonny stopped.

Sonny placed his tattooed hands on the marble desk and removed his hat, crown down, upon the flat surface. He looked skyward, as if for guidance. It was the same marble, he knew she was thinking, that Rita Hayworth and Barbara Stanwyck had fingered as they had checked in to the resort in past years. He was sure that he was disrespecting it by simply making himself comfortable.

" *Wanda*," Sonny said, and half smiled, "the dog is not your concern. I saved the dog's life, and, because of that, he has adopted me. I haven't even named him. You and I can both see," and he turned here towards the animal, "that he is a 'him' because he has a *dick*. When my daughter does name him, I'll be sure to let you know, since I see that is important to you. I'm now the resident investigator for the renowned Starlite establishment and, while it may be against the *written* rules, it turns out that I'm the one who enforces those rules." He rubbed then at the teardrop tattoo at the top of his right cheek as if it itched, *before* again making eye contact. "So, in other words, if you have an issue with someone breaking the house rules, be sure to come to *me*. If you have an issue with me breaking the house rules, be sure you *don't*." Sonny slapped the marble then, twice, and turned and rehatted himself. Wanda shook her head and chose to misunderstand and took to reorganizing.

He and the dog rode in the Merc with the windows down, as if somehow breezy 108 degree heat is better than stagnant 108 degree heat. And it is, actually, but like the equivalent of actual hell versus perceived hell. Both are ridiculous in any real sense. Sonny smoked a Chesterfield and exhaled out the open window. They headed towards Cathedral City and a poker game there. The passing sky was a vibrant, silent blue and the palm trees underneath it hung suspended on skinny fibrous stems like heads with exploded hair.

He searched the radio as he drove and found a home with "Cold, Cold Heart" by Hank Williams and so he turned that up. The dog sat panting in the back seat. Sonny smoked, exhaled, and sat sweating up front.

He parked in the lot at the Pecos Club and dog and man together walked to the rear entrance, the dog moving his legs up and down quickly in an attempt to momentarily avoid the hot concrete. Sonny knocked three times and a man opened the door a crack and peered out, squinting as his eyes adjusted to the brilliance outside.

"Lemme in, you fucker," Sonny said.

The man peered through the vertical slit a second longer than was required and then said: "Ahhh, Sonny Haynes. Of course. I did not recognize you. You've gotten so much uglier since last we met."

The man had jokes, Sonny found. "What's your name, again?" He asked this though he knew well the man's name was Fortunato, a Cuban who had somehow ended up in California, propping games for wealthy Italians and Anglos. It all made sense if you didn't bother to think about it.

"My name is what your mother called me last night, brother," he breathed, in accented tones.

"My dear Irish mother has been dead for 45 years, you fucker," Sonny answered. "So I'd *love* to know what she had to say." He walked through the door as it opened, stopping to make sure the shepherd followed. "The girl been doin' alright?"

Fortunato nodded as he opened the door and responded to the question, but added: "well. Yes. But there is plenty of competition today. Not just the vacation contingent. But some rollers. Maybe not very good, though. But she holds her own, you know that...", the man said, flipping his hand askew, and the moment passed.

Sonny bristled at this, as it was unusual to hear that Katie wasn't cleaning up at any regular poker game unless it was by design, but continued into the dimly lit ballroom slowly, the shepherd following behind on the diametric rug underfoot.

Fortunato, upon seeing that a dog had loped behind Sonny as he entered, said: "Umm, Mr. Haynes, sir. We don't allow dogs in here..."

Sonny turned then, and said, "Oh, it's no problem. I mean. This fucker just follows me everywhere. I can't seem to get him to stop. If you want to try, have at it," and continued towards the game. Fortunato made one investigative step upon which the loping dog turned back upon him and raised a lip to reveal a glint of incisors and the hint of canines and Fortunato stopped cold and the dog continued on.

Sonny had to walk through the main ballroom, which featured a faux-renaissance piece on the ceiling and plush shell-shaped booths and generally looked like somewhere good steak was served during business hours, and continued into the backroom which featured a poker table, two more set up for blackjack, another for baccarat, and a roulette table.

The only area with anyone present was the poker table, and six people there, including the dealer. Sonny pulled a chair from a blackjack area and sat bitch on it, adjusting his hat upwards to watch the cards. He sat distance enough from the table so that it was understood he was not in the game, and the dog curled about his feet. He lit a Chesterfield and watched, silent. His daughter, or at least what each of them considered such, was sitting 4th, or, from him, at nearly 12 o'clock at the table. She had her hair in a ponytail that pointed upwards and only accentuated the freckles that ran rampant over her nose. The others were men, of course, two hatted, two with the dignity to put theirs aside, with hair slicked into parts. Sonny avoided eye contact. He knew that Katie didn't want him here, didn't want him 'checking in', but he also knew that the Italians had some heavies in town this week. It was his job to make sure they didn't take in some poker. That could only go badly—she would win then, easily, and they would be insulted by a woman who could *do* something, they would default to physical affects, he would displace joints and bones, etc.—it could only go sideways. He was, in effect, playing damage control.

Funny enough, she won enough hands and the men about her just grumbled. They picked up their hats with some enthusiasm and squashed them on their heads and the day was done. Sonny pretended not to notice. Then Katie was by his side, smile wide. She did this without any self-consciousness. She was 17. As if there were nothing else.

"You won again," he said, wanting it to be a question but both knowing better.

"Yeah" she said, rolling her eyes and smiling sideways and pulling cash into a leather satchel. "This was an easy one. I expected more. You know those days when they start easy and you keep expecting it to get harder but it never does?"

Sonny tried to remember one of those.

"Well, it never did. I was laying low the last couple of hours thinking somebody was going to bring something new. Nope, *easy peasy*," she finished, scrunched her nose, and smiled widely and it was all a joke.

Fortunato held the door open as the three of them exited the establishment. Sonny leaned in close as he passed, and said, "you're from Cuba, yeah," more statement than question, "you keep fucking my dead ma I'm gonna have to do the same for yours." He hit the man on the chest then, as if in jest, though it pushed the man back two steps. "All's fair, and such..."

Katie stared out the open window as they drove the 111 west into Palm Springs. The wind whipped about the cabin and the shepherd's tongue lolled and Sonny removed his hat and let his hair fly about his head.

"You've gotta name that dog, kid," he said.

Katie turned her head, as if to answer, but said nothing.

"It's weird having a dog named 'dog'," he continued.

She smiled at this. "Yeah. I've been thinking Zeus."

Sonny inhaled and flicked the smoke out the window and exhaled and looked at her without expression.

"You know me," she said. "Always reading. There's this book, *History of the Gods.* And he's worthy, right?" She looked at Sonny then, for confirmation.

Sonny nodded then, his hair whipping about in the hot air. "He's a beast," he answered. "Zeus is fine. You let me know if that's your final answer."

Sonny eased the Merc into the reserved spot in employee parking at the Starlite and sent Katie with the bag and the dog to their suite. Sonny went to his office set off from the main desk and removed his .45, and placed that and his worn brass knuckles in the top drawer, closed it and sat in the swivel chair. Spun once. Twice. Home, again. Of a sort. The air conditioning unit raged in the corner and the small genius there. He was thinking of the bottle of Four Roses he kept in the bottom right drawer. He was thinking of the dog and how Katie had taken to him so quickly. He was thinking of his dead ex-wife, and the bloody sheets and the splintered bedframe, and the chorus of the frogs at night...

A man tapped Sonny on the jaw. No one did that, of course, *ever*, but Sonny had fallen asleep and was drooling on his desk blotter and the man had awakened him. These small failures. Sonny shook his head and tried to clear whatever remained.

"You must be Mr. Haynes", he said. His voice was all pulse and accent. German maybe. "My name is Schneider. My associates lost some money earlier today. I am here to recoup said funds." He smiled then, and his smile was more grimace than fun. Then it was gone. He had blonde hair slicked in a part and wore a smart two-piece suit. It wasn't bought where Sonny bought his.

Sonny smiled, because that's what he had learned to do in these situations. Smiled at the odds. At the limitations. At the ridiculous circumstance in which he found himself. He reached then, pulling back the top drawer for his brass knuckles. They were not there. Nor was his .45.

"I took the liberty of removing your knuckles and your handgun," Schneider said, and shrugged. "I have heard a bit about you, you see. And while I found it rather funny you were taking a little nap at your desk, I still took it upon myself to remove said articles so as to not distract you from the task at hand." He put his palms on the desk, here, and stood, looking down at Sonny, who, he was pretty sure, still felt a bit of drool hanging from the right corner of his mouth.

"Tell me where the girl is, or where I can get the money. Either works," Schneider said, hands still on the table. Every time he said 'the' it sounded like 'zee', and it brought back memories for Sonny.

Sonny laughed then, in the absence of a better option. Laughed into the black. At it, in fact. "What money is that, exactly?" He asked, and looked at the blonde man. "And what girl? You see many girls hanging around this mug?" He gesticulated about the office and its surroundings. "I mean, I know they're plush. But what the fuck. You must be dumber than what dropped out a dog's ass, bud. And Shneider, a Kraut name, collecting for some Wops? You must've—" At this, his own brass knuckles caught him high on his forehead, as Schneider brought his right hand down in a brutal arc that Sonny recognized only an instant before he recognized nothing at all.

***

Sonny woke then, in a start. There was a spray of blood on his desk blotter. That was his, unfortunately, and, of course—but it took him some seconds to process that. His office door was closed. He head was 5 times too big and throbbing and felt as if Jesus himself had slapped him silly while he drank bourbon from a tap at the virgin Mary's tit. He tried to stand but found the process altogether unhelpful and fell backwards into his chair. He tried to think but it may as well have been quantum physics. He knew one thing: Katie, money, his suite. Three things, then. He had to somehow accomplish THAT, which, he had to admit, given his present condition, seemed unlikely. He grabbed the arms of his chair with his hands and remembered how his pops in Tennessee way back when had told him that if you didn't finish a thing you started, oh fuck. He couldn't even remember it. It had been important, once.

He stood then, put his hand against the wall to balance himself, and thought here on the process. It was like putting together a toddler's puzzle, and he was struggling. He had to leave his office; walk through the lobby; possibly engage someone at the front desk (*please God no*); exit through the right rear entrance and walk an outside walkway some 300-400 feet to their suite. He must remember a key, in case. He raised an index finger in celebration of this realization as if he were someone else and then felt in his right front pocket and found it there. His head pounded on and he felt his forehead and a lump there. Perhaps a racquet ball, hoping to be a softball. He reached for his fedora on the hat rack and found it on the third try and placed it on his dome, covering the bulbous addition to his forehead. His hat slanted low and to the left, like he had forgotten how to dress himself, but if he could maintain a regular gait through the lobby, he may just make the outside walkway. As for the gun and knuckles, it was what it was at this point. Had to move forward. Had to get to Katie.

He took the three steps to the office door and it was a journey. He felt for the desk, the wall, then the handle. Then the handle turned and he had to cross the lobby. There were people out there, in suits and dresses and with luggage on carts and bellboys whisking about. Sonny felt as if the world were moving at twice the speed he was. He did, however, manage to lean on the office door frame and plot the voyage. He hoped to be more accurate than Columbus, though he had his doubts. He set out, then, across the expanse of blue carpet like so much Oceania. He took a step towards the front desk, which was a half-circle that completed the lobby and placed his left hand on that and used it as a fulcrum and anchor and support of everything that has ever mattered until he reached the line of people in the middle and smiled then, which he hoped looked less like a shitfaced massacre than he imagined, and took the rudderless steps in the hopes of getting between some of the masses. It is possible that he clipped a small child but by the parent's reaction, even by Sonny's severely delayed understanding, it seemed as if the child was put to blame. Sonny reached back onto the desk and followed its curve with his left hand and he finally ran into the exit door. Literally.

He pressed onto the lever and was outside and without desk or fulcrum he swayed and pressed forward and imagined he must have looked like the drunkest man alive. At some point he reached a door, only to realize it was the wrong door as he banged into it, unable to stop his aimless momentum. His head was no longer throbbing, it just simply felt like another appendage entire—if it were possible to excise the whole thing and start over, he would have. Finally, he found the right door. 12. Not a particularly difficult number, one would think, to find.

The key slipped right into the hole and Sonny regarded this with some amazement before he turned the knob and looked about. The scene inside took some reckoning: a man bleeding from both the head and the thigh was on the floor, face down, completely motionless; the shepherd was hunched and growling at him with a crimson glow in the light; Katie sat on a bed with a broken lamp in her lap. His knotted head looked about at this and tried to take it all in. Then, each in its time, he held his hand out to the dog, and said, 'shhhh' and the animal recognized like for like and wagged his tail and came forward and Sonny then leaned to the man and saw it was Schneider and removed his own brass knuckles from the man's hand and his .45 from the man's coat pocket, as well as a .22 in the man's ankle holster, and smiled as gently as he could to Katie as he sat on the bed next to her and asked, "Hey, how we doin', sweetie?"

She looked up then, though not entirely at him. Did not answer.

"Looks like you may have hit the bad guy on the head with that lamp, yeah?", he said and smiled. "That was *amazing*. This guy," and he pointed at the kraut on the floor here to remove any confusion, "came to take the money you won earlier."

He leaned over to her and placed his hat on the bed while placing his two hands on her cheeks and lifting her face so that their eyes met. "You see the second head I'm trying to grow?" and his eyes motioned in the direction of the bump that seemed to have taken over that side of his head for the moment. "He did that, too."

Katie, as blank she seemed, flicked her eyes towards the bump and smiled, once, quickly, then immediately showed concern. "That doesn't look good," she said, and shook her head, staring at it now.

"Yeah," Sonny agreed. "It also feels like somebody has transplanted another head onto mine and I'm carrying both of them around. And one of them is *literally* nothing but pain. Like, the small head is trying to take over the big head with pain alone." He grimaced at her then, which he hoped would pass for a smile, and continued: "but the important part is that *you're okay*. That's what matters. I'm *sorry* it took me a while to get here. Thank you for hitting the bad German man." He removed the broken lamp from her fingers here, and placed it on the floor.

"The dog bit him. Bad. In the leg," she said, then. As if in confession.

"Well," Sonny said. "the dog is a stud. We talked about this before. He's not gonna let dumbshits like that hurt you. Yeah?"

He stood then, still holding her hands in his. "Hey, you okay, sweetie?" he asked.

She looked at him then, her brown eyes lucid and set. "Yes. I'm okay." She shook her hands and arms then, as if in an effort to remove something. Then looked at him again. "I'm fine. And yeah, his name is Zeus."

Sonny smiled at this, and pet the head of the shepherd who had come to sit beside him. "Well. Okay then. Hey, Katie, you know if we have any aspirin?" he asked.

Sonny drove north to the unincorporated areas of the desert in the Merc with Zeus in the backseat. The day had cooled to a moderate 90 and the sun was setting along the pacific. The windows were open and he passed under the 10 highway and flicked his cigarette towards the dying light as *Crazy Heart* by Hank Williams played on the radio. He barely noticed the thumping in the trunk as they rode.

They pulled off the road some miles west and they bumped and rolled along the dirt roads until they stopped by a wash set some twenty feet deep by decades of winter rains, now simply a gulley of sand. A cloud of dust set into the night as the Merc pulled itself up. Sonny kept the lights on and walked to the trunk with Zeus behind him and popped it. The man inside was still bleeding into the trunk and the whites of his eyes shone wildly in the darkness. Sonny reached in then, pulled the man out roughly by his shoulder and set him against the bumper. The red rear lights of the Merc bookended the scene, country radio still playing. Sonny sat then, Indian style, and ripped the tape from the man's mouth, and they were face to face. Sonny lit a smoke as Zeus sat beside him in the sand.

The man, Schneider, spit once then into the sand and took some deep breaths and finally brought his face up and met Sonny's gaze.

"Hey!" Sonny said, jovially. "So you were saying, money, girl?" He gesticulated about, the embertip of his smoke miming the trail of a firefly. "You find 'em?"

The man looked at Sonny and his expression went dark and sat there.

Sonny laughed shortly then, an altogether joyous and singular thing. "Okay, so, here's where you say you're sorry, and we move on", Sonny said, and exhaled his smoke. "Problem is, you see where you are. This sand, you aint leaving it." He gestured then, to the sand and sand and sand about.

Sonny looked at the man, and shrugged. The dog dozed. The sun set, slowly, and all about the desert a thing not unlike slumber carried itself forth and the new sounds and movement it carried piggyback. The cigarette dangled from Sonny's lips as he pulled the .45 from his belt and the man followed it with his eyes.

The Merc now sat like a lighthouse in the landscape, lonely and alone.

I Want to Be With You Always by Lefty Frizell began on the radio and Sonny sighed. "Well, shit. This here's a good one. Damned if I'm gonna waste it on you." And he shot the man in the right knee. The blast was sharp and loud and echoed briefly and the man twisted to the right and shouted once, long and howling.

"Walk on that," Sonny said, and stood.

The man rolled and shouted again and grimaced and the piano bars rolled in the song in the Merc's speakers and he turned his face to Sonny and shouted, "you'll die for this!" which sounded slightly like 'zis' to Sonny who chuckled and said, "sure. But you're gonna die now." Sonny shot the man again then, in the chest, who heaved forward once against the blast and bucked once then lay still.

The song finished shortly thereafter with the crying of a steel guitar and then it began with *The Rhumba Boogie* and Sonny looked at the dog and said, "see, now this one I don't like," and opened the driver's door and turned off the radio.

He walked back to Schneider then and nudged him. He moved like any corpse, anywhere. A sluggish back and forth. "My head still hurts, by the way, fucker. A lot." He placed the gun then back into his belt and pulled a knife from his back pocket and cut and removed the tape on the man's hands, then reached down and picked the man up by his shoulder and heaved him down into the wash.

The body hit and rolled and rolled and finally skidded to a halt in the sand. Sonny balled up the tape in his hands and he and the dog sat looking down into the darkened gulley. He reached down with his left hand and placed it on the dog's head, softly.

"So yeah," he said. "Looks like your name's Zeus. Get used to it. And thanks."

POCKET KINGS

Palm Springs, Summer, 1951

Sonny Haynes wore the relentless pressure of the needle on his forearm and looked skyward to the tattoo flash artwork posted on the ceiling of the shop. A large fan crouched on the floor and another overhead whirred impotently in a vain attempt at cool. The artist broke for a moment and wiped the forearm clean and begun anew, the electric whine and hum of the gun like a song without melody. Katie, his sort-of daughter, sat crosslegged in a chair to his right, *The Day of the Triffids* open on her lap. She held the pages down in a hopeless battle with the fans. Her German shepherd, Zeus, lay stoic beneath her, one eyebrow twitching, then the other, in turn. Sonny looked at the girl to get her attention, but she was rapt in the tale of a blind populace amidst ravenous and malevolent environs. He often found that getting tattooed, besides the general numbness and dull pain, the loud static of the gun, and the hours of sitting, brought with it a sense of reflection he rarely found anywhere else. And so he sat there in his wifebeater, in the stifling heat of the Cathedral City night, the anchor slowly taking shape on his left forearm, the .45 in his lap, and thought of the fractured, circuitous route his life had taken and which now found him, astonishingly even to him, somewhere near a figure of respect in the underground community. He shook his head once at the absurdity of it, ran a hand though his pomaded hair, pulled the smoke from behind his ear, and lit it with practiced efficiency with the zippo in his right hand. The front door of the shop opened then, and the bell rung above it, heard even above the buzz of the gun and the circling blades of the fans.

Zeus stood, Katie looked up from her book, and the artist stopped and swiveled in his chair to see a short and very round man in a black suit remove his fedora and place a heavy-looking valise on the shop floor. He took a handkerchief from a rear pocket and wiped his brow and replaced the hat. He had a small moustache running the length of his top lip and it broadened as he smiled. "You must be Sonny Haynes," he said.

Sonny removed his cigarette and pulled a loose piece of tobacco from his tongue. "What gave me away," he asked. The truth was, Sonny had long ago lost the ability to blend in anywhere, except maybe in the main pop of a prison. He was covered in ink, and even when he kept his sleeves buttoned and his collar fastened, the teardrop hanging pendant from his right eye, the sparrows on his neck and the 'good luck' on his knuckles, not to mention the horseshoe and crown of thorns on the back of his hands, made the process altogether unlikely in this enlightened year of 1951.

The man moved forward with his hand extended and Zeus exited forth a heavy and extended growl and the man stopped abruptly and looked down at the dog, unsure of what to do.

Sonny looked at the man, ignoring the dog. "What do you want? I don't need a lawyer, and, obviously, you're a lawyer," he said.

"How did you—"

"The bag. Only lawyers carry those kinds of briefcases. You may as well advertise it," Sonny said, by way of explanation. He looked at the artist and said, "hey, gimme 10, will ya."

The artist swiveled left and stood then and placed the gun on the table and went to the front desk of the shop. Sonny stood as well and placed the .45 in his belt and exhaled towards the ceiling. "So? You come here and find me, interrupt what I'm doing, and now you've got everyone's attention," he nodded towards Katie and her dog.

The man came forward again, arm extended, and again Zeus growled, though this time Sonny turned to the animal and gently put his left hand on its muzzle and shook with the attorney. His hand was soft, and plump. Like a dumpling, Sonny thought.

"My name is Winston Watts. I, uhhh, have a proposition for you, Mr. Haynes. You were recommended to me by Saul Bernstein, the Hollywood director whom I understand you are acquainted. A client of mine, and an actor of *his*, has a delicate situation which has been brought to our attention. We were hoping to engage your services so that you could go to work on said situation. It would require your utmost discretion, of course."

Sonny smashed the soldier into the ashtray and lit another. He exhaled and smiled then. It was a rare sight, that smile. Katie looked at it like it was something altogether inexplicable. "Fuckin' old Saul," he said, and chuckled briefly. "Alright. You've got 5 minutes. I'm interested."

The next afternoon, Sonny sat smoking a Chesterfield at his desk at the Starlite Hotel and Resort, at which he held the position of House Dick. He looked up at the brown lady that stood in front of his desk, impatience rolling off of her like heat waves.

"They stole something—my Chanel handbag!—and you've got to look into this!," the lady exclaimed. She was white, wealthy, tan enough to use leather conditioner, into her mid-40's, attractive a decade ago, everything that told Sonny this was a nightmare before the first word.

"So...your handbag is missing, correct?"

"Aren't you listening at all! I mean, YES, my handbag is missing!" she shrieked, with emphasis on the necessaries. "It's black. Patent leather."

Sonny wrote this down. "Is there anything else missing that you have noticed?"

"No. Not so far." She pronounced far like fahhh, as if the letter R was a thing without handle.

Sonny removed the cigarette and itched at his tattooed eye. "Ok, so what makes you think it was the hotel help?"

The lady leaned forward then, and placed both fists on the desk for emphasis, "because she's a Mexican gal. I've *seen* her. It's a Chanel bag. Do the math, pal."

Sonny leaned back and exhaled his cigarette and did the math. It didn't add up. Maria did those rooms, and she was amazing. Everybody in the Starlite knew she was next in line to run maintenance.

"You know what," Sonny said, and winked a tattooed eye towards her, "I'll take a good look at it. If what you say is true, I'll get your property back to you. This, uhh, Chanel handbag." He stood then, and exhaled. "Room 232, right? Mrs..."

"Goldberg," she answered.

"Of course," Sonny said, in reply.

Sonny sat on his couch, not smoking. He didn't know what to do with his hands, he found. Katie sat in a side chair, and Zeus lay at her feet. The actor, an early-20s kid named Johnny, sat in a director's chair across from Sonny, who had bought the chair because he thought it had been a good piece and then realized no one liked sitting in it. Now this kid was.

"Okay, so you've got attorney-client privilege here, since I've been hired by Saul's lawyer as an investigator, and that, therefore extends the privilege to me. The dog is a dog. The girl reading is hearing nothing and I'll be taking notes. So I need you to be honest here. This is not an interview. You don't need to convince me of anything. Just tell me what happened, and why you're here."

The kid was beautiful. He looked up and his eyebrows clinched and a lock of hair fell upon his forehead and his sky blue eyes met Sonny's and it was all too much. But life is not a scene.

Sonny stood then, and pointed his unlit Chesterfield at the kid. "Okay, look. You are, by nature, a liar. We both know this." He extended his cigarette at the kid then for agreement but received none. "You lie for a part, you lie to the girls (he looked then at Katie, who seemed strangely fixed on the boy), and you lie for a living."

Sonny put the cigarette in his mouth and looked down at it in annoyance as he realized it was still unlit. Katie chuckled at this, and he gave her the stinkeye and put it behind his ear. "I get that. It's your job. You're an actor, for Christ sakes." He tried hard not to roll his eyes. "But here's the deal. This is not a role. The director you are currently working for, and a lawyer that works for him, have come to me because they're concerned about you. I, and I want get this straight beforehand, don't give a fuck about you."

The young man flinched at this.

"But Saul is a friend of mine. So I'll help you. But you've gotta be honest. You aren't here for no reason. So I need to hear the reason. And it needs to be legit. If it's not," Sonny said, and looked over at Katie, who was still focused on the actor, "then you can save your own ass."

Sonny sat back down again and twirled his still unlit cigarette: "And here's the thing. You can lie to Saul. You can lie to your girl. You can lie to your agent, shit, lie to your priest. Don't care. But if you lie to *me*, you're fucked. From what I understand, you've got one chance. And I'm it."

The kid looked down for an indefinite amount of time. In film, it may have been profound. In reality, Sonny found it unnecessary and annoying. "I screwed up," he said, finally, and looked down. As if somehow everyone in the room did not realize this was the sole reason they were all together. "I owe some money to some people," he finally said.

Sonny rolled his eyes. "Okay. Lots of people owe money. I owe money. Who give a fuck. Why is this important?" he asked.

The kid stared straight forward. "Because I owe it to a guy named Angelo." He gesticulated for affect. He looked at Katie then, with an expression that bordered on desperation or sadness, Sonny couldn't tell which, and added: "And he's owned by Guiseppi Enzo."

"*Oohkaaay*," Sonny said, hoping that neither the kid or Katie had heard his breath catch. Knowing that what the kid said was the honest truth because very few truths could have been worse. "Okay. So how much did you lose, and what exactly did you lose *in*?" Sonny asked.

The kid looked up then. And the hope contained therein. "Well, sir. It was 10 large, by the end of the night. And it was poker."

"Poker?" Sonny asked.

"Poker," the kid answered, and Katie lay *The Day of the Triffids* on her lap with a slap and she and Sonny exchanged a single glance, and the game was afoot.

Sonny had learned long ago to be proactive with the world and its subtleties and apologize later for whatever toes or feelings or loss of limbs his transgressions and their consequences demanded. He knew, or at least thought he did, that Anna hadn't stolen anything from the Goldberg's room. Thus, he had the bellboys keep a close eye on room 323, and would receive daily updates for the bargain basement price of $3 a day. According to the night manager, The Goldberg's were a decadent Los Angeles couple, and the husband was Ira, a prominent architect. He was in the Palm Springs area working, scouting locations for clients, and was gone most days. His wife, Ava, she of the leather skin and allergy to the letter R, was mostly either taking in the Palm Springs shopping, lunching with other ladies who wore Chanel handbags, or was at the hotel in her suite. They were booked in 323 for another week. As the hotel investigator for the Starlite, Sonny was steadfast that no Chanel handbag would go missing under his watch. He didn't have the time or interest in doing the leg work himself, of course. That would be a galactic waste of time.

So it was no surprise then when Ricardo, the bellboy who was Mexican but tried to pretend he was not (he had explained to Sonny that he got better tips when people thought he was Italian and not Mexican), told Sonny that Mrs. Goldberg had been visited earlier by a young gentleman not named Ira Goldberg.

Sonny sat at his desk and took in the information. He feigned shock.

"He still there?" He asked, when his shock was past form.

"Think so," Ricardo answered.

Sonny pulled a roll of bills from his pocket and removed a $5, and slipped it across the desk. "Nice work. Come get me when you see him leave," he said, and winked. The kid walked out. Sonny wasn't sure why he had done that. Winking to another man was a strange maneuver, and left much to chance—particularly in this corner of the planet. It was a habit he was not fond of. Like actors, doing anything with, well, *acting*. But he found himself doing it nonetheless. He puffed at his Chesterfield but it had long since gone out.

Sonny walked to his suite and turned both situations over in his head. The next time the kid was approached about the money, he would attend the drop. That he had decided. The handbag, well, that seemed a conundrum which he imagined had a much simpler solution, though he had little evidence to fortify that position at present. He turned the key in the door lock and entered the living area and to his surprise found Katie and the kid sitting across from one another, each with a fan of cards in hand. Zeus stood quickly and trotted over to greet him and he placed his fedora on the hatrack.

"Hey, whatcha doing?", he asked, and while an explanation seemed rather unnecessary, it served as a placeholder for the question he wanted to ask.

Katie looked up at him then. "I'm teaching the kid something about cards. You lose 10 large in one night, you need lessons," she said, and her tone implied that the whole thing should have been rather obvious.

"The kid?", Sonny asked, and looked at the kid. "Kid, how old are you?"

Johnny looked and him and blew a lock of hair from his forehead and said, "I'm 23, sir."

"So you're 23." Sonny nodded at this. "Kid, the girl across from you—who just referred to you as 'kid', is 17 going on 18." He said this as if this should explain some mystery that all of them had been wracking their brains over. They both looked at him as if he said words that made no sense and went back to their cards. Sonny threw his hands up and went into his bedroom, the dog trailing him.

With his feet on the floor, he lay back on his bed and stared at the popcorn ceiling of his hotel room suite. He had worked out a deal with the Manager that he and the girl stayed free of charge as long as he was on the job, and it worked for all parties. He was pretty much on call 24/7 for the manager and the well-heeled clients of the Starlite (although, truth be told, there was little to do on a daily basis and he often worked outside jobs to fill his time), while he received a two-room suite he never had to worry about cleaning or catering to the never-ending demands of ownership. It was a marriage that worked. The dog was not supposed to be on the premises, of course, but he had gotten the job on a reference from Saul, and it was clear that the business that Saul sent the Starlite from actors or crew on either set or vacation, catering to the 90-mile rule Hollywood had instituted, far outweighed any issues Sonny brought with him. At least so far. Thus the unorthodox family and its contingencies.

The popcorn ceiling offered few answers, Sonny noted. He heard Katie in the living area explaining particulars of poker to the kid, though he could only make out sporadic words. He spread his arms wide on the bedspread and stretched them. The phone rang then, a jarring and overlong jangling, that Sonny nearly jumped for simply to make it stop.

"Haynes here," he said into the mouthpiece.

"Mr. Haynes, this is Winston Watts. I have some information I have been asked to forward to you."

Sonny instinctively smoothed his pomaded hair that had gone rogue from his sitting up from the bed and pulled out a small notebook he kept in his sportcoat pocket and grabbed a pencil on the nightstand. "Shoot," he said in response.

"Do you know the Desert Air?" he asked.

"Yep," Sonny answered, falsely. Everybody in the Palm Springs area knew the Desert Airpark and Air Hotel. It had opened earlier that year to fanfare and ribbon cutting and enough media to bring the likes of Hughes and Sinatra. It had an air strip, a heart-shaped swimming pool, and enough bars to end the drought. Yeah, he knew the Desert Air.

"A man named Gino is expecting Johnny this evening at 9pm in the Lanai Room at the Desert Air," Watts said. After a pause, he added: "I trust that you won't let him go alone."

Sonny laughed quickly at this. "He won't be going at all, Mr. Watts."

"I'm not sure that a meeting of this sort should be ignored, Mr. Haynes," Watts replied quickly.

"It won't be. I'll be there. I'll make sure that Gino is given alternative options," Sonny said. It sounded to both men as if he might say more, then he didn't. There was silence on the line.

"Very well then," Watts said, finally. "I trust that you will take care."

"I'll give you a call tomorrow and let you know how it went," Sonny answered, and hung up the phone. He lay back down again on the bed and immediately sprang upward at a knock on the suite door. So much for rest.

The dog trotted behind him as he walked from his room to the front door. Katie and the kid continued playing cards. "Don't get the door or anything," he said sarcastically. Katie smirked widely at him in knowing rebellion and went back to her fan of cards. Sonny cracked the curtain on a side window and saw that it was Ricardo.

He cracked the door. "What's up?" he asked.

"That man, in 323. He left just a couple minutes ago," Ricardo said.

"Which way?" Sonny asked. "Parking lot, or front door?"

"Front door. He asked me for a taxi," he said. "He's probably still there."

"Excellent, Ricardo," Sonny said, and tapped the man on the shoulder. He grabbed his hat and left the suite at a jog, Zeus at his heels.

2.

Sonny sat in the Merc and idled at the exit to the Starlite parking lot. He had a clear view of the entrance from here, and could see the man waiting in front for a taxi. Ricardo had identified the man when he returned from Sonny's room to the valet area by a quick point and nod in the man's direction. He was a tall gent, over six feet, and looked tan and muscular, with a large roman nose and strong jawline. Sonny figured he was popular with the ladies, in particular the widows and unhappily married and their Chanel handbags. All four windows were down and it was still hot and Zeus sat panting in the back seat, though Sonny doubted it was over 95. Moderate for early summer in the Coachella Valley. Sonny adjusted his hat further back on his head and searched the radio dial while he waited. He settled on the baritone of Billy Eckstine as "I Apologize" blared from the speakers.

A taxi cruised into the half circle drive and the man entered the rear seat. The cab exited the opposite side of the drive and Sonny pulled out into traffic to follow. He gave the taxi a wide berth, as the yellow of the cab was easy to keep track of as it cruised east along the 111 towards Cathedral City. Once inside the city limits the taxi made a left and headed north towards the arterial 10 freeway. The neighborhoods that passed went from single-story ranch houses on large lots to fenced homes with debris in the front yards and wood boards on the odd window and finally to ramshackle two-story apartment complexes and cars on the street that seemed to serve as both home and vehicle. The cab stopped in front of a building with a sofa on the sidewalk in front and the man exited. He stood and removed his hat and walked to an iron stairwell on the right of one of its two buildings. Sonny idled a block behind and watched as the man produced a key from his trouser pocket and opened the red door and went inside.

Sonny drove another half block and parked the Merc. He rolled up all four windows, and he and the dog exited and walked to the complex. There were two stucco buildings, each an opposite copy of the other, with a small courtyard in the middle. Besides the sofa on the sidewalk for one's seating pleasure, the yard featured a rusty car bumper that lay in the weeds and a metal barrel with a blackened grate on top used for grilling, Sonny figured. There was a picnic bench missing the seat on one side and two palm trees in need of trimming. The sign in front proclaimed *Desert Oasis*, of course, and incomprehensible the difference between expectation and reality.

The two of them walked to the building on the right and then the stairway on the right of that. Sonny felt quickly for the heft of the .45 holstered on his left shoulder underneath his suit jacket and, finding it exactly where he imagined it, fitted the brass knuckles in his trouser pocket onto his hand. He knocked three times on the door with his left hand and waited.

He raised his hand to knock again when the door cracked open slightly. He saw half of the man's face there.

"Yeah?" the man said, as way of greeting.

"Hello sir, I need a few minutes of your time," Sonny said, and slowly moved his left foot towards the door opening as he spoke.

"You selling something?" the man asked. Then, noticing the German shepherd for the first time, "Why the fuck you got a dog with you?" He took a closer look then, and his eyes widened briefly as he realized that the man on the front stoop had a teardrop inked beneath an eye and more tattoos on his neck and hands. The dog did not fit either and no encyclopedia salesman in the history of encyclopedia sales looked like this man and the scene was wrong and he was, again, late to the dance.

Sonny had by this time lodged his foot in the opening of the door and smiled. "Yeah. A little slow there. Back away from the door, fuck head."

The man had panic in his eyes for the briefest of seconds and then seemed to square himself and recognized that the die were already cast. He tried to close the door in a halfhearted attempt and Sonny's foot stopped it and then he put his weight behind his right shoulder and the door flew into the man's face and he fell backwards onto the carpeted apartment floor as the door flew wide open.

Sonny entered and the dog followed. The man groaned and touched the side of his face. "You could have just opened the door. Saved that pretty face of yours," Sonny said, and closed and locked the door behind him.

The apartment had a couch with a metal ice cooler serving as coffee table and a linoleum kitchen table with three chairs and a radio on it and water-streaked wallpaper and carpet the color of vomit. The air was still and stale and the window had tape covering the crack that ran lengthwise and all about sat a crouching weight completely bereft of hope. The man settled in one of the chairs and held a plastic bag filled with ice to the side of his face. Sonny sat opposite him, his business card on the table. They stared at each other.

Sonny pulled at his left lapel so the man could see the butt of the .45 in the shoulder holster and lay his right hand on the table, knuckles still affixed. His left hand pushed the card across the table to the man.

He looked at it briefly, then again. "Okay, shit. What do you want? You don't want me to go to your fucking hotel no more, I won't go! What the fuck." He looked injured, as if Sonny was just a messenger and the world had hurt his feelings, his eyes pleading and angry and helpless all at once.

Sonny looked around the kitchen, and the living room that it opened to. "You got a beer?" Sonny asked.

"What? No, man. There may be a soda pop or two in the fridge," the man answered. Sonny stood and opened the fridge and bent down and reached in for a bottle of RC Cola. He looked around for a bottle opener, and, upon seeing none, placed the cap at the side of the table and held it there as his right hand slammed the bottle down and the cap popped off. He sat back down and took a long sip.

"I figure this is your gig," Sonny said, finally. You find rich, older, unhappy tourist dames and you bang 'em." He nodded the RC bottle his way at this. "And that's probably not such a bad business. Maybe they pay you. Everybody gotta make a living. I'm not here to shit on yours." He nodded then, as if confirming something to himself. "But as the house dick of the Starlite establishment, we have a certain...decorum we'd like our guests to expect and maintain. I'm not sure you meet the standard there."

The man looked across at him and wondered how this tattooed clenched fist of a man could possibly lecture anybody on decorum but said nothing. He looked around the kitchen, then at Sonny. "Okay, fuck man. Like I said, I won't come around there no more!" He said, somewhat desperately. He removed the ice pack and moved his face around and said, "this *hurts*, by the way."

"What's your name," Sonny asked. Then put his hands out in a universal gesture of stop. "Doesn't matter, actually. What's the name you gave Mrs. Goldberg?"

The man scrunched his brow and looked up and Sonny. "I always use Anthony. Well, mostly. So yeah. Anthony."

"Last name?"

"They never ask for last names. It's one name, light a cigarette, buy a drink, walk with my hand on the small of their back." He looked out the scarred window. "That's all it takes, most of the time."

Sonny grinned and played with the business card on the table, turning it over and over. "Well, you aren't welcome at the Starlite anymore, Anthony. You're smart enough, and creampuff enough, to not test that I think," he said, more to himself than the man across from him. "But here's the thing. I have a customer who is missing a bag. An expensive bag. And while I don't particularly care for her taste in bags or in men, I have a responsibility to find that bag and return it."

The man's eyes narrowed for a second and he said, "I don't know nothin' about no bag, man. The ladies pay me cash. We both have a good time." He sat back and adjusted the ice bag on his face.

Sonny looked out the clouded and taped window. "I don't believe you," he said, finally. "I think you take whatever you can take. When they fall asleep, when they're in the shower. On the balcony. Whatever. And then you pawn whatever you get. And they can't much complain about it, because their husbands might get suspicious. But *this* lady, see, this lady comes to me and blames *the maid*." He picked the business card up again and began playing with it. "And I know the maid, and the maid is a good lady. Got a family. She doesn't steal handbags. I think you do." He put the card back in his jacket pocket and exhaled. "So I'm going to ask you again. Where's the purse?"

The man's expression ran the gamut over the coming seconds. It was as if he were in an acting class and he was supposed to express every emotion in 10 seconds. Anger, sadness, panic, resignation. Finally he dropped the ice bag on the table and stood up. "It's in my room," he said.

"You're smarter than you look," Sonny said, and stood.

He walked to the room and Sonny and the dog followed. The room was small: single bed, small closet, beat up chest of drawers. The one extravagance was a full-length mirror inset on wooden legs. The bed was unmade. The window here did not have any tape or cracks, so there was that. The man got on his hands and knees and began rummaging under the bed.

Sonny slid the knuckles off his right hand and reached across his body for his .45. "Whoa there, cowboy. Make sure that whatever comes up from there is only a purse." The man stopped, and looked up, eyes wide.

"Jesus, man. Relax."

"In fact," Sonny said, "move." The man got up and looked at Sonny, uncertainly.

Sonny bent down and tossed the mattress to the side with one hand. Then he flipped the box spring over, so that just the frame remained. On the floor was a bevy of goods: handbags, furs, a sequined dress, a cigar box. He bent down and flipped the box open: a collection of earrings and pearl necklaces and cufflinks and gold and silver chains stared out at him. Sonny looked at the man, but said nothing.

"Grab the handbag you took from Mrs. Goldberg," he said as he stood. The man bent down and grabbed the gold chain handle of a patent leather bag with the iconic label on it. He handed it to Sonny. "And that. What is that?" Sonny asked, and pointed to a fur.

"That's a mink stole wrap, man," the man answered. "That'll fetch a nice price."

"Where'd you get it?" Sonny asked.

The man thought for a moment. "The Racquet Club," the man answered. "Older blonde. Crazy fuck."

Sonny nodded at this. "Good. Screw the Racquet club. Grab that too."

"What the *fuck*, man?" The man spread his arms in the universal gesture.

"My daughter will dig it. Or, you know, I could step in the other room and call the cops. I'd *love* to hear you explain this," Sonny answered, and feigned a step towards the living area and the phone there.

The man exhaled a "Fuuuuuuuck," and leaned down and grabbed the wrap.

At the Starlite, Sonny locked the door to his office and hung his sportcoat and the wrap on the hat rack and placed the handbag in his desk drawer and sat down. Zeus sat in the corner and rolled onto his side. Sonny put his cap toe boots on his desk and his hands across his stomach and leaned back. His watch told him it was 6pm. He had three hours to get to the Lanai Room. He reflected briefly on the fact that he had left his 17-year old charge with the kid actor and the possibilities there. He struggled with these things: he was not her father, but felt he owed a debt to her late mother and should take care of her; she was a good kid, with a good head on her shoulders, but she was 17.

Almost 18. He knew what *he'd* have been doing when he was 18. There was nothing for it.

Suddenly he shot forward from a dead sleep and his eyes opened wide and it took some seconds to place where he was. He looked at his watch, blinked until the hands made sense, and saw he now had less than an hour to get to the Lanai Room. He picked up the phone and rang his room and Katie answered after four rings.

"Where you been?" she asked.

"Had some business to take care of," he answered. "The kid still there?'

"Who? Oh, Johnny? Nah. He left a long time ago. Had rehearsals or something. Zeus with you?" she asked.

"Yeah. Actually, could you pick him up in my office? Take him for a walk and feed him? I got an appointment over at the Desert Air in a bit. You don't have any games tonight, right?"

"Nah. Tomorrow at the Chi Chi, I think. And yeah, okay. I'll be there in a sec." She paused, then asked, "You get that handbag back?"

He hated that he could keep nothing from her. He knotted his eyes with his thumb and forefinger and nodded. "Yeah," he said, finally.

"She was messing around, huh?" She asked, and on the other end of the line Sonny shook his head.

"I just can't keep anything away from you, can I, kid?"

"Nope," she answered. "I'll be over in a sec."

"Ok. How's the kid's poker skills coming along?" he asked. The ten large question. Said Elephant, said room.

"Swell. He's starting to get it. Not the quickest on the uptake though. He should probably stick to looking good rather than thinking, y'know?"

Sonny laughed at this. "Yeah, I do," he said. "Come on over."

Sonny walked to the lobby from the self-parking lot at the Desert Air. Having to make a potential getaway and running to your car is a much different prospect than running outside and having to then wait for a valet to bring it. Once inside, a lei of fresh flowers was maneuvered over his hat and about his neck by a hostess. He looked at it awkwardly and asked for the Lanai Room. He hadn't yet been to the Desert Air, had only heard of it, and it was something to see, he decided. It took up 300 acres of space, and it seemed like the lobby comprised a tenth of that by itself. He passed the Compass Room Restaurant and Bar, which featured a floor to ceiling wall of windows that overlooked the airstrip, until finally finding the Lanai Room Cocktail Lounge. The room was a semicircle and draped in red. Tiki masks and Polynesian prints dotted the walls and booths were set about the outside of the room as a large bar dominated the middle of the space. His watch said it was 8:50.

Sonny ordered an iced tea and sipped at his drink. It was in a faux coconut and seemed to have more straws and accoutrements than ice cubes. There was a large red straw, a red plastic sword with a cherry run through, and an umbrella. He removed some of these and looked about the room. He was looking for Gino. Sonny figured he'd be alone, or with one other greaseball, and they'd take a booth. Nobody can come up from behind that way. And he knew Gino was waiting for the kid, so he'd be watching for the entrance.

So there Sonny was, watching people who were watching people. It took a minute, but he found them. There were two of them, in a booth, with an excellent view of the entrance, spending far too much time craning their necks. Sonny palmed his coconut and made his way over to the booth. He quickly and without hesitation slid onto the red plastic next to the smaller man, assuming this was Gino. If Gino were the larger man, he would not have needed to bring a smaller man with him, or so Sonny figured.

"Hey! We're sitting here. You got a problem?" The smaller man asked, as he was being pushed towards the middle of the booth by Sonny's weight. The big man looked unsure of what to do; there were no instruction booklets handy.

Sonny put his coconut on the table and lifted the lapel of his sportcoat with his left hand so they could see the butt of the .45. The big man immediately began reaching into his coat, and the smaller man put a hand on his arm to stop him.

"I'm here with a message for Gino. You Gino?" Sonny asked, nodding towards the smaller man. He was short, had black hair smoothed back from a widow's peak, the wisps of a mustache evident. He had small, intelligent eyes and ears that were slightly large for his head.

"I'm Gino. But we don't want no message. We want our money," the man said, with bravado enough for the whole room.

"Yeah," the larger man seconded. He had a mustache and a double chin large enough to use for a handle and wide-set eyes perched above full-moon cheeks. He did not look dangerous, but he did look stupid. And one was usually good enough for the other.

"And lookit this guy," Gino said, pointing at Sonny, "tattoos all over himself." He shook his head at this, as if it made no sense.

"Well, it must be a sad day for you then when you realize that you get me instead of money. But hey, here's the deal," he drank iced tea from his coconut here, "you took ten large off of a kid that doesn't know how to play poker." Sonny looked at both men then, one to the next. "And, while I think there may be ethical issues there, he's obviously an idiot."

The big man smiled at this, so Sonny figured he was using small enough words.

"All I'm asking, is you give the kid an opportunity to make it back. The kid doesn't have 10 large. He just doesn't."

"That's his fuckin problem," Gino interjected, all machismo.

Sonny nodded at this. "Well. Yeah, it is, actually. You're right. But now it's also lots of other people's problem too, because he can't pay it, and we can't have him disappearing, or having some scar on his face, or teeth pulled out, like you fellas like to do sometimes," the big man smiled at this, happy with the reputation apparently, "because the studios got money invested in the kid. He's starting a movie soon, right out here, even. Joshua Tree, 29 Palms area," Sonny pointed north with the thumb of his left hand, as if somehow if they looked that way, they could see the set. With his right hand, he affixed the brass knuckles in his trouser pocket and moved the hand under the table.

"Look, pal. I don't give a shit about none of this. I need ten grand. In my hand, or we do to *you* what we'd do to him," Gino said. "You get me? And then after we do you, then we *still* get the kid. So why are we talkin to you here?"

Sonny looked down briefly and then smiled at the little man. "*Yeahhh*, I don't think that would go well for you." He smashed his right hand sideways into Gino's crotch and felt the metal knuckles collapse the soft tissue of his ballsac until he felt bone. The pelvis, he found himself thinking, offhand. Gino immediately groaned and his head went down to the table and hit it involuntarily. The big man started to rise and his thighs hit the table and he was reaching beneath his jacket for his piece. Sonny heard the small man next to him heaving air into his lungs and exhaling heavily and realized he was sobbing.

A waiter walked over to the booth, and found a scene: Sonny was grinning up at him, the little Italian had his head on the table and appeared to be crying and the large Italian was crouching uncomfortably with his hand reaching for something in his jacket. "Is everything okay here, gentlemen?", the man asked.

"Never better," Sonny answered. He looked over at Gino, and said: "Never mind him. That rum punch you got hits you like a ton of bricks! And this gentleman across from me is just reaching for his wallet. He'll be handling the bill." He smiled up at the waiter, full of genuine innocence. "I'll have a refill of iced tea though, if you don't mind." The waiter looked over the table once more before prudence got the better of curiosity. He nodded once and walked off.

Sonny leaned down then to Gino, who was still gasping for air and drooling on the linen tablecloth. "You know The Pecos Club, Cat City? Where Fortunato runs the games?"

Gino exhaled loudly, spittle flying from his mouth, and nodded.

"Be there Friday, 9 o' clock. The kid gets a chance to win his money back. He loses, we'll cover it. Then I'll take his teeth out myself." Sonny patted the back of the man's head twice as if he were a child, and stood.

"Nice seeing you boys. Let's catch up again on Friday," Sonny said, and nodded to the big man, who was still somehow caught in the grip of indecision, unable to decide whether or not to pull his piece in a crowded public place, and nobody to tell him what to do. Finally, he removed his hand from his pocket and leaned down to Gino and Sonny turned and walked away. He passed the waiter on his way out, and grabbed the coconut off the tray. "Turns out, I'll take it to go," he explained, and left the Lanai Room sipping his iced tea awkwardly, doing his best to maneuver around the new drink umbrella.

3.

The next day was Thursday and Sonny started the morning off by putting ointment onto his new tattoo, which itched like a motherfucker. Pieces of it had scabbed over on the edges. While he was getting ready he decided it was a transition day—he'd deal with the Goldbergs today, make all the necessary phone calls, finish the paperwork he'd been putting off for weeks, and prep Katie and the kid for the practice game tonight at the Chi Chi and the real deal tomorrow at The Pecos Club.

In his office, he called the front desk and had Ricardo sent over. When he arrived, he told him to come get Sonny, and Sonny alone, as soon as Mr. Goldberg came back today. Ricardo said he would. Then he called Melvin, and arranged for him to escort the kids to the game tonight and sit in. Next was another phone call, this time to Fortunato at the Pecos Club, getting the game set for tomorrow evening. He gave him the attorney's name and number for financing. Then again he called the front desk and this time had them send Maria in. She arrived minutes later, and the two of them discussed the day's events in Sonny's office. Finally, he looked at the stack of paperwork he had been avoiding, sighed once, and dove in.

It was late afternoon when Ricardo knocked on the office door, breathless, and reported that Ira Goldberg had just arrived in the back seat of a taxi. Sonny removed a $10 from a stack of bills and folded it once and handed it to Ricardo. "Excellent. Go find Maria—she should be in the laundry room, about now—and have her meet me at 323," Sonny said. Ricardo dashed off. Sonny opened the drawer and removed the Chanel bag and walked out of the office.

When he arrived at the room Maria was sitting outside on a bench looking nervous. "Hey, easy peasy," Sonny said, and smiled to put the young lady at ease. "We don't let these people say things about us just because it's convenient for them. Right?" and he cupped her shoulder and handed her the bag. She did not smile but she nodded with determination.

Sonny knocked on the door then. Before he could knock again the door was opened, and Ava Goldberg glowered out at the two of them. Then her eyes caught the handbag in Maria's grasp and she gave a knowing smile, full of malice and victory.

"May we come in, ma'am?" Sonny asked. He wanted the husband as witness for this.

Her eyes twitched, some decision there, and then she opened the door wide, and said to the room behind her, "Honey, that investigator has found my Chanel bag. I *told* you it was the help," and she motioned the two of them to enter, closing the door behind them.

Sonny and Anna walked into the room, a suite not terribly different from the one in which Sonny lived, minus one bedroom, and they stood in the living area. Maria looked as comfortable as a lamb in a lion's den.

A tall man in a shirt and tie stepped out of the bathroom and he put his arm over his wife's shoulders, and said, amiably, "That was some quick work! So, what's this all about, here?"

Sonny smiled and introduced he and Maria. Then he got down to business. "So, your wife came to me and told me that her bag had been stolen, and seemed quite sure that it was Maria, here, who does your room. Now, knowing Maria the way I do, I thought, *nah*, but hey, I got a job to do, so I'm gonna do it." He smiled then at Ava, and continued: "So I used my not inconsiderable investigative talents and tracked the bag down. It was in the possession of a man named Anthony over in Cathedral City, who cuckolds rich wives and widows at some of the local haunts and tends to have some sticky fingers afterwards...," he paused here, and Ira's expression changed and he removed his arm from his wife's shoulders, whose own expression was turning red in anger.

"Now—," Sonny continued, and it was here that Ava broke in—

"That's preposterous!" She exclaimed, as much to her husband as to Sonny and Maria, "I don't know what you're talking about! If anything, this maid of yours stole my bag and gave it to this vagabond of a man—"

Sonny, ever the voice of reason, continued: "Well, ma'am, I'm sure you're correct, but I did follow the gent from the 300 wing of the hotel back to his apartment, from where I extracted your bag to return it. So, while I wouldn't venture to guess as to why he may have been here, I can assure both of you that Anthony was indeed on the premises. More than once, it seems. He has been barred from the property," Sonny added, looking at Ava Goldberg, "so he won't be returning."

Ira rubbed the stubble on his chin and turned his back on his wife, walking swiftly to the sliding glass door before turning around. "Good *lord*, Ava," he said, and his voice was a mixture of disbelief and fury.

"Anyhow," Sonny went on, "I figured the least I could do was have Maria, who is in *charge* of the room, and, as you can see, is quite innocent of the accusation pressed upon her, return Mrs. Goldberg's bag to its rightful place." At this, Maria placed the bag onto the couch and grinned widely. Ira Goldberg slumped in the nearest chair and put his face in his hands. Ava went to him at once, but not without first giving Sonny a glare that could have frozen the swimming pool.

"You folks have a nice night, now," Sonny said, and he and Maria walked out and closed the door behind them. As soon as the door closed, they heard voices within, one pleading and the other plaintive and resigned.

Maria smiled up at Sonny and he winked at her and turned and walked back to his office.

Katie was a poker prodigy. She had been playing at men's tables, and taking men's money, since before she needed a training bra. Already, she was a figure of reckon in the Palm Springs area—and, being that she was just about 18 and female, Sonny either went with her to games or had Melvin accompany her. Melvin was an acquaintance of Sonny's and somebody who would be considered a friend if Sonny was someone who had friends. As it was, Melvin was a black, born-and-raised Coachella Valley native, had a PI license (something Sonny had yet to find the motivation to do himself), was fluent in Spanish, and was a wiry 5' 9". So even if Sonny *hadn't* liked the guy, there were plenty of reasons to keep him around. Many of the places he could go and questions he could ask, in Spanish no less, if Sonny found himself unable to do likewise, and, of course this being 1951, the opposite was true as well.

At 8pm that evening Melvin sat on the couch in the suite. Sonny sat across from him in a chair. Not the director's chair. They had already discussed the events for this night and the next, and were going over it once more to be on the same page. Melvin would escort Katie and the kid to the game at the Chi Chi tonight; getting in would not be an issue as the staff there, like so many other Palm Springs and Cathedral City establishments, knew him over many years; the kid would play, Katie was there as 'support', or, in other words, the 'girlfriend'; being that the kid was a semi-known actor, nobody would question that; the two of them had worked out subtle signals that she would relay over the course of the night to help him on certain hands, as they had been working on both subtle tells and tutoring throughout the week. The idea was that if they were caught tonight, no problem, they'd come home with their tail between their legs and come up with another plan for tomorrow night. If they got caught tomorrow night, they might not come home. Meanwhile, Sonny was heading to The Pecos Club tonight to meet with Fortunato and make sure the particulars were set for tomorrow evening.

When Katie came out of her bedroom, she had on a crème-colored strapless dress that accentuated her light brown skin, one of the few benefits she received from her deadbeat Hawaiian dad. She had her hair done up in a style that Sonny could only imagine was held by bobby pins and magic alone.

"Amazing," Sonny said.

"Wow, Melvin said, his baritone adding extra syllables to the word.

"Hey," Sonny said to Melvin, who smiled broadly.

She walked into the room carrying a clutch and sat near them. "You guys are stupid," she said, and rolled her eyes.

"That's my girl," Sonny said. "Takes a compliment with the best of 'em." He stood and walked then to his bedroom and when he returned he was carrying the mink stole wrap. "For you, madam," he said, and placed it about her shoulders.

"Holy crap," she said. "Really?" She felt it with her fingers and looked at him sharply. "Where'd you get this?"

"It just fell off a truck," Sonny answered. "You'd be amazed." He saw Melvin rolling his eyes at this and Katie scrunched her eyes at his obvious fib and she stood and looked in the mirror, turning this way and that to see it better.

At that there was a knock on the door. It was the kid, and within five minutes they two of them had left with Melvin. They were in good hands. Ten minutes later, Sonny and Zeus were gone as well.

The next morning Sonny and Katie were sitting across from one another at Louise's Pantry eating pancakes and eggs. Katie had a short stack with sausage and slathered the pile in syrup. Sonny had one large hotcake and two scrambled eggs.

"I couldn't believe how well it worked!" Katie said, in between bites. Her black hair was in a loose ponytail and slightly wild. "The first half of the night," she swallowed, eyes getting large, and sipped her orange juice, "I mean, I gave him instructions but he was generally doing okay. We hung in one hand big because I was sure the guy was bluffing, and he was," she smiled at this, then forked another mouthful of pancake. "Anyways," she continued, mouth full, "when he was up five bills I cut if off altogether. Just let him play. He ended up losing a couple, think he ended up with three bill carryout, but hey, it worked." She paused then, looked at her remaining pancakes and her eyes got big. "Plus," she added. "We've got an indicator, so even when I do things that may seem like signals, like a cough or itch on my nose, if there is no indicator, it's irrelevant. Like I said, it worked."

Sonny had been listening intently, and nodded at this. "Nice. You done good, kiddo. You think there's a worry for tonight?"

She sipped more juice and considered this. "Sure. First, we need to make sure that nobody there tonight knows me."

"Shouldn't be a problem," Sonny said, quickly. "I talked to Fortunato last night and we know all the players there. There's the kid, a cop, two dago's—both in the life, and a high roller from out of town. I'll be there, Melvin will be there, the attorney, Winston, will be there, shouldn't be an issue."

"A cop?" She asked, her eyebrows raised.

Sonny chuckled. "Yeah, I know the guy from way back in LA. He's with the Sheriff's now. Loves a good game. A little insurance policy."

"Huh," she exclaimed. "Okay then. What about the dealer?"

"Fortunato is having the guy come in from LA. He works a lot of the Hollywood games, from what I hear."

She nodded, her head moving up and down in a slow rhythm. Sonny nodded then too, and Katie smiled at him, the trail of freckles across her nose seeming to spread with her grin. "What?" she asked.

"You nervous?" he asked.

"Not yet. But I will be," She answered, continuing to grin as she said it.

They arrived at The Pecos Club in two cars; Melvin had driven the kid and Katie in his Jeep Station Wagon, and Sonny had taken Zeus and followed in the Merc. They parked at opposite ends of the mostly full lot and met Watts, the attorney, who had been sitting in his Cadillac. Watts walked up to Sonny and they shook.

"Mr. Bernstein sends his regards, Mr. Haynes," he said.

"Does he, now?" Sonny said, and lit a cigarette. "Let's see if he sends his regards when the night is done and he doesn't have to cover ten large from one of his dumbass actors," he continued, and exhaled through a grin.

"Are you familiar with the setup in this establishment?" the lawyer asked.

"Very," Sonny answered, and knocked on the door. Fortunato greeted them and hands were shaken and introductions made. Fortunato was a tall Cuban who had navigated a circuitous route northwest and found himself in the Coachella Valley in California running a steakhouse and music club that fronted late-night illegal gambling for wops and tourists and Hollywood folks observing the 90-mile rule.

They walked through the kitchen, where Fortunato made it clear he was unhappy that Sonny had yet again brought his dog, and were escorted into the back room, thus avoiding the main ballroom and dining area. The room contained two blackjack tables, a roulette setup, another for baccarat, and the poker table. Chairs were stacked up along the walls, and Sonny and Melvin removed enough of those and placed them far enough outside of the poker area to be taken as witnesses and not participants. The dealer was a small man in a vest with a severe part and a mustache, and was already seated. Gino also sat at the table with a drink in front of him, and another man sat next to him, a bigger man, with an alcoholic's nose and not enough sense to have yet removed his hat. There was also Cliff, the sheriff, who wore an open-collared Hawaiian shirt and winked at Sonny when they made eye contact. Finally, the roller from out of town took up the end of the table, in a three-piece suit and black-framed eyeglasses and pomaded white hair. The big greaseball from the Desert Air sat in a chair behind Gino for moral support, no doubt. Katie, in the dress and mink from the night prior, walked Johnny to the table and whispered in his ear as he sat, for what looked like well wishes. She came over and sat near Melvin and Sonny.

Gino raised his head and looked at Sonny and said, "Jesus, you had to bring a spook and your fuckin dog?," and the men he brought with him broke into grins and laughed at this. Melvin made eye contact with Sonny, who looked at Gino and winked and the night began anew.

Poker is an affair best suited for those with strong bladders and unlimited attention spans and it was not until nearly two thirty in the morning that the dealer packed up the chips and offered the used cards, dead now to any real game, up to any taker. Each of the parties went their separate ways in all manner of spirit. The sheriff had bowed out early, and while his attendance was a plus, he had to get up early for work and so left around midnight. In the end, the kid had won back the majority, though not all, of the money he had lost to Gino. The roller from out of town walked out the biggest winner and was gone within minutes of the game ending. The attorney handed Gino $1500 in cash and walked to Sonny.

"Well done, Mr. Haynes. Mr. Bernstein, and I should say the producers and executive producers of the film as well, will be quite happy to pay less than a fifth of what was originally owed." He shook Sonny's hand, and nodded to Katie. "I see why Mr. Bernstein spoke highly of you, though I must be honest it was hidden to me at the beginning of our affairs."

"Well," Sonny said. "I'm an acquired taste. Takes a while." Melvin was putting the chairs back in their stacks and Fortunato was paying the dealer and the night had come to a close. The three Italians began to walk out.

"Hey, Haynes," Gino called out. "Be seeing you," he said, and he turned and exited to the parking lot.

Sonny turned to the attorney. "Watts, I'm wondering if you'll do me a last favor."

Watts turned his face to Sonny and raised his brows in expectation.

"Could you drop Katie at the Starlite and take the kid wherever he needs to go? I have some business to discuss with Melvin," Sonny explained.

"Sure," Watts nodded. "No problem."

Sonny leaned to Katie and whispered in her ear and she and Johnny left with the attorney. Fortunato had begun turning off the lights and Sonny gave him a mock salute from across the room, and Fortunato nodded in return. Then it was just Sonny and Melvin and Zeus in a mostly darkened room, the curtains that lined the walls cast in horizontal shadows. "Hey," Sonny remarked, "maybe

I head to that exit," he motioned his head towards the rear door, "and maybe you go back through the kitchen and out the side door."

"Always trying to make me go out the side door," Melvin quipped, but he understood the play.

Sonny smiled and lit a cigarette and stood in the dark room as Melvin went towards the kitchen.

It was no surprise when Sonny walked the lot to his car and found the three Italians leaning against the trunk of his Merc. The lot did not have lamps and instead only the bowl of stars above and he could barely see the features of the three men, although he could see the gleam of a shotgun in the big man's hands. Zeus growled low and long and Sonny placed his hand softly on the dog's muzzle. The embertip of his cigarette glowed in the night and his right hand held his .45.

"Boys," he said.

Gino pushed himself off the car and pointed at Sonny. "Hey circus freak, you think you can steal almost 10 grand from me and just walk away?" he asked. He began pacing, and Sonny realized it for what it was. He was working his way up to courage.

"Not really. In fact, I'd have thought you were an even bigger punk than you are if you had let me just walk," Sonny said, and exhaled into the night air, the plume dissipating slowly in the heat.

"Let me tell you something, pal," Gino said, and walked towards Sonny and pointed at him here, "You don't know—"

It was at this point that Melvin emerged from the darkness and hit the big man with a blackjack at the base of the neck. He immediately dropped the shotgun and it clattered on the cement. Melvin leaned over the man on his knees and followed up with two more heavy blows and the man went onto his stomach with a groan and lay motionless. Sonny raised his .45 at Gino's face and walked forward and pushed it into his nose so that it was bent awkwardly and walked him backwards into the back of the Merc. The third Italian with the alcoholic nose had begun to reach into his jacket pocket but had seen the play on his boss and Zeus had growled and trotted forward and the man removed his hand, then put both of them out as a show of universal resignation.

Sonny exhaled his cigarette into Gino's face and asked, "I don't know *what*? Who I'm messing with? Is that what you were going to say?" He flicked his cigarette end over end into the darkness and continued, "yeah, I know *exactly* who I'm messing with."

Gino managed a whimper and said, "Don't—don't do this...I'll pay you back! I'll give you whatever you want."

Sonny moved the barrel of the gun onto the man's forehead and tapped it there twice. "Hear that, Melvin, whatever we want. Interesting."

Gino reached into his pocket and shoved the cash the attorney had given him at Sonny. He grabbed it with his left hand and pressed the muzzle into the little Italian's forehead harshly as he counted off five one-hundred dollar bills. He handed them to Melvin, who walked over and grabbed them and put them in his jacket pocket. Melvin then stepped to the other man and pulled the firearm roughly from the inside of his lapel.

Sonny pocketed the rest of the bills. "Both of you, turn around, hands against the car," he said. They did as they were told. "Mel, frisk em, keep whatever you want." Sonny walked over to the dog and patted his head and popped open the trunk. When Melvin had finished taking cash in a tooled leather billfold and a switchblade and an ankle revolver from the men, Sonny brought down the butt of the gun on the crown of each of their heads. They fell like puppets whose strings have been cut. Zeus walked over and smelled the men. They stood there in the darkness, and Sonny holstered his .45 and lit cigarettes for each of them and they surveyed the assembled humanity on the concrete. "Well," Sonny said, "help me get 'em in the trunk."

They both looked at the big man then, and knew the job would be a taxing one. "Fuuuuuuuck," Melvin said as he exhaled.

When the men were stacked one upon the other in the trunk, Sonny slammed the cover shut and shook Melvin's hand. "You good?" Sonny asked.

"Am I good?" Melvin said, and smiled, his teeth shining brightly in the darkness. "Sheeeeeit, man. You know how to put some money in a brother's pocket, Sonny." He laughed and felt the wad of cash, and his new billfold, in his jacket pocket. "Yeah, I'm good."

"Hey," Sonny said. "Go by the Starlite, will you? Go through the lot and into the backside of the wing," he said by way of explanation for the black man to go unnoticed to his room at this time of night.

"Yeah, I know the way," he said.

"Tell Katie I'll be late."

Sonny drove the dirt road south from Palm Springs, onto Agua Caliente land, and what some here called the Indian Canyons. There was nothing but sweeping silence and starlight and sand in every direction. Zeus lay prone across the back seat throughout and the headlights bounced before the wrathful darkness ahead. If there were any disturbances from the trunk, they went unheard.

THE CONSORTIUM

Palm Springs, 1951

Sonny Haynes, House Dick for the Starlite Hotel & Resort, was throwing crumpled pieces of paper into the corner trash can of his office when he picked up the ringing telephone. Janice from the front desk said, "Mr. Haynes, there's an English gentleman here to see you."

"How do you know he's English?," Sonny asked.

"His accent," Janice answered. It was a good answer.

A few moments later, a man walked in. Thin mustache, expensive gray suit, derby hat. He and Sonny exchanged a glance and he sat in the chair opposite. Placed his hat on the desk. Sonny, generally distrustful of the human race besides a handful of people, had his .45 aimed at the man's balls under the desk. His left hand smoked a Chesterfield, and it looked, and felt, awkward.

"Mr. Haynes," the man began, "I'll get right to the point. A man from our company came here a while back. His name was Schneider. He came here to collect some winnings from, well, I believe, *your daughter*." He said this last bit as if it were incomprehensible.

Sonny continued smoking awkwardly with his left hand. He exhaled across the desk, hoping it reached the man. "Yup. I remember him. He was a kraut. I was sitting here thinking, why the hell is a kraut collecting for some wops. It made no sense." He smashed the fallen soldier into the ashtray and made a mess of it.

The man across from him smiled then, but it was a smile saved for children in a dean's office. "You see, I represent a *consortium*," he said, and actually brought his fingertips together in an A frame. "We, shall you say, collect on moneys lost that should not have been, and/or games that were not properly represented."

Sonny stuck his lips out and did not answer. He had no idea what consortium meant, but he was good with context, and had this fucker actually used and/or in a sentence? He itched the inked teardrop under his right eye, then gave a grimace. "No," he said. "You represent people who are pissed they lost money. That's it. Poker has no house. There is a room, a table and a dealer. You play the other players."

"And you, I understand, have quite a good one here," the man said, and smiled. Sonny smirked at the man, not because he was correct, and he was, but because he had just writ his own death warrant in bringing up his adopted daughter.

Sonny lit another cigarette. The palm trees outside his window swayed slightly in the dusk. "Schneider came here. I told him to fuck off. He left, and I think you need to do the same. If you don't," and he winked here, "I'll be happy to show you out." This was untrue, of course, Sonny had shot Schneider once in the knee and then again in the chest and rolled him into a desert ravine, but, he figured, *details.*

*

Sonny didn't know much about life. He had loved once, deeply. She was dead. Had been a homicide roach in LA. That was long gone. But what he did know, and of this he was certain, was that when faced with a threat, you never retreated. You hit first, and you did it with such force that a response was unnecessary.

Sonny tailed the English guy and his driver, who happened to run about 275—Sonny was excited about that—to a bar in Cathedral City as the night blackened down. Sonny had only been to this spot once, but knew the owner—Ralph, he thought—fronted poker games a couple times a month. It was a crappy joint off an alley, but the parking was solid, and nearly empty. The English guy and the driver parked and walked in, Sonny backed into a spot mostly covered by foliage and watched. And watched. And then watched some more. Stakeouts were a blast.

At some point, he took a switchblade he had in the glove box and punctured the two front tires of the Cadillac, then pissed in the bushes.

He walked back to the Merc and watched some more. He awoke when the back door to the bar slammed. The bar owner—Ralph, he was sure now—trailed the men but he was in bad shape. He had obviously been knocked around some and was bleeding from the mouth, Sonny could see. The English guy and the mammoth driver stopped at one point, and Sonny furiously rolled his window down to see if he could catch any of the conversation.

"You can't just come in and—", the man probably named Ralph said, and he fell to his knees.

The Englishman walked towards him in the way that Brits have when they see they have been given the upper hand, spinning an umbrella—Sonny figured it couldn't possibly be an *actual* umbrella, who the fuck carries an umbrella in Palm Springs, for chrissakes—with a slow, heel-first confidence. He had a briefcase in the other hand. Sonny already knew he was going to kill the English guy, but now he knew he was going to enjoy it.

The Englishman, had he given a name? Sonny couldn't remember. He didn't think so. It was probably something like Henry or Richard or Jonathan. No nicknames for those fuckers. The Englishman walked up to probably Ralph and bent down and said something to the man. Sonny couldn't hear it, though he bent his ear in hopes. He opened the Merc's door then, and walked behind the trunk and kept in the shadow of the foliage and made his way to the rear of the Cadillac.

The owner was still on his knees in the middle of the parking lot as the Englishman and his large driving monkey got into their Cadillac. Sonny stayed in the shadows. The car chortled to life, and they pulled out, turning right in the lot. Sonny followed. It was perhaps 15 feet before they realized something was wrong with the tires, and Sonny then stepped forward and shot the driver twice with the .45 through the window. No use in wasting any time on a guy that size.

The Englishman opened the passenger door and began running. Sonny let him run. He had learned that long ago, on the force. Let them run. They are only hoping to outrun the legs of consequence, and they have neither the stamina or ability to do it.

He ran out of the lot. He ran up the next block. Sonny walked behind him, hoping he had taken his umbrella. He had not, Sonny saw. What the man did not realize, of course, and that Sonny did, is that he was running into the foothills of the San Jacinto mountains, and that the residential streets were behind him. Beyond that were prickly succulents and rocks and rattlesnakes. He almost wanted to leave him. But he didn't.

Sonny found the man sitting on a curb, blocks past any houses, the last curb before the foothills, wiping his brow with his handkerchief and breathing hard. His derby was lost to the night. He looked up at Sonny in an attempt to maintain his dignity.

"The Consortium—" he began.

"Fuck your boy scout troop, King Henry the 5th," Sonny said. The man looked confused.

Sonny pointed the .45 at him and the man put his hands up immediately.

"Jesus," Sonny said, "do you have no respect at all? You go around taking people's hard earned fucking money in the name of some bullshit organization and don't even have the decency to die right?"

The man winced then, and his mustache twitched. Sonny bent his knees at that point, hopeful that he could raise them again, and whispered, "You don't deserve a head shot." He stood then, both knees popping audibly, and shot the man twice in the belly and left him to die.

When he got back to the parking lot, Sonny took some effort in moving the monolith in the driver's seat over and then backed the Cadillac into a spot. The briefcase was in the backseat, and he grabbed that.

He banged his fist loudly on the back door of the establishment. The door opened and the man he had seen on his knees was there, eyes wide.

"Here's your cash, bud," Sonny said. "I didn't open it, didn't take any, don't want any." The man took the briefcase. Sonny lit a Chesterfield and peered down at him, exhaling into the night sky.

The man was a small guy, maybe Russian. Mostly bald.

"Ralph?" Sonny asked.

The man looked at him, confused.

"What's your name?" Sonny asked.

"Alexei," the man answered.

"Got it," Sonny said. "I was close. I mean, Ralph, and Alexei, practically the same." He shrugged, then turned and walked to the Merc.

PAY THE DEVIL

Palm Springs, Winter, 1951

The house investigator for the Starlite Hotel & Resort in Palm Springs, California, sat at his desk flicking matches, both blackened with use and those previously untouched, at the trash can in the corner. He was not a good shot, he found—twelve for forty is a poor percentage in just about everything but hitting in baseball. Nevertheless, like gamblers and optimists and others of that ilk who value potential over reality, Sonny Haynes was sure he had now figured out the proper technique for tossing the tiny torches. It was then, of course, that his office door flew open and his not-daughter but almost, Katie, walked in and collapsed in one motion into the chair across from him. Sonny spent a second filled with horror and shame, as if he were a teenager again and his father was finding him behind the barn with the neighbor girl, or with a cigarette he would later vomit from, or the whiskey bottle he had taken from the pantry, which, coincidentally, would also lead to vomiting. The devil's hands, and such, he found himself thinking, as he composed his face into something resembling the concept that she had interrupted some important work.

"You forget about knocking?" he asked.

She shrugged, then looked at the sprawl of matchsticks that lay about the trashcan, then back at him and smiled. "Another busy day investigating for the Starlite, I see," she said, and nothing else was needed.

Sonny leaned back in his chair and put his boots on the desk and thumbed the fedora back on his head like he imagined Marlowe would have done. He scratched at the tattooed tear below his right eye. "What's up, kiddo?" he asked.

She shrugged again. She had recently turned 18, and shrugging was a thing. It was what she did when there was very clearly something to be talked about but it had to be coaxed out, like a scared dog with a piece of meat.

"Okay," Sonny said, to fill the silence. This parenting thing, going on three years now, was not something he found himself particularly adept at. Hopefully he was better at it than flicking matches at the trash can, he found himself musing, but still not something that came naturally. "Well, how's work?" he asked, in hopes that would break whatever seal existed.

Katie had begun working part-time at the library some months ago, and she seemed to enjoy the work. She had always been a bit of a book nerd, truth be told, and it seemed to suit her. She didn't *need* the work, of course, she was a poker savant and had been sitting at, and taking money from, men's tables since she was 13, but the job gave her something to do, since the late-night poker exploits were usually only a couple of nights a week, depending on the amount of mobster and Hollywood tourists vacationing in the desert at any given time.

"Oh?" she exclaimed, jarring her back to the conversation. "The library?" she asked, though it was not a question. "It's good. Keeping me busy, and Miss Anna," that was her boss, "she's been giving me some new responsibilities," she said, and smiled, though it was a false smile, and disappeared as quickly as it had appeared.

"Well, that's good," Sonny said, lamely. "What games have you got set up—"

"I've made this new friend," she interrupted. "She's a nice girl, I think. Though I guess it won't look that way now," she added, quietly, more to herself than to Sonny.

"What's her name?" Sonny asked, and lit a cigarette with one of the few remaining matchsticks in the box. He exhaled towards the ceiling and looked at her.

"Her name's Faye," she answered. "She's from Florida. Only been out here a few months." She nodded at this, in confirmation.

"Florida, huh?" Sonny answered. Now there's a crazy fuckin' place, he thought, but kept to himself. "How old?" he asked, cigarette dangling from his seam of lips now.

"Just turned 19. Last month, actually. Remember that night I went out with a few girlfriends?" she asked. He found that he did remember such a night, and nodded at the recollection. "Yeah, well. That was to celebrate her 19th. Anyways," she said, and stopped. She looked away and did not continue.

Sonny removed his brogues from the desk and leaned forward and placed his elbows on the hard top. He had the cigarette in his right hand and the embertip glowed orange in the office, some small fire alight. He rubbed his face with his left hand, then his neck, and both tattooed swallows there. "Okay, look, bug," he said. Bug was short for Katiebug, which was a nickname. "You've got a job you like. You've got a friend. From Florida," don't roll your eyes, he thought, "named Faye. These are all good things," except the Florida thing, he thought, "so why does it seem like we're talking about a funeral here?" he asked. He wanted to say, I've got work to do here, but he knew that she knew that would be a lie. He wanted to say, this is boring the shit out of me, but, whatever parenting instincts he did have, well, they told him that wasn't such a swell idea either.

"She's pregnant," Katie blurted out, and looked at him with a guilty expression, her lightly-browned skin still alight with the redness of blushing.

Sonny, with a practical mind about such things, said, "well. That happens. Good for her, I guess. Who's the chum?"

"Okay, see," Katie started, and she pointed at him and scrunched her nose and her freckles bunched up and said, "this is why I kinda didn't want to tell you. I figured you'd freak out."

He sat back again, and his mouth opened wide and his arms spread in the universal gesture of '*look at how cool about this I am*' and said, "now why would you think that? I don't even know this girl."

"Well," she brought both her knees up on the chair then, and wrapped her arms around them, "the guy is married."

Sonny knitted his brows together then, then unscrunched them. "Well, that's a bit of a pickle, isn't it," he asked, not asking.

"Yeah," she said. "And," she started, then looked at him as if she really didn't want to say the next part, then did, "he's a preacher."

"Ohhhkay," Sonny said. He nodded, but it was not a nod of confirmation. More a nod of aggression at bad news. Katie knew the nod.

"I didn't want to tell you," Katie said. "In fact, I wasn't going to," she added, "but she went to him last week to talk it over and he told her to get rid of it, and that if she didn't, she wasn't allowed to come to the church anymore."

Sonny smiled at this. He was quite a fan of hypocrisy, but religious hypocrisy was without question his favorite variation. "Which church would this be?" he asked, still smiling. His cigarette had long since gone out but he had failed to notice.

She shrugged again, but this time it was the resigned, '*why not?* shrug, as opposed to the '*I'm in a deep shell within myself and won't come out*' shrug, so that was good. "That one near the cove. Baptist, I think," she said, then added, "he's one of the head guys."

"Name?" he asked, simply, still smiling.

"Bob, something or other," she answered. "I think. I've never met him, or anything."

He stood then, and stretched, seeing for the first time that the cigarette in his hand had long gone out and so unnecessarily stubbed it into the ashtray with a collection of its brethren. He picked up the match he had used to light it and tossed it at the trashcan, where it bounced off the rim and landed on the floor. Twelve for forty-one, he thought. He put his right hand on Katie's shoulder and said, "you did the right thing," and smiled again what Katie thought of as his 'creepy smile' and walked to the hat rack. He checked for the brass knuckles in his pants pocket, then put on his shoulder holster, checked his .45, and slid a black-checked sportcoat over it, winked at Katie, and walked out the door of his office without another word.

Once in his black Mercury, he drove east on route 111 under the bulk of mountains that rimmed the southern horizon.

*

Cathedral City held the unenviable designation of being second-class to Palm Springs in virtually every category besides illegal activity, in which it was held in some esteem by those in the know. The city was a thin slice of the valley, running from the 10 freeway on its northern boundary, there beset by lower-middle class working neighborhoods and questionable apartment complexes, to its southern rim of 'The Cove', a more upscale neighborhood fitted neatly into the foothills of the San Jacinto Mountains and home to many modernist architectural indulgences and a burgeoning arts community.

The First Baptist Church had been built some five years prior, a majestic and striking building, and sat at the base of The Cove, in many ways a symbolic and figurative antechamber one passed through to enter the neighborhoods beyond. Sonny parked the Merc in the mostly empty church lot and sat in the car. He slowly finished the cigarette he had been smoking, exhaling out the open window and towards the overcast sky of the early afternoon. The drive over made him realize that this had been an impetuous decision, to put it mildly, so he decided to let the situation breathe a bit. He ran a hand through his pomaded hair and rehatted himself, pulling the fedora's brim low on his forehead as he started the Merc again.

He parked this time across from Nat's liquor store in Cathedral City and entered through the double doors. Bottles of every hue and variety of the happy poison welcomed him. He raised a hand in greeting to the man behind the counter. Sonny had a difficult relationship with booze, as he had been on and off the wagon intermittently for some years now. He was, by all accounts, a terrible and sometimes violent drunk, but there was always the chance that next time he wouldn't be. Never know until you try. Having to play caretaker to Katie had helped, however, as he found that the role of father figure meant more to him that he would have previously given it credit for. He had a blowout every once in a while, but otherwise he had handled himself with aplomb in recent years. He smirked at the thought, then paid for the pint bottle of Four Roses and put it in his coat pocket. For a rainy day, of course.

The man behind the register was a swarthy, dark man named Anthony. Sonny figured him Spanish or Italian but had never asked, despite being acquainted with him for some time now.

"Melvin in his office?" Sonny asked.

"Yup," Anthony answered. He nodded towards the back room as if Sonny hadn't been in Melvin's office at least twenty times before.

Sonny lit a Chesterfield and walked through the plastic curtain that separated the store from the storage room. The room was stacked high and low with boxes and there was a set of stairs attached to the wall on the right side and he climbed those. At the top was a door with frosted glass, and a name embossed on it: Melvin Easley, Private Investigator.

Melvin was a rarity on many counts, being a black licensed PI, an owner of Nat's liquor, fluent in Spanish, and, perhaps most unlikely, a friend of Sonny's. Sonny knocked on the door, opened it, and stuck his head through the crack he had created.

Melvin looked up from his desk and smiled. "I thought I recognized those steps. Sounded like a bear was coming up here," he said, and smiled. Melvin was a dark-skinned man, with a thin mustache that matched his wiry frame.

"Got a few minutes?" Sonny asked.

"Yeah, man. I'm just going over next week's schedule for this place. Nothing pressing," he said, and swept the paperwork aside on his desk. "Take a seat."

Sonny entered and did as he was told, hanging his hat from the chair.

"What do you know about the Baptist church over near the Cove?" Sonny asked.

Melvin leaned back in his chair and looked towards the ceiling. He had spent the entirety of his 38 years in the Coachella Valley, and there was little that went on at this point, illegal or entirely on the level, that he didn't know at least something about. "Well," he said. "You mean First Baptist?" he asked, but continued quickly, "I know the man of the cloth there—good man, from what I understand, I know that there has been some chatter in some circles of some...political issues with the church, and I know that the only interest *you* have in religion is wanting to smash its teeth in," he leveled his gaze at Sonny and the two men locked eyes, briefly. "So what is this about?"

Sonny waved a hand in the air, dismissively. "Ehh. I don't know yet. I heard a rumor about the head guy there—and I heard it from Katie," he explained. "So I didn't question it when normally I would have. And that bothers me. I went over there to hang him upside down and see what fell out, then thought better of it." He looked out the window, where the palm trees that lined the street bent in the northerly breeze that swept down the slopes the San Jacinto mountains. Neither man said anything for a time.

"Anyways," he continued, "I'm glad I did. Doesn't seem right."

"Okay," Melvin said, and nodded. "Like I said: from what I know, dude is alright. But hey, we both know that don't mean shit half the time. You want me to ask around? Shouldn't take me but a day or two."

Sonny looked down at the desk in thought. Then, finally: "Yeah, could you?" Melvin started to answer but then Sonny asked, "Is he married? You know?"

"I believe so, yeah." Melvin seemed to consider it, then continued, "Yeah. He is, actually. In fact, I think she works in the church with him, unless I'm getting that mixed up with someone else."

Sonny drove the Merc northwest on the 111 and again entered the heart of Palm Springs. It was a balmy day, a winter mixture of breeze and easy heat and overcast, with the necessary humidity it brought in tow. He parked the Merc on the street near the corner of Palm Canyon and Tahquitz Canyon, that being the home of the Welwood Murray Memorial Library. It was a stout one-story building, built in the common southwest stucco and red tile design, with the entrance facing the corner directly.

He entered the double doors and walked to the reference desk, where he recognized Anna, the head librarian. He had met her once before, when Katie had first started working here and she had brought him by for introductions. Her reaction to seeing Sonny that first time had been an interesting one. Sonny was used to being stared at, even gawked at—between his general bulk, overall demeanor and, even in a sport coat and trousers, the still evident tattoos that covered his neck and hands and the teardrop that hung pendant from his right eye, these things had years ago made that the norm. The general reactions were often surprise or disgust, depending on the person's age and tax bracket. Anna, however, had that rare third reaction—one of interest, and perhaps, even naughtiness. This had not been lost on him—he may have been a widower, but he wasn't yet dead.

She saw him walking towards the desk and stood, her hand outstretched. She was a comely woman of perhaps 35, with auburn hair and eyes that were intelligent and bright. Sonny nodded as he approached, then took the extended hand and shook it. He wasn't quite sure whether he was supposed to kiss it or shake it, but the latter of the options certainly seemed the safer of the two. Despite his once having been married for some years, and what most would consider a fair amount of interest from the opposite sex before and after, Sonny generally felt like an inarticulate gorilla when in the presence of a pretty lady. Fortunately, this was work related, and that somehow made the process easier.

"Miss Anna," he said, by way of welcome, his gravelly voice at a normal volume. He heard a 'shhh!' from somewhere in the room and remembered that they were indeed in a library. He reddened and Anna smiled sympathetically and she whispered, "Hello, Mr. Haynes. Nice to see you again—to what do I owe this pleasure?"

He whispered back, hoarsely, "Can we talk a minute?"

Anna nodded and turned to a young lady who was also behind the desk, he supposed another young librarian-in-training like Katie, and Anna whispered something in her ear. Anna then straightened, motioned with her hand to follow, and they made the walk to her office.

Anna's office was what one might expect of a librarian. There was a sturdy desk with what looked like order and delivery forms, a schedule pinned to the wall, bookcases filled meticulously and completely with books, and a picture of what looked like a younger her with an older couple and another young man. Sonny presumed it to be a family picture. He sat across from her and lay his hat, crown down, on the desk.

"Now, then, Mr. Haynes. What can I do for you?"

Sonny had debated with himself on the ride over whether he should get right to the point, or come at this delicately. Looking at Anna now, he realized that the decision was an easy one.

"Katie told me this morning that one of the girls in your employ, Faye, I think her name is, is with child," he said.

Anna smirked at this. Of all the reactions he had thought of, that one hadn't crossed his mind. She said nothing, which was another thing he didn't expect. He was liking Miss Anna more by the second, he found himself thinking, albeit grudgingly.

"So," he waded back in, since no one was talking, "I was wondering if you knew anything about that."

Her smirk turned into a full smile and Sonny nearly fell out of his chair.

"I'm assuming that you mean in her specific case, and not just the simple act of general procreation, Mr. Haynes," she said, her smile never leaving.

Sonny reddened and she laughed quietly and smiled at him sympathetically. Again. Twice now, in the same visit, he thought.

"I'm sorry, Mr. Haynes, I'm just having some—"

"Please, ma'am. Call me Sonny," he said.

"Okay, *Sonny*. Call me Anna. Ma'am is for my mother. I'm just playing around a bit. Yes, I'm aware she is with child. I try not to get into my employees lives too much, these young girls," she waved a hand at this admission, "but that Faye is a little spark plug, I will say that."

Now it was Sonny's turn to raise his eyebrows into a question and wait for her to continue. Anna opened a drawer and pulled out a cigarette, then lit it. "Would you like one?" she asked.

Sonny waved her away and pulled the pack of Chesterfield's from his pocket, then lit one quickly. They stared at each other and smoked. She brought a small glass ashtray from the drawer and placed it between them. "Katie has mentioned that you do investigative work for people, is that correct?" she asked.

Sonny exhaled out the side of his mouth and nodded. "I help people gather facts," he said, and shrugged. "Sometimes I help people out of jams," he continued, and screwed the cigarette into his seam of lips.

"You'll have to tell me sometime how you got into that line of work," she said, and the light that flashed in her eyes when she said it was enough to make Sonny adjust in his chair.

"Now, a few things I will tell you, and this is really all I know," she said, and gestured, both hands outward. Smoke rose from the cigarette.

Sonny nodded, prodding the conversation forward.

"Faye has only been here for a short time—oh, I don't know, six, eight months, maybe. I have noticed that she and Katie have gotten close. I have also noticed that she has had multiple gentleman callers here at the library in that time. Not that I am anyone to judge someone's wild streak, let me tell you," she chuckled at this, more to herself than anything, "but I'm talking four or five different men, and not always age appropriate, either, shall we say," she added.

Sonny took a small notebook from the inside pocket of his sportscoat and opened it to a blank page. "Any names, or ever recognize any of the men?" he asked.

She thought, briefly, then nodded. "One of the first was a policeman, because he came into the library in uniform. A couple of times. But that was...months ago. The most recent, and the oldest, is a balding man. A small man. I've seen him in the papers, I believe," she said, and smoked.

"The newspaper?" Sonny asked.

"*Yes*," she answered, but the admission stretched on as if it were much longer than one syllable. "He came in—strange too, almost like he was checking on her—and didn't stay long. But they did have a whispered 'argument' in the nonfiction corner. I couldn't hear anything, of course, but it was clear that they certainly weren't discussing dinner plans."

Sonny jotted some notes down and nodded. "And when was this?" he asked.

"Maybe two weeks ago," she said, and stubbed her cigarette out in the ashtray.

"Okay, Anna. Thanks for all this," he said.

"Mind if I ask about your interest in this?" she asked, and cocked one eyebrow.

"Oh, I just want to make sure the kid isn't mine," Sonny deadpanned.

Her other eyebrow shot up and for a split second she looked stricken. He had gotten a real reaction from her, for the first time in the meeting. Sonny smiled then, a big, wide smile on his big, wide face, and she threw the used matchstick on the desk at him, feigning horror.

He picked the matchstick off of his sportscoat and exhaled a lungfull of smoke towards the ceiling. Then he explained: "I'm just a sucker. Normally I'd say something along the lines of 'I can't tell you because of client confidentiality,' but in this case there is no client, as of yet. Katie told me about—the situation, but then she gave me some information that didn't seem right. It didn't jibe. So I figured I'd look into it." He shrugged at the admission, and began to stand.

"Well, you know, this information isn't all *free*," she said, and smiled, her eyes again flashing briefly. "Dinner, Friday night. Pick me up at 7, you choose the place."

Before he could react, she removed his notebook from the desk, and scribbled something in it. Handed it back. "Here's my address and phone," she said, and looked at him coolly.

Sonny grinned, and he could tell it was a look of pure idiocy without even seeing it but he couldn't stop himself. "I, uhh, look forward to it," he stammered, and stood, hatting himself.

He left the room then, not looking back. His steps seemed to be particularly light as he strode, and he seemed unable to think clearly. The ridiculous grin was still affixed as he pushed his way through the double doors.

When he reached the Merc—he didn't remember walking through the library proper or the front doors—he reached into his pocket for the keys. A man approached quickly from across the street, his leather-soled footfalls on the concrete announcing his arrival to Sonny a second beforehand.

Sonny stopped what he was doing, the fleeting intoxication gone immediately.

The man leaned on him heavily from behind, and pressed close, their hats touching, and said, "A lotta questions aren't worth asking, bud."

Sonny smiled at this. This was his comfort zone, his happy place. "You have no idea what you're doing, do you?" With this, he elbowed the man sharply in the chest, then reached back, grabbed the man behind the head by a handful of oiled hair and smashed his face solidly into the top of the Merc's metal doorframe. The man's nose splintered audibly and a fan of blood shot across the driver's window. He then walked the man around the car, still holding him by the handful of hair, and threw him harshly onto the sidewalk, where he lay, moaning and bleeding. Sonny walked to him and frisked the man for a gun, but found none.

Sonny picked up the switchblade knife that lay in the street near his car door, assuming that was what the man had held against his back. He pressed the button and the blade disappeared into the handle and he pocketed the knife. He then started the Merc, and glanced once towards the library. Anna was standing at the window, expressionless, her jaw held thoughtfully in her hand. Then she waved.

"Jesus, what a gal," Sonny said out loud, to himself, as he turned the corner at Palm Canyon.

*

Sonny returned to the Starlite then and set about at the tasks he was actually paid for. He had two notes on his desk when he returned. The first claimed that there had been reports of a Mexican stalker roaming the halls, reported by a Mrs. Johannson. Sonny knew that this would simply turn out to be Miguel or Noe, both maintenance guys here at the hotel and so he balled the report up and threw it towards the trash can, missing badly.

The second report was a missed phone call from Melvin.

He picked up the phone and dialed. "Hey, that was fast," he said, when Melvin picked up.

"What can I say, man—some of us are good at parts of our job other than smashing dude's faces in," Melvin said.

Sonny chuckled at that. "Yeah, well, what'd you get?"

"Baptist dude's name is Bob Givens. Wife is Charlene. They both on the level. Nice folks, from what everybody says, unless being boring is a crime nowadays," Melvin said.

"Okay. Guess I'm glad I didn't hang him upside down then," Sonny said, and heard Melvin chuckle on the other end of the line. "Anything else?"

"Oh yeah," Melvin answered, and sighed audibly into the receiver. "Man, when you step into it, you get your whole boot in there, don't you?" He paused briefly, then continued: "So Bob's been under a lot of stress lately, sounds like. He's a deacon, okay. And the Baptist church is owned by him and his wife. It might say 'the First Baptist Church Association' on the paperwork—that's the congregation, but all that really means is him and his wife. They *are* the congregation."

"Okay," Sonny said. "You're just a fount of knowledge today, aren't you?"

"And you know where that church is located—right at the opening of The Cove," Melvin explained, "so the word is that there are some big Catholic mucky mucks that want that property and that...I don't know, *presence*, I guess, because of the location."

"Let me guess," Sonny said, "so the mayor, or city council, or chamber of commerce, or whatever, is forcing them out."

"—and Bob won't sell," Melvin countered. "Dude did a sermon last week with two black eyes."

"And the teen pregnancy is the next step. To ruin the guy's reputation in the community," Sonny said, and rolled his eyes. "Doing God's work," he said, sarcastically. "Thanks, Mel. I owe you."

Melvin laughed at this. "Gimme a holler if you need me," he said. And hung up.

Sonny was following up on the nonexistent 'Mexican Stalker' case when Katie appeared in his office doorway.

"Whatcha upto?" she asked.

"Mrs. Johannson has claimed there's a Mexican stalker roaming the halls and courtyards," Sonny said, with mock concern.

"Probably just Miguel," she said. He smiled at that.

"What about you, kiddo?" Sonny asked.

"Have the day off at the library. And no real games anywhere until Friday night. So...reading. Talking with friends. You know," she said, and rolled her eyes as she did, "all those pressing social engagements for an 18-year old."

"Hey. Take a seat a minute," he said, and motioned to one of the chairs across from his desk. She sat, looking questioningly at him as she did.

He leaned back in his chair and looked at her.

"You're being weird," she said.

Sonny nodded at that, and thought, yeah, maybe so. "So, I want to tell you a couple things. This case," then shook his head, realizing his error, "this *situation*, that you told me about. I've been moving pretty quickly on it. I wanted you to know that I went by the library today, talked to Anna," he held his hand up here, to deflect any angry teenage glances that might come his way. Instead, Katie looked on with interest, but no discernible emotions. "I wasn't sneaking around, or checking up, I just needed to find out what I could about Faye—so I did," he said, simply. "Had nothing to do with you," he added.

Katie nodded at this, slowly.

"So, I want you to tell me everything you know about Faye and her situation," he said. "Earlier, you gave me the abridged version. Turns out, I need you to give it to me unabridged. As best you can."

She scrunched her nose at him. "Umm, okay, I guess. I don't know that much though," he said, and looked towards the ceiling in thought.

"That's fine. Just let me get to know her a little," Sonny said.

She shrugged. "Okay, well. I've only been working at the library for a few months, so anything before that...I mean, I know she moved here from Florida about eight months ago," she started—

"Do you know why she moved here?" Sonny interjected.

"I asked her one time, she said something about a bad boyfriend back there, and she's got an aunt that lives out here. Figured it would be a new start—something like that. Anyways, she got the job at the library," Katie said, then admitted, "and like I said, I don't know much except for the last couple months, really."

"Okay," Sonny said, and nodded. "Tell me about those then."

"She had been dating a cop—," she said, and smirked and nodded in acknowledgment at the admission, as Sonny had made it very clear that she could date anybody she liked as long as he was not a cop or an actor, and continued, "and maybe someone else too, when I met her. I mean, she seems to like dating. I don't know. Anyways, she had broken up with those guys and she started going out with a new guy. She was kinda secretive about it, though."

"Did you ever ask about him?" Sonny asked, whereby he proceeded to light a Chesterfield and subsequently miss the trash can with the wayward match.

"Once or twice, but it was like she didn't want to talk about it. So I left it alone, you know?" She shrugged, again. "And then like a month ago she mentioned this pastor guy. Then a couple weeks ago I found out about the pregnancy. I mean, that's it." She sat up straight and recollection flickered into her eyes: "Oh, well, and then she said that the pastor said that terrible thing to her. But that was like 2, 3 days ago. It was on my last shift with her. But yeah, that's it."

Sonny nodded at the information. "Okay. Have you ever met her boyfriend, or the pastor guy?" he asked.

"Nope," she answered, quickly.

"Okay," he said, and exhaled towards the ceiling, "have you ever mentioned me to her? What I do? Where we live? Anything like that?"

She looked at him questioningly for a moment, then said, "Yeah, I guess I have, some. In fact, yeah—I definitely remember one conversation where it came up. Why?"

"Well, katiebug. There's a pretty strong indication at this point that—well, I think that maybe she was using you to use me," Sonny said, and let that hang there.

She looked at him with a scrunched expression that unfolded as the realization set in. She bit her lower lip in consternation. She was a bright kid—that was not lost on Sonny.

"Melvin is pretty sure that the pastor has no idea who Faye even is—I think the goal was to get you to tell me, and then for me to shake the guy down. Hard," he said, and then added: "which I almost did."

She looked crestfallen with the news.

"Not great to feel used, is it?" He asked, though the question seemed as much to himself as to her. He stood and walked over to her in the chair and put his hand on her small shoulder. "Don't get used to it, but this won't be the last time, either."

"Well, shit," Katie exclaimed, and though Sonny wasn't crazy about the declaration, he thought it fit the situation well enough.

Katie and Sonny sat in the living room of Mr. and Mrs. Bob Givens, in the small house they owned behind the Baptist church at the base of The Cove in Cathedral City. Sonny had worked homicide in Los Angeles for nearly a decade before descending into his current life, and experience can be taken for wisdom at times. This was one of them. Not one minute after sitting down with this middle-aged couple with their antique coffee table and hand-knit doilies and earnest, kind faces, was Sonny completely convinced that neither of these people not only didn't know Faye, but that this conversation in and of itself was going to cause a stone bruise that would take some time to heal. He felt bad having to be the messenger, of course, but they needed to know what larger political and religious forces were trying to do—to not only their congregation and property, but now to their reputation as well.

When they left, Bob and Charlene walked them out on the front steps. Charlene took Sonny's hands in hers, and said, "Thank you for letting us know this, Mr. Haynes. You are indeed doing the Lord's work. We need a champion, it seems, and while you may have not offered up for the part, the Lord has seen to it to show you the way."

Sonny smiled at this, completely unfit at the moment for a suitable response that did not require sarcasm or outright laughter.

Katie, generally better with both etiquette and the English language than Sonny, said, "we're just very sorry to have to bring you the news, Mrs. Givens."

Mrs. Givens smiled sadly at Katie and said, "I know you are, sweetie. It's writ all over your face. Thank you. Now, if you don't mind, Bob and I here have a lot to talk about."

Bob's eyes had taken on a yellowish cast as the two black eyes from the week prior had begun the healing process, and he put his arm over his wife's shoulders and they turned into their house, closing the front door behind them.

"Well, that was fun," Katie said, as they walked to the Merc, which was located in the parking lot in front of the church.

"Yeah," Sonny responded. "A friggin' party."

There were two men sitting on the Merc when they turned into the main lot. Sonny recognized them both as standard issue goons, monkeys in suits sent to pass along a message.

"Sonny—", Katie said, as she noticed them.

"*Yeeeaahh*," he replied. "Just keep walking."

When they were about ten feet away from the car, Sonny stopped and put his hand out to halt Katie as well. "I suppose y'all are sent by Jesus himself," Sonny said. "Let me guess. I need to stop asking questions, or else there will be consequences. One of you waves a gun at me, talks about how I don't know how things work around here, and leaves me with a black eye or a busted nose. That sound about right? I set the scene for you?"

In Sonny's experience, whenever there were two thugs, the stupid ratio was always at least 1:1, although at times it affected both of them. In this case, he saw that it was indeed 1:1, as the man on the left smiled and stood, while the thug on the right side of the car looked like he needed an instruction manual to proceed.

Lefty put his hands out in a gesture of *'hey, we're just hear to have a friendly conversation'* and took a couple of steps forward. "Okay, bud. You've made your point, now let us make ours. Be a professional, handle this right, and the girl here stays safe and nobody ends up shot in a church parking lot."

Sonny had no reason to like Lefty, of course, but he did appreciate how calmly and accepting he was of the situation. He had to hand it to him. Sonny nodded at the man. He locked eyes with him and reached slowly into his sportscoat, coming out with the .45, dangling from his thumb and forefinger impotently. Then he reached into his pocket and removed the set of brass knuckles. He placed both items on the trunk of the Merc, and walked slowly towards the man, hands out wide.

Righty came quickly around the Merc and grabbed Sonny's two hands and put them roughly behind his back. Sonny glanced once at Katie, whom he saw look at the weapons on the trunk, and shook his head once at her, a clear sign to stop thinking what she was thinking. That would get them both killed.

Lefty took two steps towards Sonny and delivered a brutal body shot, getting his body weight behind it and twisting the hips expertly. Even as the air left him and he gasped for breath, Sonny knew the man had been a boxer, professionally trained. As he was looking at the concrete, wondering why his lungs couldn't find any air in a world filled with it, the uppercut caught him flush on the cheek and eye socket, and the stars that came with it danced in his vision and then he was falling down a well.

He woke to Katie's face staring down at him. She had been crying, so of course his first reaction was to ask if she was okay, which was met with snorted laughter.

"Am *I* okay?" She started crying again and grabbed a lock of black hair hanging in her face and attempted to put it behind her ear. She wiped the tears from her cheeks and stood, unsure of what to do.

"Gimme a minute," Sonny said, and exhaled heavily. "I'll be fine."

And he was, given time. When he stood, he found his weapons still on the Merc. He holstered the .45 and put the knuckles into his pocket. He felt and heard glass on the concrete, under the soles of his brogues, and looked down. Then at the Merc. The back window on the driver's side was broken. He shook his head in disgust and muttered, "asshole."

Sonny looked at Katie then, his wits about him. "You okay?," he asked.

She nodded, and, seeing the glass at his feet, said, "One of the guys busted that and said, this is for Mickey."

Sonny assumed Mickey had been the one who donated the spray of blood onto his car window yesterday. "Was it the stupid-looking one?" he asked.

"Yeah," she said, nodding. "His partner got on him about it too, as they were getting into their car."

Sonny attempted a smirk at that, but found that his face hurt too much to accommodate the request. "What do you say we head home, kid? We'll order room service," he said.

They sat in the Merc and Sonny inspected his face in the rearview mirror. His cheek and eye socket would definitely swell and bruise, he saw, though they only hinted at it now. "Sorry about that whole scene, kiddo. A part of the job sometimes," he said, and looked at her. He turned the key in the ignition and the engine fired to life. "Anyways, so much for being the *Lord's champion*!" he joked, and, despite the pain involved, laughed out loud at which Katie joined in as they cruised west on Highway 111 towards the Starlite as twilight came on.

*

They both ate room service cheeseburgers and watched *I Love Lucy* on the hotel television. They laughed at times, and it kept them distracted from the swelling on the left side of Sonny's face. There are boxers that swell, and there are boxers that bleed (Irish, for sure), and while Sonny did not find himself among those lucky few who get paid for practicing the pugilistic arts, he certainly swelled like one. He found himself looking at the hallway mirror and thinking he could be mistaken for a pufferfish, when the phone rang.

"Hello," he answered, on the first ring. It was a reaction.

"Mr. Haynes," Anna said, and Sonny responded, dumbly, "that's me."

She laughed then, and it was both welcoming and silly. As if anything he could have said would be suitable. Which was excellent, because he found himself thinking that anything he had to say at present would fall short of even the most basic standards. With the phone to his ear, he looked again in the mirror to his face: his hair was pomaded back but stuck out in arrows wide, his cheek and brow pulsed and bulged, his chin wore a two-day stubble.

"You asked in my office if I remembered a name," she said, through the receiver. "Of the older, balding man. The politician," she continued, by way of explanation.

Sonny looked away from the mirror, nothing good happening there, and nodded. "Yeah. The guy who visited Faye," he said, in way of recognition.

"McCorman. That's what I've seen in the papers, anyway. McCorman," she said. "I saw his picture in the paper again, today, then put name to face, and it came to me." She paused, then asked: "We're still on for Friday, yeah?"

Sonny smiled at that and nodded, none of which she could see. Thank goodness. "7 pm."

"Tell Katie 'hi' for me," she said, and hung up the phone.

He pulled the receiver from his ear and looked at it. Nodded once, and hung it up. Then he walked to the bathroom to take a very hot shower. Everything hurt.

*

Sonny knocked on the door of room 118 the next morning. Noe, Miguel, and Katie stood in a half circle behind him.

Mrs. Johannson answered, her blonde hair an explosion explained only by the combination of bed head and hair spray. Her face scrunched beneath it.

"Ma'am," Sonny's southern roots coming forth at the right time, "I've brought forward the potential conspirators with regards to your room issue," he said.

She took a moment then, and brought two hands to her cheeks, as if they were cold compresses, and said, "well, it's about *time*, Mr. Haynes. You can't imagine what Wilfred and I have been going through...," and then she pointed, rather certainly at Noe, and said, "HIM, *he* was the man...", and stopped there, finger still extended.

Katie, who had not been introduced but was among the four, grinned fully at Sonny and turned her face, a teenager with nothing positive to say. Sonny very gently guided Mrs. Johannson's pointing finger and smiled. It looked like a grimace, but it was a smile, nonetheless. "These are our maintenance men, Miguel and Noe," and he pointed his chin at each of them. "They make sure that the pools are clean and have the proper amount of p.h. and chlorine, that the ice machines are well stocked, that your showers and toilets are functioning properly," Sonny said, and, for some reason, it struck him as funny. The privilege of it all. He held his hand to his nose and mouth to extinguish a chuckle. "They are employees of the Starlite. They are not following you, nor do they have any access to your room when you are in it," he said. "Do you understand?" he asked.

Mrs. Johannson again attempted to bring some order to whatever chaos had composed itself on the top of her head and nodded, once. She did it to Sonny only, disregarding the rest of them, and closed the door to her room.

Sonny smiled and slipped both Noe and Miguel a $5 dollar bill for their trouble and they all went their own way.

When Sonny and Katie walked into their hotel suite, the phone was already ringing.

"Hello?" Sonny asked, when he reached it.

"My man," Melvin said. He gave Sonny McCorman's private address.

"You need me?" he asked. Sonny chortled into the receiver, then said, "gimme two hours."

*

Sonny drove the Merc south and smoked. The windows were down, and, of course, one was broken entirely, as he flicked ashes out into the balmy, starlit evening. He parked the Merc around the block and walked to the address. He met Melvin two houses down in the front yard. One of the interesting aspects of Palm Springs is that the city, along with many of its surrounding areas, are vacation and resort spots. This leads to many of the houses being vacant for much of the year. So, no neighborhood watch. And sometimes, no neighbors at all.

"Got anything?" Sonny asked.

He could only see reflections of light on the contours of Melvin's black face in the darkness, but there was no disguising the eye roll. "One meatball near the front. Another inside. That's all I've seen," he said.

Sonny smiled. Probably the same two. Big greaseball. Smart boxer. This was okay. "Alright, look," he said. "I've got this." He looked at the glass monstrosity of a house and nodded. "If I need help, come get me."

He took a step forward and stopped, then looked back. "If I'm dead, don't leave me there. Lord knows what they'll do to me," and smiled in the darkness.

The two men waited a long time. Nothing happened. The only thing moving was the occasional shooting star. Sonny was crouched in darkness on the front porch and Melvin was across the street until finally the big Italian opened the front door and lowered his shotgun and lit his cigarette. Sonny and Melvin watched him smoke. The thing about smoking: it's not a short journey. It's not a shot of whiskey. It takes time.

When the big man exhaled smoke and turned his back towards the north and the stars there, Sonny stood quickly and in two steps he had released the blade of the stolen switchblade and punched furiously at the back of the man's neck, 4, 5, times. His body slumped without ceremony, the shotgun slipping from his left hand and the lit cigarette was dropped into a potted succulent. Melvin quickly crossed the dark street and Sonny entered the open front door.

The house was a Palm Springs marvel, as so many were. A combination of modern and ridiculous and so much glass and sharp angles. Sonny heard Melvin dragging the dead man into the foyer behind him. No use attracting attention out on the porch from the lack of neighbors. That was good thinking.

Then he and Melvin stood, stock still. The house ticked. A clock in the kitchen to the left provided the soundtrack. There was music upstairs, they both heard, but muted. A few voices, also, in muffled but sharp tones. Too many doors, and carpets. The song, however, was clearly the new Nat King Cole single. "Too Young" was the title, and both men slowly made their way up the spiral staircase.

"Answer me, my love" came on next, and the two men found themselves at the top of the staircase, crouched. The music was louder here, and the upstairs foyer was mostly empty. It looked like a house nobody had ever bothered to move into. There was, however, a light from the bedroom at the north side of the property. Both men heard noises from within, at least two men and a woman. Sonny and Melvin spread to the edges of the foyer, one on each side, their backs to the windows that framed it, and caught whatever darkness they could.

The record ended and the needle was raised and the speaker popped one last time.

"I'm done!" A female voice yelled from inside the room. "I'm keeping my baby! And not raising it around your bullshit!" she exclaimed, loudly, in a southern drawl.

Sonny and Melvin looked at each other in the darkness and she burst from the door between them. Then she turned, once, and while neither Sonny or Melvin knew why she was leaving, it was very clear to both of them that she wasn't stopping. A man came from the room then, Sonny recognized him even in darkness as the boxer, the lefty, who had cleaned him in the parking lot, and he caught the woman in the half-dark by the arm. Sonny could only assume at this point that the woman was Faye, and the boxer cold-cocked her with his left. Her head hit the floor before any other part of her body, and he found himself thinking, *at least he didn't punch her stomach.* There was that, at least—assuming she wasn't dead, of course.

Sonny stepped from the corner darkness then and shot the man once in the throat with his .45. After the experience in the parking lot, his imagined revenge had included beating this man senseless and saying something witty and then looking into his eyes as they faded. Instead, the man stumbled around the foyer briefly, holding his neck as if to keep in its contents, and fell, face first onto the carpet. Sonny felt a bit cheated by the whole thing, but it was short-lived.

Sonny and Melvin quickly made their way to the room and there found a man sitting on the edge of the king size bed holding a .45. The politician McCorman *was* a small man, mostly bald, with round spectacles on a gentle face. When they entered, he looked at them without reaction; He saw them both, then didn't.

He sighed, audibly. "I loved her," he said, softly. It was barely audible.

Sonny crouched in front of him, .45 at the ready, while Melvin continued moving towards the man's flank, his pistol aimed squarely at the politician.

"Your goon out there just tried to kill her," Sonny said. "So, not sure how—"

The politician shouted, then, an unintelligible vowel of loss. The clap of visceral pain echoed slightly in the mostly empty house. His eyes, however, stayed focused on the carpet below.

"Okay, okay," Sonny answered, quietly. "So, why don't you hand me the gun," he said, imagining himself the world's worst psychologist.

McCorman looked then at the two of them, looked at them like he hadn't seen them before. Like they were brand new. Then he put the .45 into his mouth, and, without hesitation, pulled the trigger. The blast was obscene in the silence and painted the ceiling above and the wall behind him in blood and skull and brain matter as the man's body flopped backwards onto the bed.

Sonny and Melvin looked at each other once, each with wide eyes, their ears ringing in the silence.

"Well, that went sideways," Sonny said, and made an expression that said, *you never can tell, can you?*

He stepped forward and walked to the bedside table. He picked up the wallet that was on it—inside was $2400. He took $1400 for Faye and his own retainer, handed Melvin an even grand. They left the carpeted room on tiptoes, as if any sound was some form of desecration.

In the upstairs foyer, Sonny knelt by Faye and checked her breathing, which was strong and normal, although she was still quite unconscious. He then picked her up, being as gentle as he could. Even pregnant, she was a little thing, he found himself thinking.

The events on the rest of the night moved quickly. They drove to Nat's liquor, which was Mel's place, and gave Anthony $100 to drive the still unconscious Faye to the ER at Desert Regional, the newly built hospital in Palm Springs—neither Sonny or Mel wanted their faces or license plates associated with whatever investigation might follow. Sonny put the remaining $300 into Faye's wallet and stuffed it into her purse before they left. Anthony then dropped her off, made up a story about finding her like this—told them he thought she may be pregnant, but he wasn't sure, and got the hell out of there the moment she became the center of attention.

The next day was Friday, and the morning was a cold one, with an angry wind coming off the slopes of the San Jacinto Mountains that gave a heavy lean to the palm trees lining the streets. Each of their exploded heads bent south in unison.

The swelling around Sonny's eye had begun to dissipate, but what it now lacked in size it had gained in color. It was the hue of a plum with yellow edges—it was a good look, for someone in his profession, he thought and chuckled, as he looked at the mirror after getting out of the shower. It was going to be a great look for his date that night.

Sonny had told Katie a few of the details about the night prior, though not everything, and then called Anna and let her know about the condition of her employee as well. Both women had agreed to visit Faye, so then it was no surprise when there was a knock on the door that morning. Anna was there to pick Katie up, and they were headed to the hospital together, a pair of concerned librarians.

Katie opened the door and Anna looked in and saw Sonny in the background.

She smiled. " *Wow,*" she said, when she saw his eye. "You do that just for me?"

"Yeah," Sonny answered, with a grin that hurt. "Did I overdo it?"

She shook her head and said, "see you tonight, cowboy," to Sonny and then looked at Katie. "Ready, kiddo?"

Katie nodded and looked back at Sonny and smiled, and the two of them were gone. Off to see pregnant and beaten Faye, whose beau had blown his brains all over the popcorn ceiling when he found himself alone and forsaken, screwing over the Catholic Church as he did. *What a world*, he thought. And then: *fuckin' Florida.*

When he got to his office, there was a note on his desk. Apparently, Mrs. Greenberg had seen a Mexican stalker roaming the hallways. Sonny started to roll his eyes but found that hurt. He looked out his window at the leaning palm trees, then tossed the note onto the desk and expertly lit a Chesterfield. He tossed the match at the trash can, making it easily, and leaned back in his chair, tipping his fedora back on his forehead as he did.

TANGO WITH THE DARKNESS

Palm Springs, Spring, 1952

Sonny Haynes, house investigator for the Starlite Hotel & Resort, sat at his desk reading the morning edition of *The Desert Sun*. He had awoken that morning angry, as dry drunks will do from time to time. His dreams that night had been of his late wife, and his sleep was fitful and each time he fell asleep into the same dream. He hadn't had a drink in some time now, despite the rampant thirst for one, and despite the pint of Four Roses in his office drawer and the fifth in a kitchen cupboard in his resort suite. And so that morning he had said 'good morning' to Katie, his adopted daughter, trying to hide his anger, and then he dressed and drank a cup of coffee angrily and walked to his office with his dog in tow. Now he was smoking angrily, and he exhaled towards the ceiling, where a cloud had begun to accumulate.

There was a knock on his office door. Two raps. Sonny's German shepherd, Zeus, who was laying in the corner, raised his shoulders from the ground and his ears perked like a pair of antennae.

"Yup," Sonny answered, angrily.

His office door opened then, and Noe entered. He looked about the office and immediately began to cough, while simultaneously pointing at the window. Sonny nodded at this, placed the newspaper on his desk and stood, still smoking, and raised the window.

Noe was a Latino maintenance man of somewhere between 35 and 45, short in stature but looked shorter in his dungaree overalls, and his face wore a mustache that belonged in a hall of fame, somewhere. He had worked at the Starlite for many years now, Sonny wasn't sure of the number, and had never been anything but steady for the resort. Fact was, Sonny couldn't recall ever seeing him in his office before this.

"Mr. Haynes," the man said, as he stood in the doorway. "I, ummmm," His hand came up in a universal gesture of '*I'm not sure how to say this...*'

Sonny grinned, and, given his requisite anger, it was an ugly thing that more resembled a grimace, and motioned for the man to sit. Sonny Haynes was a big man, wide and thick and with tattoos virtually everywhere there was noticeable skin. But he was also a smart man. Sometimes.

Noe sat in the chair across from the desk and he put his hands on his knees, and sat bolt upright. If there was a more obvious way to appear uncomfortable, Sonny hadn't seen it.

Sonny stood then, and asked Noe to do the same, who looked at the bulky man as if he were crazy, but accommodated the request nonetheless. Sonny shook his head side to side, his neck noticeably cracking, as if that could start the day anew. Then he pulled out his pack of Chesterfield's and shook two loose.

"Smoke with me," he said, and lit both cigarettes and both men sat, again. Because clearly, more smoking was what was needed. It was a strange moment, but Sonny hoped it was a new start.

Sonny leaned forward on the desk. "Noe, look. You've been here long before I ever arrived. You do a solid job. What's up?" he asked, hoping to alleviate the man's discomfort, then smoked and exhaled upwards.

Noe smoked and exhaled quickly. "Mister Haynes," he started, his accented English heavy and unsure, "I say this only because you have been good to me," he finished, and smoked quickly, again. As if it were a race to the finish.

Sonny inhaled and exhaled, nodded thoughtfully, flicking his ash into the Starlite-embossed glass tray on the desk, then scratching at the tattooed teardrop at the corner of his right eye.

Noe snuffed his cigarette, only half finished, into the same ashtray. "Room 212," he said. And then he moved his neck in a circle like there was a kink in it, obviously feeling unequipped to express in the words of a foreign tongue the urgency and lack of comfort he felt. In Noe's expression, Sonny saw uneasiness but more than that, even some desperation. An imploring quality that, in its turn, made Sonny uneasy as well.

The house dick sat back in his chair. His fedora was on the hat rack, but he wished it was on his head so he could push it back. Then he locked eyes with Noe. "Okay, room 212" he said, and nodded once. "I'll take a look."

Sonny didn't often go into people's rooms when he knew they were presently being used. There was something particularly invasive it about that he found unnerving. It wasn't that it was illegal, per se, as his duties dictated that he had both the authority and even responsibility, given probable cause, to investigate potential nefarious activities on the grounds of the resort. He just didn't like to do it. This was, however, the only time Noe had ever alerted him to anything, so he checked with housekeeping, and found that the room had been empty earlier that morning.

After knocking on the door and getting no response, Sonny walked around the walkway to the courtyard side of the plaza and found the backside of the same room. He had the very short universal nub of a key for sliding glass doors, and he used that to enter room 212 in the early afternoon, pushing aside the two sets of blinds. Normally, upon entering this way, one sees the standard Starlite glass table a small television on a tripod stand, and a couch. That would be the normal thing.

Room 212, however, had a very different feel to it today. Most noticeable, he supposed, was the Nazi flag pinned on the wall behind the television, although the three M-16 assault weapons that lay on the couch and the multiple, neatly stacked clips of ammunition on the glass table were not standard Starlite equipment either. There were also numerous assorted flags stacked one atop another draped over the back of the couch, the crossed sign of the confederacy on top of the pile. Stacked about the room were identical hard cases, and Sonny recognized their purpose immediately. He knelt and clicked one open, and inside there were five neatly packed and displayed M-16 rifles like on the couch. He counted the boxes and came to 20 large ones, with an additional 10 smaller cases that each held three neatly packed Smith & Wesson .357 revolvers. There were smaller cases still that held boxes of ammunition and additional clips. After taking inventory, Sonny stood and took in the scene. He had a lot of questions and nobody to ask.

Okay, Sonny thought. Okay, Noe.

He pulled the walkie-talkie off of his belt then and said, "maintenance, please bring five of the rolling laundry bins to room 212, asap."

He grinned then, and found suddenly that he wasn't angry anymore. The day was getting better already.

*

The Starlite Hotel & Resort was one of a handful of establishments in the Palm Springs area to have earned a reputation as a destination spot of some distinction. It had been built some ten years prior and had managed the trick of seeming older and yet inextricably modern, a place to both see and to be seen. It did not hurt, of course, that both of its owners were industry icons, and therefore much of its clientele featured the Hollywood set and those who hope to catch a glimpse of that type. It was not uncommon for actors and actresses, both established and up-and-coming, to be seen walking across the red carpet in the formidable lobby, its windowed and sunlit entrance leading to the renowned semi-circular front desk, looking as much like a futuristic airline check-in as hotel lobby. And while it couldn't compete with The Desert Air, the newly-built, tropical themed resort to the east that boasted some 300 acres and its own airstrip, The Starlite certainly held its own.

The manager of the Starlite Hotel & Resort was a man named Harry Schein. Harry and Sonny didn't necessarily get along, they just ignored the fact that they didn't. Sonny was put in place at his position by Saul Bernstein, the Hollywood director who was co-owner of the resort, whom Sonny had once helped out of a jam. Meanwhile, Harry was related by family in some oblique way to the other owner, whom Sonny had yet to meet. So while neither man had made much of an effort getting to know the other, Sonny had, until this day at least, assumed they were playing for the same team.

He found Harry in the lobby, attending to two men who were checking into the resort. Sonny leaned against the semi-circular front desk and watched the proceedings. Sonny guessed the two men were in their late twenties, both of them thin and handsome. He assumed they were both actors, as they carried that bland, attractive look that does not change in any camera angle. One looked faintly Hispanic with a whip of black hair slicked back while the other was very Anglo, blonde with high cheekbones. Harry was chatting them up and shaking hands, having bellboys attending to the luggage and escorting them up the red carpet. Sonny assumed they were gay, or at least switch hitters. His time working Los Angeles homicide had introduced him to the idea that many in the Hollywood lifestyle fit that description, but his time out here in Palm

Springs had cemented it. Not that he cared. The least of his worries were what people did in their own bedrooms. It was just a thing to be noticed; come investigation time, it could save quite a bit of energy eliminating certain avenues.

Harry Schein was unlike the two handsome young men he was walking the aisle with. He was short, Sonny put him at 5' 6", with a monk's balding halo and rimless spectacles. What he lacked in stature he made up for with enthusiasm however, smiling and laughing at the guests jokes with an attentiveness that gave Sonny the creeps. Hell is other people, of course, and Sonny knew that he couldn't do that job any more than Harry could do his. And so it goes.

Sonny knocked on Harry's office door a few minutes later. He was beckoned inside and there walked towards Harry at a massive wooden desk. The room was quite large, at least three times the size of Sonny's office, with windows looking out into the courtyard and the pool there, and signed pictures of Hollywood elite on the walls. There were two bookcases as well, both filled mostly with large hardbacks, although Sonny doubted that Harry spent too much time with the written word. There was one framed item that caught his eye, and when he saw it, he veered from his path in order to look closely. It was an architect's rendering of the layout of the Starlite from above.

"Never seen this," Sonny said.

"Is that right," Harry answered, but it wasn't a question. "Mr. Haynes, I've got a busy day in front of me..."

Sonny turned around and walked to the desk and sat, heavily. He lit a Chesterfield and glowered across the desk at the bespectacled man. "Okay then, Harry. I'll get right to it. I need whatever information you have on whoever is staying in room 212. Don't tell me you don't have it, 'cause one of us does, and it ain't me. Second, I need to know why I was not *told* of not only who said individuals are, but who you got to help them bring in nearly 40 cases and boxes of assault rifles, handguns, and ammunition into our hotel that *I am supposed to be protecting*." His voice carried with it an intensity and anger that could not be mistaken. Harry, to his credit, looked unperturbed. "And last," Sonny continued, "whatever cut you're getting, you're offering me half, or I am going to make this *very* bad for you." This last comment got to the manager a bit, and Sonny saw his eyes flash with either fear or anger.

Harry looked down in his lap briefly, and steepled his fingers on the desk. When he looked up, he spoke: "I'm sure I have no idea what you're talking about, and how dare you accuse me of impropriety. I'll have you know—,"

"Wrong play, chief," and Sonny slammed his palm down on the man's desk. The man jumped in his chair, startled.

"And just how do you know about these supposed weapons?" Harry asked.

"An anonymous tip," Sonny said, and smiled. It was a wide smile, and one that held more than a hint of malice. But the goal was to make sure this didn't get back to Noe and make life difficult for him. Sonny ashed into the glass tray on the desk and leaned back. "I'll tell you what, though, Harry. I was a homicide roach for nearly a decade in LA. And you know what guilty people all have in common? They get caught up in the details. They're never surprised there *was* a crime, because they already know that. What they want to know is how it was found out, or who the witness is, or who told. Just like you." He exhaled and smashed the cigarette into the tray. "You're not concerned with the fact that we have almost 40 boxes of weapons in our hotel, you want to know how I know," he said, and shook his head.

He stood then and itched at the teardrop tattoo under his right eye, the ink on his hands and knuckles becoming prominent as he did so. "So, here's the deal. At this point, you're fucked. You have no leverage. You're in bed with some fascist clowns who probably sleep with their flags every night. You did that, not me. I, however, now have their guns." Harry's eyes bulged at this, as if the depth of the situation was finally dawning on him, like the eyes of a drowning man at the last second realizing he won't be able to make the surface. "And they are not getting their guns back until they talk to *me*. However you handle that situation is," and Sonny waved a hand in the air here, "very much up to you," he said, and smirked, then turned and walked to the door. Still facing the door, he said, "and if you ever try to run a scam like this behind my back again, I'm raising a black flag on you." He opened the door then, and as he did so he ripped the handle clean from the wood, exposing a large, ragged hole.

As he walked through the lobby to his office, he stopped at the front desk and placed the door handle on top of it.

A blonde in a powder blue sportcoat and skirt looked from him to the handle, a nervous smile on her lips.

"Hey Janice," Sonny said, "Mr. Schein's gonna need a new door." His face gave a scrunched expression that said, *what can you do?*, and continued walking the lobby towards his office.

For the rest of that day, Sonny set up some of the particulars. First, he called Melvin Easley, a local private investigator whom he partnered with at times. He let him know the details, and the play. Melvin confirmed that he would be ready and available when the call came. Sonny then called Chief Thompson, head of the Palm Springs Police Department, and they set a time to meet.

The next morning, Sonny and Katie slid into the Merc. The engine started heavily, then settled into a guttural, deep-throated rhythm reminiscent of something more visceral than taking the two of them to breakfast. Sonny had been driving the sled since he had worked security detail for the notorious Sanchez, a Mexican drug dealer and all-around sporting gent. He had worked his way up the security ranks with a brutal combination of wanton violence and feigned loyalty until he was the personal bodyguard for Sanchez whereupon he set up a drug deal that didn't exist, shooting and running over the dealer, taking the trunk full of zeroes over the border and back into California. He probably wasn't very welcome in parts of Mexico, upon reflection, but he kept the Merc as a trophy. He felt a kinship with the Merc, and had so far changed the plates three times and knew he would drive it until it died on him like the horse he recognized it for.

It was not yet 9am but the thermometer would read nearly 75 degrees already in Palm Springs, and they drove highway 111 southeast towards the diner, where they were to meet Chief Thompson, the head of the Palm Springs police. The windows were down and Sonny exhaled lungfulls of Chesterfield smoke out of his window while Katie held her arm out of hers, bending and cupping her hand as she guided it over and around the tops of the palm trees in her vision as they passed. It was a glorious Southern California morning, the desert air carrying with it an herbal sweetness with the elevated rim of the San Jacinto mountain range shepherding the road below through its foothills as the Merc slid into the parking lot of Kay's Diner.

Chief Thompson was a wiry man of perhaps 55, with hair that resembled silver more than white, a salt-and-pepper mustache that harkened back to his original hair color, and a bearing of so much patience that he seemed to slow things down around him. Sonny and Katie slid into the booth across from him and sat.

The sheriff was studying the menu as if he had never seen it before, although he was a regular here.

"Haynes," he said, and nodded. "Katie," he said, and smiled, genuinely, which was returned in kind. If he was surprised Sonny's 18-year old daughter had accompanied him, he certainly didn't show it.

"Chief," Sonny said, in reply.

They all studied their menus. "Young lady," Chief Thompson said, "I understand you're working at the library now. How's that going?"

She put the menu down and looked at him. The sun slanted in seams through the blinds, accentuating the freckles that ran across her lightly-browned nose. Her birth father had been Hawaiian, and her brown skin and black hair was the only thing of worth he had passed down. "I'm enjoying it," she said. Then added, "Miss Anna has been great." Miss Anna was the head librarian, and a sometime dating partner of Sonny.

The chief nodded at this, his mouth shaping itself into an approving seam. "And, I'm sure you're not still taking all the marks in the illegal poker games set up around the valley?" he asked.

And yes. She was. On the regular. "I'm not sure I know what you mean," she said, and smiled, squinting at the sunlit window. Sonny smirked at this, and the chief turned his gaze there. "So," he said, "what's what?"

Sonny was about to answer when they were interrupted by the waitress. They placed the order. When she had gone, Sonny said: "There's a situation I just want to keep you abreast of. Could end up being nothing. I removed a large cache of weapons from a room at the Starlite. And a bunch of Nazi, Nationalist crap. I'm pretty sure it's gonna end up being used in an arms deal somewhere in the valley. I'm guessing not Palm Springs, so it might not even fall under your jurisdiction. But since it started here, I figured I'd let you know."

The waitress brought three cups of coffee and placed them steaming on the table. The chief put enough cream and sugar in his to make it something else entirely, while Sonny and Katie drank theirs black. The whole while, the chief did not speak. The chief was not a stupid man. He knew very well of Sonny's past, and not just the outsized reputation.

He sipped his cream and sugar drink, the bottom of his mustache turning tan as he did so. "Okay," he said, finally. "Well then. I appreciate you letting me know. I've been a lawman long enough to know that what we have here" and he motioned with his first two fingers between Sonny and himself, "is an unorthodox situation, you might call it." He rubbed at his chin. "I'm also quite sure that you're not telling me everything I need to know about this situation. I also know that you're not gonna to tell me everything, regardless of any hemming and hawing I do on my side of things."

Sonny sipped his coffee and said nothing.

"Tell me why I shouldn't just send over a truck and confiscate the weapons," the chief asked, sipping his khaki colored beverage.

Sonny tilted his head at this, as if that thought had not yet occurred to him. "Well. Because you're a smart man, Chief," Sonny answered, and lit a Chesterfield. He exhaled towards the ceiling. "You go in right now, you'll get some thirty plus boxes of weapons. You involve your department in the situation, and everything stalls out. You end up with some weapons you don't need and likely lose all the players that are involved." Sonny ashed into the tray and the waitress brought over the three dishes. Katie's was a pile of pancakes higher than the plate was wide. Both men looked at it with interest before continuing the conversation.

"Look," Sonny continued. "Let this play out. Like I said, I've talked with Melvin—"

"Easley?," the Chief asked.

"Yeah. The PI," Sonny answered.

"Good man," the chief answered, and nodded.

"—and he guesses that the only place these fuckers would do something like this is up near Yucca or Twentynine Palms. They've got sanction there. That's Riverside Sheriff's Department, anyway," Sonny said, and rolled his eyes. The dereliction and widespread abuses of power in that department were well known to both outlaws and lawmen alike in Southern California, and the northernmost parts of that valley may as well have been the Old West.

The chief leaned back, drinking his coffee.

"So, I figure, let this thing play out. Whatever happens, I'll keep you in the loop," Sonny said, seemingly finished. Then he added, waving his cigarette: "Because you know I ain't involving RSD if my life depended on it," He said. He smoked the end of the cigarette and smashed it into the tray. Then he opened the bottle of ketchup and put some on his scrambled eggs.

The chief looked at the process as if that were the more interesting part of their conversation, then nodded, once. He said: "You know the White Sox are coming here for Spring Training this year."

"Yeah?" Sonny said, between bites. "Let's catch a game."

"Yep," the chief said, cutting a piece of sausage in half. "Let's do."

*

Back at the Starlite, Sonny knew the moment he entered the lobby that the two men sitting across from one another at a side table were waiting for his return.

Nobody had told him as much, but Sonny had gotten very used to the type of clientele that utilized the resort and its amenities.

These men were not that. One, dressed in a black suit with a red tie, could possibly have passed if he were alone. He wore his hair slicked straight back, and looked impatient while trying to act as if he were not. The other man, however, Sonny recognized immediately. He did not know this individual, of course, but he was of a mold Sonny had dealt with his entire life. He wore a blonde flat top, shaved nearly to the scalp. His jawline was cleanshaven with a mouth that turned down at the corners, and his shirt had short sleeves. He wore a tattoo on one forearm, Sonny was sure that would be military, most likely Navy. He had eyes that seemed to settle on people with mild disapproval and linger there, as he rolled the toothpick he kept in his mouth from side to side. He had seen this type as a kid in Tennessee, oftentimes wearing a badge and trooper hat. He had seen this type when he worked as a cop in Los Angeles, and then as a homicide dick. It is not a type given one locale, despite the stereotypes. He could be found in the wetlands of Florida or in Appalachia just as easily as in the trailer parks in Idaho or the suburbs of LA. The accent may vary, but the mindset never did. He may as well have had PECKERWOOD tattooed on his forehead. Sonny figured as he approached them that the suit was clearly the business end, and the peckerwood was the contact with his own kind.

Rather than pretend otherwise, Sonny aimed to see the situation out straightaway. He walked towards the two men and grabbed a chair as he did and spun it around and sat at the table. "Y'all lookin' for me?" he asked.

The two men looked at him, and both smiled, but each wore his differently. The man in the suit's was warm and wide, understanding that business was in the offing. The man in the flat top grinned, his toothpick peeking out of the corner of his mouth, and said: "Now why you think we'd be lookin' for you?" The 'for' came out 'fer.' Without waiting for an answer, he asked "You the house dick?"

"Because, men like you don't come here for another reason," Sonny said, simply, answering the first question. He lit a cigarette without offering one to either of the others.

The two men looked at each other, and the flat top said, "Now, what you mean men like—" but the man across from him stopped him with a motion and continued smiling.

"Mr. Haynes," the man in the suit said. "It is Mr. Haynes, is that right?"

Sonny nodded, but said nothing. The cigarette smoke lazily rose in front of his face.

"My name is Caldwell, and this man here," he motioned towards flat top, "is Jenkins. We understand that you may have something of ours. We also understand that you have done nothing *wrong*, at this point, but merely your job as the resort investigator." He paused there, not finished, it seemed, but pausing nonetheless.

Sonny said, "yeah, I took your toys." He waved his cigarette and exhaled.

"Yes," Caldwell said, with a slow and understanding nod, "good of you to come out and tell us. No games!" he said, and pointed at Sonny. "I like that. Well, as I'm sure you can understand we'll be needing those back, with of course whatever provisions you choose to provide." While his words in themselves provided no threat, they also gave no option. He was a man whose orders he expected to be followed. He sat back in his chair.

Sonny smashed his cigarette into the glass ashtray on the table, then scratched at the teardrop under his right eye. "Okay," he said, finally. "Here's the thing though. Whatever you're paying Harry, I get double. It's not my fault you cleared it with the wrong guy," he said, and winked at Caldwell.

Sonny drove the Merc east on highway 111 later that day. The sun had begun its descent and was thus partially hidden behind the peaks of the San Jacinto mountain range, shading large swaths of the valley below. The day was still warm, but fading, as a desert coolness had begun to lace the air, encouraged by the shadows. The windows were open and "Cry" by Johnnie Ray was on the radio. Sonny exhaled skyward and mouthed the words he knew as he drove east into Cathedral City. "Cry" gave way to "Wheel of Fortune" by Kay Starr, a new favorite of Katie's, Sonny mused. He decided he would ask to use Anthony as a tail for the coming work, as he parked the Merc at the curb in front of Nat's Liquor.

Anthony was the counter man at Nat's, a tall, swarthy gent who seldom smiled and had a partial beard ten minutes after shaving. He was also an ex-con whom Melvin had known since he was a kid, so was trusted when tasked with certain responsibilities. Sonny raised his hand in welcome as he entered and Anthony nodded.

"May have some work for you. Simple tail job," Sonny said, and two-finger pointed his way with an unlit cigarette at the man. Anthony creased his lips and slowly nodded. Not much of a conversationalist, Sonny thought. He walked through the plastic curtains into the back room, stacked high with boxes of all manner of spirits and cigarette cases, and up the staircase along the wall to Melvin's office.

The door was open so Sonny poked his head in. "Got a minute?" he asked.

Melvin was looking plaintively at a chalkboard he kept in the office. He nodded, and waved Sonny in, still staring at the board, which had dates and numbers Sonny assumed were shipping and delivery dates. Melvin was an anomaly in any number of ways, being a bilingual black licensed PI in the Coachella Valley was a thing unto itself, but also a business owner, albeit one whose dealings with the chamber of commerce were cloaked in false paperwork and fabrication, to say the least. He was a small, dark-skinned, wiry man with a thin mustache and close-cropped hair. He was also one of the only men on the planet Sonny considered a friend.

Melvin finally nodded at the board, wrote two figures down on the yellow legal pad in front of him, and looked at Sonny. His lips were puffed out and he was nodding, with a *'what can I do for you?'* expression written all over it.

Sonny took off his hat and hung it from the hat rack. "Just came by for a quick chat on the gun deal," he said.

"Okay. What do we know?" Melvin asked, and spread his hands wide.

"It's gonna go down soon. The clowns who brought the cases aren't planning on making a vacation out of it. They're only checked in for another day or two," Sonny replied. "They came by today to get their toys back. I made it easy for them."

"You gave 'em their guns back?" Melvin asked.

"For a hefty price," Sonny said. Melvin chuckled at that.

"You tell Thompson?" Melvin asked.

"He knows," Sonny said. "I'll call him when it's done."

"And you wanna use Anthony as the tail?" Melvin asked.

"You're a fuckin mind reader," Sonny said, and lit a Chesterfield. Melvin nodded.

"It'll either happen out in Imperial County or up near Yucca," Melvin said. "Way too much action around here." He looked at the chalkboard again, and kept his eyes on it as he continued, "plus, the guys that are into this kind of shit are bottom feeders. They live in places they can hide, like cockroaches. They don't spend too much time 'round normal folk, 'cause they know normal folk recognize them for what they are."

It was Sonny's turn to nod. Truth was truth.

*

The next day Sonny sat in his office and looked over two reports that had been filed by occupants of the hotel. Both had been given to the front desk and passed on to the house investigator. One man, a Mr. Thornberry, had complained that his tires had been slashed in the parking lot. Sonny made a note to look into that one. Not much he could do about it, he figured, but still not something you want on the property. He would take a look at the scene, apologize to Mr. Thornberry without the Starlite accepting any responsibility, and see to it that an auto shop with whom they maintained a relationship would provide tires at a deeply discounted rate. The second involved a Ms. Smith, who was convinced that her neighbor in room 204 was 'ogling' her from his partially shared deck. Sonny blew air out of his mouth and rapped his fingers on his desk. Out his office window, he saw the flowering heads of palm trees leaning north in rhythm with the desert winds sweeping down the face of the San Jacinto Mountains.

The phone rang. He picked it up after a single ring.

"Mr. Haynes, it's Janice, from the front desk. Those men you asked me to remember?"

"Thanks, Janice. Yeah. What about them?"

"Well, Daisy is checking them out right now," she said, almost in a whisper. Sonny could imagine her, not 100 feet away, holding her hand over the receiver as she spoke, and smiled.

"Excellent. Thanks, Janice." He hung up the phone and immediately called the pay phone down the block, where Anthony had been parked in his Oldsmobile. Anthony picked up after the 3rd ring.

"Yup," he answered.

Sonny said, "They're checking out now. They'll be loading up probably in the parking lot—"

"I'm already ahead of you. I'm watching it. The valets are loading the black cases into a big white pickup right out front," Anthony said.

"Jesus," Sonny said, and rubbed his forehead. "Not exactly discreet."

"Not sure these guys are the sharp end of the spear," Anthony said, and Sonny chuckled, not just at the truth of it but also because he had never heard Anthony express more than one syllable answers to anything.

"Alright, well. Keep a tail, give them distance. Mel and I will be ready to move."

"Yup," he said, and hung up on his end.

Three hours later, Sonny Haynes and Melvin Easley drove highway 62 north and then northeast towards the high desert. Dusk had settled in, and the Merc barreled through the mountain pass before dropping into a long straightaway. Before them sat first Yucca Valley and then Joshua Tree, with the National Park directly southeast from the highway. It held more land within it than the state of Rhode Island, yet, like much of the desert that surrounded it, was inhospitable for all but the hardiest of men and creature alike.

This portion of high desert was similar in landscape to Palm Springs, but without any of the creature comforts. Where Palm Springs was a Mai Tai in a tiki room, complete with red plush booths and artsy island décor, the high desert was hot moonshine in a mason jar from a rusted still. Air conditioning had not yet been invented in this part of the valley, and, unlike its ritzy cousin to the south, the well-heeled Hollywood crowd did not come here, nor were they welcome. And they knew it.

Sonny's phone call with Anthony had been short but intriguing. It seemed Anthony had followed them from Palm Springs up past Yucca and the Pioneertown turnoff, into Joshua Tree, and then north on a dirt road with a wooden sign with HARKIN painted on it. Maybe a ½ mile up, the truck turned into a fenced property with a one-story dwelling and a dilapidated barn. Anthony continued driving on the dirt road to avoid suspicion, and waited some time before turning around and heading back. He reported that there were a number of vehicles, maybe five, inside the fenceline, but was unsure as to how many of them were functional as opposed to simply being a part of the landscape at this point.

The intrigue, however, came just before he hung up. There had been another tail. A black sedan with two men, who had followed behind Anthony to HARKIN and then he saw them again in a vacant lot as he turned to go south on the 62. They had not followed him on the return route.

Sonny stopped for gas on the straightaway they had dropped into after the mountain pass. It was early dark now, and the wind had kicked up and blew stinging sand across his face as he leaned against the Merc and tried lighting his cigarette. After the third failed attempt, he gave up.

He sat back in the driver's seat, as the attendant finished with the fill up.

"What do you know about these guys?" Sonny asked, after finally finding success with his lighter. He started the Merc and pointed it north. Melvin had been born in raised out here in the desert, and little went on, legal or otherwise, that he did either know about or have a way of finding out.

"What you mean, *these guys*?" Melvin asked.

"This outfit," Sonny clarified, but looked sideways at Melvin. He knew Melvin had known what he meant.

"These guys?" Melvin asked, and blew out a breath. "Just a bunch of ignorant peckerwoods with ties to some church out in Lancaster. Anglo-Saxon Christian Congregation, or some shit like that. Same folks in cloaks and hoods, different name," he said, looking out the window into the darkness.

Sonny said nothing to that, but continued smoking, and exhaled out the open driver's window.

"This ain't nothing new, man. You know that—you from the damn South," Melvin said. Sonny did know, and nodded to show that he did. "Funny shit is, people think it's only down there," Melvin said, and shook his head. "Y'all been trying to get rid of us forever. You know California tried to ban black people from coming and living here?" he asked, and looked at Sonny then, his eyes big and incredulous.

Sonny barked out a half-laugh, and looked at Melvin. "No, I did not know that," he said, a smile on his lips. It was obviously not funny, but the absurdity of it, especially in juxtaposition to the Tennessee of his youth, left him without another reaction. "They did not," Sonny said, his voice lacking any conviction whatsoever.

"Numerous times, man," Melvin said, continuing. "It never got all the way through. But it was there." He paused. "And Oregon did it. They fucking did it," he said, and the words hung there like a bad breaking pitch. He nodded his head as if to confirm the fact.

Melvin exhaled then, a long breath that seemed to carry with it things at which Sonny could only guess. Then he said: "So, *these guys*? Like I said, just some peckerwoods with a bad idea."

"Bad ideas can get a man hurt," Sonny said, and flicked his cigarette out the window.

*

We got here too late. That was the thinking of both men as the Merc approached the property on the dirt road with the headlights off.

They were each thinking this because the windows of the Merc were down and as they approached the fenceline two things were made very clear: first, the barn was lit up brightly and too easy to find, and second, there was gunfire all over the place. The desert night was alight with it. "Sounds like a damn firing range," Sonny said.

He brought the Merc to a halt in the weeds on the shoulder of the road and the two men looked at each other. They exited the car and crouch-ran to the fenceline, looking in. There was what looked like a house, fairly small, front porch, without any light. There were the numerous cars about, as Anthony had mentioned. They saw the white pickup. And there was also a black sedan, it looked like a Cadillac from this distance, parked near the barn, which had large doors open on both sides, north and south, and plenty of light coming from within. The barn was perhaps fifty yards from the two men. Another shot rang out and a man stumbled from the south opening of the barn and turned, took three steps and fell flat, like a puppet whose strings had been cut. The man's hat spun off and pirouetted to a stop in the dirt beside him.

Then it was silent. Almost jarringly so. They could hear voices from inside the barn, but could make out no details. The gated entrance was some fifteen yards up the road and they jogged that and Sonny said simply, "I'll take the south door," and once through the gate the two men darted in opposite directions and into the shadows as far from the light emanating from the barn as possible.

Melvin went around the house and stayed in the shadows, finally crouching behind an abandoned vehicle. It was an old Model T that was missing the front left tire and had weeds higher than the headlights. He knelt there and peered around the front grill. Sonny, for his part, had stayed near the south fenceline and used the dark as cover. He ran crouched to the Cadillac and knelt behind the right front tire. He assumed this was the same sedan Anthony had seen tailing him. He assumed that they were Italians, and mobbed up. The Coachella Valley was seen as a neutral site, since guys from all different families and locations of the mob used it as a vacation spot for themselves and their families, and any violence committed to one another here was seen as off limits. But this, well, this would be seen as an open hit, since these guys weren't mobbed up, so would instead be seen as some local peckerwoods getting out of line. He also assumed that these contractors had no fear whatsoever of the situation, since they drove their car right onto the property and parked not fifteen yards from the barn. Sonny twisted his neck around the front grill and looked towards the lighted barn entrance.

Sonny and Melvin had opposite views from each side of the barn, but the scene each man saw was the same. The Italians had seriously underestimated the situation, and things had definitely gone off the rails here. There were bodies on the ground, at least three of them, possibly more, since neither man could see inside the barn in its entirety. There was a man, presumably one of the Italians, hanging by his wrists in the middle of the barn. He was shirtless, and had been brutally beaten. His eyes were bruised and swollen, his nose was bent, and his mouth hung open off-kilter over a chin covered in blood. It looked like he was wearing a mask. A swastika had been cut into his chest. There were four men that could be seen, none of them paying particular attention to the hanging Italian at the moment. There was also a fourth dead man laying no more than ten feet from Sonny—the one who had been shot as they parked the Merc. Sonny looked closely at the man and recognized him as Caldwell, the man he had met at the Starlite. The businessman who brokered the deal. Inside the barn Sonny saw Jenkins, the peckerwood with the flat top who had been with Caldwell at the resort. He was drinking from a can of beer and laughing heartily at a joke another man had told. Sonny nodded in recognition as the scene played out in his head. This had been a classic double-cross with the added bonus of the Italians showing up. So the boys had had some fun at their expense, probably made Caldwell watch, then Sonny imagined Jenkins had shot him when he had asked for payment.

Sonny looked in the barn again and saw that the four men were sitting on the boxes and crates of guns, talking amongst each other and laughing. Relaxed. They all had cans of beer in their hands. Two of them wore a-shirt tank tops while the other two wore white t shirts. There was Jenkins, of course, with his blonde flat top, but two of the others were blonde as well. One was bald and had a swastika tattooed on the back of his head. He saw handguns stuck in the rear waistband of two of the men. Obviously, there were guns all over the place, what with the boxes and their contents, but there was no way to tell if any of them were loaded. Sonny walked to the rear of the Cadillac, making use of the darkness, and ran quickly to the side of the barn. His .45 was in his right hand as he moved quietly along the outside wall towards the open door and the light that issued from it.

He had no way to communicate with Melvin, but assumed that he was watching and once he saw Sonny enter through the south opening that he would back him up from the North. He certainly hoped so, at least. Sonny had been in these situations, on both sides, more times than he could count, and he had but one way of dealing with them: create surprise by acting first and with more force than others expect. By doing that, most men will recoil—and then you know immediately who in the room needs to be dealt with next. So when Sonny reached the edge of the doorway, he peered once around the edge, saw where the men were, turned, and fired, without hesitation or warning.

The bald man with the swastika on the back of his head and a wifebeater on was thrown backward as if by an invisible hand as Sonny's .45 hit him squarely in the chest. The gunshot was deafening in the high-ceilinged barn.

He was dead before he hit the ground, his can of beer falling into the dirt, its contents pouring silently out of the opening. For a time, nobody moved. The men, Jenkins sitting on a crate, two other blondes standing, were frozen with shock. Then, as if a director had called 'Action,' many things began to happen at once. Sonny went to a knee and fixed the .45 on one of the blonde men and fired, his shot taking the man high on the shoulder and spinning him backwards and sending him over a crate. Jenkins, sitting on one of the crates, raised his hands, which were empty, and started shouting something, although Sonny could not make it out with the rush of blood in his ears and the temporary deafness from firing twice in this enclosed space. He saw movement towards the other barn door and both assumed and hoped it was Melvin, but could not focus on that as the other blonde man had pulled his gun from his waistband and simultaneously fired twice while backpedaling. The first shot hit the dirt near Sonny's right foot and he was unsure of where the second shot went but heard the whizzing of it and knew it had been very close. He stabilized his position and shot. The man's head exploded and he fell backwards, a pink mist hanging like a cloud where the man's head had been.

Then everything stopped. He still had not been able to figure out where Melvin was. He heard moaning from the ground behind one of the crates and remembered the blonde man he had taken in the shoulder. Jenkins sat on the crate, a bemused look on his face. It was not the look of a scared or shocked man. His hands were still up, and he was still talking.

"Shut up," Sonny said, and walked towards the man on the ground. There was a .357 on top of the crate, which Sonny grabbed and tucked into his belt. He saw no other obvious weapons and took another step so he could see around the crates and there saw the man moaning and wheezing man on the ground. The damage that a .45 slug does to the human body, in particular the chest and head area when hit directly is not for the squeamish. This man seemed to have lost much of his upper left chest and shoulder area, now so much exposed meat and innards. He was bleeding badly and Sonny knew there was no chance for him. An ambulance, if called, would be at least 30 minutes, probably more, in arriving out here in the hinterlands. He kicked the pistol the man had gripped in his right hand some feet away into the dirt and turned to Jenkins.

"Nice little double-cross you had going, here," Sonny said.

Jenkins smiled. "Like you should be talking," he said. "Seems to me like you made out all right."

Sonny looked again at the north door. Still no sign of Melvin, whom he knew to be reliable. He didn't like it. Looking back at Jenkins, he said, "They're gonna send you up for this."

"Nahhh," Jenkins said, and shook his head. "That's what I was telling you when you was shootin' the place up like the OK Corral. I'm a federal informant." He stuck a toothpick into his mouth, and continued: "I'm protected," he drawled.

Sonny took a couple of steps back and took the scene in. It was something to behold. There were six bodies now on the ground, one shirtless man hanging from his hands with a swastika cut into his chest, a large briefcase on the ground, some thirty crates and boxes about the barn, and multiple flags hung high from the barn rafters: Nazi, Confederate, German, American. The dying man was still moaning although it was softer now.

"What's the deal with the greaseballs?" Sonny asked.

Jenkins shrugged, and smiled back. "Wrong place, wrong time, I guess you could say," he answered. Sonny imagined there was a lot more to say but left it at that. He walked to the hanging man and felt for a pulse. There was one, but it seemed faroff and remote. He put his .45 into his shoulder holster and opened his pocket knife and cut the man down. As he grabbed the man's hands to ease him to the ground, he heard something behind him and dropped his head, recognizing his stupidity.

"You are one trusting little flower, ain't you, boy?" Jenkins said, from behind him. He was maybe six feet away. "Now turn around nice and slowlike with that Italian boy in your hands. This is gonna be a nice treat for—"

A single shotgun blast rang out and Jenkins was picked up off the floor and sent sprawling across the dirt. He lay on his back moving like an upturned turtle—slowly, and helplessly. The shotgun pellets had made a soup of his chest and he gasped for breath in desperation. Melvin walked over and stood above him, kicking the pistol from his hand. Even as Jenkins fought for life, he stared up at Melvin and those eyes carried in them only contempt to which Melvin returned a smile. "Night, peckerwood," he said.

He looked at Sonny then. "I ain't gonna say that didn't feel a little good," he said, sheepishly.

Sonny laughed at his friend. "Man, you made that close! I knew you were somewhere around here, and I figured he was as much a federal informant as I am, but I had to find out. If he was, we had really stepped in it," Sonny said.

Melvin smiled at him and looked around the barn. Shook his head.

Sonny walked to the suitcase and opened it. In it were several bundles of cash, although many were newspaper. It only had to look good, since it was a double-cross from the start. Sonny figured maybe two grand, total. He grabbed one bundle for himself, threw another to Melvin. Then he took a portion of a third and said, "give this to Anthony." He broke the bands on the rest of the bundles and threw the money into the air throughout the barn, making confirmation of the contents in the suitcase near impossible. The bills rained down like confetti, cut newspaper and twenty-dollar bills alike.

The Italian man lay on the ground, breathing lightly. "You stay here with him. I gotta call Chief Thompson," Sonny said. Melvin nodded.

Sonny stood in a diner parking lot under a lone lamplight and dialed the payphone there, looking very much like the solitary figure in an Edward Hopper painting. He got the night secretary for the Palm Springs Police Department on the second ring.

"Palm Springs PD," she said.

"I need to speak with the chief. This is Sonny Haynes from the Starlite," he said, assertively but without any aggression. Then, he added, "And who is this?"

"Oh, my name is Enid, Mr. Haynes" she said. Then: "He did leave a note on the desk here. I mean, I suppose...," she said, her uncertainty palpable through the receiver.

Sonny smiled into the phone, and squinted up at the night sky, "I suppose you better wake him up, Enid. He's gonna need to hear this," Sonny said. He lit a Chesterfield and waited for the chief to be connected.

BAD PENNY

Palm Springs, Spring, 1952

Sonny Haynes, resident detective for the Starlite Hotel & Resort, was in his office at his desk having an argument with his German Shephard, Zeus, when the phone rang. He was already unhappy with the dog, and looked at the ringing phone with the same scrunched face. Zeus barked at him, once, and that was enough; he picked up the phone. "Haynes," he said.

"Mr. Haynes, your daughter is on the line for you," Janice said, from the front desk. Sonny's scowl deepened. Not that he didn't like hearing from Katie, he certainly did, but a phone call was never good. She had met friends, gone to the movies, then Kay's Diner. What could go wrong?

"Thanks, Janice. Put her through," he said, and pointed at Zeus, laying on a blanket in the corner, "this is probably your fault."

"Sonny," Katie said, "I'm at Kay's. I'm fine. But...there are two guys following me, I think. I mean, it sounds silly. But they were at the movies, then they followed us back here. Neither Tammy or Peggy—I don't know her too well—but neither of them know who they are. And, maybe I'm being paranoid," he could practically see her shake her head in the phone booth, "but it just doesn't feel right."

Sonny thought for a bit. Then he lit a cigarette for wont of something better to do.

"Sonny?" she asked.

"Yup," he said, and exhaled. "You have fun?" he asked. With a normal kid, that question may have thrown them. Katie was not a normal kid.

"Yeah!" she said. "We saw *The Las Vegas Story*—you know me and Vegas—with Jane Russell and Victor somebody. It was good. Not nearly enough poker though," she said, and laughed. She and Sonny had spent six months in Vegas and been kicked out because of her poker skills, and that was a long story. But it was a story.

"Good," Sonny said. "So, here's what I want you to do. And apologize to your friends for me in advance. Tell them I'm going to pick you up. I need you alone. I'll head over there ASAP. You see what car they drove?"

"I did!" she said, excitedly. "It's a Chevy. Blue, I think. And they, well, they kinda look similar. Slavic, maybe?"

"Eastern European?" Sonny asked. "Russian or somesuch?"

"Maybe," she said. "What do you want me to do?"

"Ditch your friends. If you can't, okay. Come out to the parking lot in 15 minutes. Zeus and I will be there. I'm hoping your admirers will follow," he said. "Either way, we'll be there. Got it?"

"Yeah," she said, confidently. And then she hung up. Just like that. Sonny looked at the receiver and thought, *boy, she sure has a lot of faith in me.*

Kay's Diner was Sonny's favorite breakfast spot and only a mile away, so five minutes later Sonny and Zeus, who were still not happy with one another, were parked in Kay's lot with the windows down. It was mid-afternoon—the girls had seen a matinee—so the lot had only six cars. Unfortunately, there were two blue Chevrolet's. Sonny used his switchblade and slashed the front tires of both of them. *Sorry*, he thought. For someone.

Katie eventually walked out of the diner, head down, and into the parking lot. She was a small young lady, with light brown skin, black hair, and a line of freckles running across her nose, all gifts from her Hawaiian birth father. Zeus saw her and whined, tongue lolling out the open window. She had walked half the parking lot before two men turned the corner from the diner and began to follow her.

It happened like this: They walked up quickly behind her and one of them bunched her hair in his hand and they both fast-walked to the first of the two Chevy's. Sonny thought, *huh, yeah, that one.* And then: *I'm gonna break your nose for that, fucker.*

The man who held Katie's hair threw her into the backseat and the two men crashed into the front and the engine started. Sonny exited the Merc then, pulled the .45 from his shoulder holster and began walking at pace to the Chevy, not thirty feet away. It backed out of the parking spot, facing towards him now, and one of the front tire rims spun off towards the diner and the other tire made an audible pop! and the Chevy stopped. Sonny had the .45 raised at this point, and saw with no confusion whatsoever that the men inside knew two things:

One, that their car was going nowhere on steel rims; and two, they very much recognized the man in front of their vehicle.

"Out," Sonny said. "Both of you."

They pretended not to understand English, and looked at each other, seemingly confused.

Sonny, trying to avoid putting five rounds into a car in the parking lot of his favorite diner, yelled "Zeus!" and the dog jumped out the open window of the Merc and sprinted to the Chevy and both men were suddenly outside of the vehicle with their hands up. Katie had also exited the vehicle, and Sonny said, "put it back in that same spot, yeah."

Two minutes later they were all cramped into the Merc. The two Russians, maybe, were in the backseat, disarmed. Katie was at the wheel, Zeus in the middle of the bucket seat, staring backwards at the two men, growling, and Sonny was in the passenger seat, .45 draped over the seatback.

"You," Sonny said to the one who had grabbed Katie's hair, "lean forward."

The man looked at his counterpart, then did as he was told, reluctantly.

Sonny smashed the butt of his gun savagely into the man's nose, who spun backwards into the seat. Zeus barked twice and continued growling.

"Katie, drive us a few blocks away," Sonny said, focusing intently on the backseat. "Find a block without many cars. Facing the hills, if possible."

*

The setup was the same and they sat and talked. The man on the left had a goatee of blood and what looked like a bib of the same. He was still bleeding, though it had slowed.

"So, you were following a young lady and abducting her in a parking lot, for..., you fill in the blank here," Sonny said.

The man without the broken nose said, "We represent the consortium—"

Sonny banged the gun twice then against the roof of the Merc. "You guys, again?" he asked. "First you send a kraut, then a limey, now you two redheads? Well, you certainly are an international bunch, aren't you?"

The man looked at Sonny, unsure if he should continue.

Then he looked at his partner, still bleeding and not terribly concerned with the conversation, and said, "We were only told to follow the girl. Pick her up," he said, his accent strong. Whatever accent it was.

"Why?" Sonny asked.

"Because she keeps winning," the man said. Honesty. That was interesting. Sonny and Katie made eye contact and each wore a face that said, *huh.*

"And you knew me," Sonny said. "Why?"

"Tattoos," the man said. "Teardrop, near the eye. Birds, on the neck. Big guy. Every time we send somebody to collect, they disappear," he said, making eye contact with Sonny.

Sonny nodded at this. It sounded about right. Then he said, "Zeus, get in the back," and the dog hopped into the backseat of the Merc between the two men and sat growling at the uninjured man, his muzzle not six inches away from the man's face. The other man sat holding his nose together, wearing a shirt of blood.

The car was silent for a bit, besides the occasional growl from Zeus when the moment took him. Then Katie spoke: "So, you guys collect for other guys who lose their money, because they're bad at poker," she said. It wasn't a question. "And then you come here, and lose again."

Sonny thought it was a decent summation.

"So, why are you guys so bad at it?" Sonny asked. It was an honest question.

The man said nothing for a time. Then he looked up and said, "Because most people don't fight back," he paused, then. "They're either poker players or guys who front tables. They—" and he stopped there, but there wasn't really anything else to say.

Katie and Sonny looked at each other then, and they laughed. Long and hard and truly. Zeus whined in the backseat, confused.

"Alright, man, look," Sonny said. "I'm gonna give you a choice. You can disappear, tonight, like your comrades have. Like, now. Or you can take one in the knee and make sure we never hear from your organization again," he tapped the .45 to his own temple. "Think on it."

The man thought on it.

THE BEAST IN ME

Palm Springs, 1952

Sonny Haynes, resident investigator for the Starlite Hotel and Resort, had had a tough week. It started with his German Sheperd, Zeus, getting a nail stuck in his left front paw, which had led to a day at the veterinary clinic and the drugs and restrictions that went with that. Which had then led to arguments with his adopted daughter Katie, who found it ridiculous to be confined to dogsitting in their suite, provided she was 18 and wanted to be somewhere, anywhere, else. It continued with two of the rooms at the Starlite having been broken into, with nary a shred of evidence to carry into an investigation henceforth. Not that Sonny's fall from grace hadn't been both complete and precipitous, but hopscotching from an infamous LAPD homicide roach to a wanted man to muscle for a drug dealer in Mexico to being cleared of suspicion due to his connections with a Hollywood director to finally being a house dick for a resort in Palm Springs was enough to make his head spin, when he thought about it. Which wasn't often, but it was an effort. And now he had a limping and bandaged dog, a pissed off daughter, and rooms being broken into and all the while people looking to him for answers, and he had not a fucking clue. Literally. No clues.

And then today, Friday, his old sister-in-law had called him. They hadn't spoken in years. Sonny was a widower, and he had in fact been the main suspect in his wife's death at that time, thus the wanted man to Mexico bit, but Sandra, his wife's sister, had never suspected him. She had witnessed firsthand the attention and adoration he had shown her sister, and was as shocked as he was that her sister was found shot to death in bed with a jazz musician. And the phone call with her that afternoon was nice. It was...*decent.* In fact, it had been good to hear her voice, he thought. And so, with the collected detritus of the week behind him, he hatted himself, a brown Bailey fedora he had worked into shape, hopped into his Mercury, lit a Chesterfield, and drove inexplicably to The Office, a neighborhood bar.

He could not recall the individual reason for that decision, as he had not been in a bar for some time. In fact, he had not had a drink in some time. The fact that he was notoriously violent and belligerent when on the sauce was perhaps a reason for that sobriety, but if anything was clear on this Friday evening, it was that *not* thinking about decisions made in the past would be priority one.

The Office was a dark tavern with a rock façade and décor both inside and out and couldn't help but remind anyone who had ever entered its doors of a cave. The impression could not have been a mistake. It had an oak bar in a u-shape with stools set around it, and ten small, circular tables dispersed throughout with chairs attendant each to each. There was a Wurlitzer against one wall, a small stage in the corner, and bathrooms on one side of the bar. The only entrée served here was a mixture of peanuts and pretzels in bowls that were thrown about haphazardly here and there. A combination of salt on salt, intended only for thirst, with more drinks to follow. It was a dive bar, a bar's bar, and it was about to have a bad night.

*

There were two bartenders this Friday, and Sonny knew one of them. His name was Jake, and he was the owner of the place, although Sonny thought of him as Popeye, since he always wore his shirtsleeves rolled up so that his massive forearms were on display, and he wore a large USN anchor inked on one of them. Sonny had tattoos as well that covered most of the space that could be seen when he was clothed, with inkwork on his hands, fingers, neck, and the teardrop for his wife that hung pendant from his right eye.

When Sonny had entered the bar, Jake had dropped his eyes for a moment, and Sonny could read the resignation in his body language. Like some loss already acknowledged before the first pitch. They had not spoken then, however, as a cowboy band was on the stage, and the singer was an older man in a fringe shirt with a felt hat pushed back on his head, and the music was loud. So Sonny pulled up a stool at the bar, shouted 'beer and a shot!' to the second bartender, a young white kid in a shirt and tie who didn't look old enough to drink let alone serve alcohol, and the night had begun.

When the band had finished its first set, the lights turned back on, such as they were, and the jukebox began playing, but at a much lower volume than the live band had been. The song was 'Cry' by Johnnie Ray, and Sonny knew it well. Jake walked over to him then, and Sonny was finishing his second longneck and smoking. Two empty shot glasses bore witness.

"So, what brings you in tonight, Mr. Haynes?" Jake asked, picking up the shot glasses with thick fingers. He wore a flattop and had a creased, round face that looked like it had lived a little. It was also a face that could go from kind and wizened to malevolent and guarded in a hurry.

Sonny exhaled, and smashed the cigarette into the ashtray on the bar. "Just here for a few beers, Jake. Been a long week," he said, simply. And it was the truth. Or at least he thought it sounded like it.

"You been off the sauce, yeah?" Jake asked, not really asking.

Sonny said nothing to that, but scrunched his brow a bit and scratched at the teardrop on his cheek.

"You carrying?" Jake asked. This one *was* a question.

"Nah. No shenanigans tonight," Sonny said, and managed a sad smile. Then added: "It's out in the Merc. Just wanted to hear some music and drop a little poison in me." As proof, he peeled back the left lapel on his sportcoat and showed an empty shoulder holster. Jake nodded.

"Okay. 'Cause, seeing you in here, I was starting to get second thoughts."

Sonny leaned back, and lit another Chesterfield. He found himself both impressed and saddened by the reputation he alone had built in his short time here in Palm Springs, and pushed the fedora back on his forehead.

"See," Jake continued, "I'm about to be getting off—got an anniversary date with the missus," he explained. "So, I need your word—"

Sonny put both hands out in a universal gesture of defeat, cigarette dangling from his lips, "You got no trouble from me, Jake."

Jake nodded, slowly. He pointed behind him with his thumb, presumably at the other bartender. "That there is Henry. He's just a kid, but he's closed a couple times before. He'll be okay. Don't give him no trouble," he said, and turned. Then he added, "Please."

Sonny nodded back, and said, "Gimme another beer...please." He grinned. Jake reached down behind the bar and came up with another longneck.

*

The cowboy band was back on the stage playing a collection of Hank Williams hits for the second set. Sonny knocked back yet another shot of whiskey with a grim determination and turned to watch the band. His head felt wrapped in thorns. It had been ever since the phone call. The old singer leaned in towards the microphone and began a haunting rendition of 'Cold, Cold Heart.' The band included the singer/guitarist, a pedal steel guitar player, a stand-up bassist, and the drummer. The stage was small enough that it looked like it had taken no small amount of ingenuity to fit them all up there. This version of the song came from just the steel guitar and the singer with his acoustic, and it had been slowed down, it seemed to Sonny. He was no music critic, and he had no illusions about that. But it was no small feat, taking a well-known song, one that was no doubt a regular on the juke in this very room, and make it partly your own. The lament in the man's voice seemed to carry with it a sadness that Sonny couldn't help but appreciate.

When the song ended, the audience began clapping, and he saw Jake out of the corner of his eye doing the same. He also noted that Jake had changed his shirt to a flowered Hawaiian—the anniversary getup, Sonny suspected. When the applause subsided, he saw Jake lean over the bar and say something to the new kid. Henry, had he said? Sonny had already forgotten. Didn't matter. Then Jake weaved his way through the crowd and exited into the night. Sonny thought, happy anniversary, big guy.

Noticing people's actions and reactions to things is a difficult response to turn off—Sonny, having been at various times a uniformed cop, homicide detective, bodyguard, and house dick, often felt as if all he ever did was watch people. It wasn't that he liked doing it, per se, and certainly not when he was off work and unarmed and working hard at not working, but it was still there. And so, when he turned back to the bar for another round, he couldn't help but notice the young barkeep in a spirited and confidential conversation with another young man at the end of the bar. It was not a drink order. Sonny didn't need twenty plus years of experience to tell him that.

The man that young Henry was speaking to did not have a good look. Call it stereotyping, call it profiling, whatever handle you prefer, but Sonny didn't like him immediately. He was a young, skinny white guy who was too pale, his hair looked greasy and matted on his head, his white t-shirt a little too stained, his cheeks a little too hollowed out. Sonny couldn't see his teeth, but he knew those would be fucked up too. Sonny knew desperation when he saw it. Just then, words like a neon sign flashed across his brain: *I DON'T CARE.* And he didn't. He didn't want to. He couldn't unsee what was there, but for all the potatoes in Ireland, he wished he could.

He called over to Henry, loudly, sounding far more drunk than he actually was, in order to get his attention. Henry the young barkeep turned and looked back at Sonny, who said, "Another beer and a shot!" and slapped the wood bar as an exclamation point. Henry walked towards Sonny, who then made eye contact with the other young man at the end of the bar. He was obviously agitated, and he and Sonny locked eyes. The young guy's eyes were vacant. As if only partially inhabiting the body in which he found himself. Sonny looked at the bar in front of the guy—he wasn't drinking, so Sonny made the connections himself and knew then the guy was an addict. It wasn't hard to do, and it wasn't weed. This guy had graduated from that a long time ago. Henry appeared in front of him with a cold longneck and a shot glass filled with sweet amber. Sonny creased his mug into a slightly off-kilter smile to continue with the drunk façade, and nodded. Then he knocked back the shot, lit a Chesterfield, and turned around to watch the rest of the band's set. He reminded himself: *I don't fucking care.*

When the band finished, they packed up and broke down their equipment and instruments, and within minutes they were gone. The bar, which had been busy early in the night, had now thinned but still held maybe twenty patrons: a few couples, two larger parties, who had combined some of the circular tables so they could sit together, and a few strays at the bar, in which category Sonny found himself. They were young, and old, dressed everywhere from evening attire to t-shirts to Hawaiian shirts, a Palm Springs regular, Sonny had found. Women, though fewer in number, wore thin dresses in floral patterns and solid darks. It was, Sonny thought, a pretty ordinary group for a Friday night in a dive bar in a vacation spot. It was not lost on him, however, that the malcontent young man still sat at the far corner of the bar, furthest away from the bathrooms, still not drinking. Sonny muttered quietly to himself, "*I don't fucking care*," and took a sip of the most recent longneck.

He felt a presence next to him then, and turned his head to see that the western singer had returned to the bar and taken the stool next to him. Sonny smirked towards the man, who nodded in return. "You don't mind, do ya?" the man asked.

Sonny looked at the man and then his beer, and said, "Nah—have at it." Up close, the man looked even more grizzled—he wore a beard that was more gray than brown at present, and the skin around his eyes and cheeks were creased and weathered. The cowboy hat still leaned back on his head, and the fringes from his jacket whiskered the bar when he moved.

The western singer looked at Henry the barkeep and altogether motioned and said, "I'll have what he's having—and get him another too," and then looked at Sonny and said, "I saw you out here, your sportcoat and fedora, but then all them tattoos on the neck and hands 'n such, and I thought to myself, 'there's a man to talk to, you get the chance, 'cause anybody with as much opposites going on as him has lived a life. I like that."

Sonny looked down at the inkwork on his hands as if seeing them for the first time and shrugged. Henry the barkeep placed two longnecks and two shots before the two men and turned away. "You guys are good," Sonny said. "Covering Hank like that can't be easy, and you made that version of 'Cold, Cold Heart' as good as any I've heard." He sipped from his beer.

"Well, I've been playin' and pickin' here and there for over thirty years, so I hope I've picked up a thing or two by now," the man said, and nodded in confirmation to the fact. "But thanks. Hank is a good one." Then he reared his head back, as if he had just thought of something, and put out his hand. "Name's Earl."

Sonny put his beer down and the men shook. "Sonny," he answered.

"So, what brings you into this cavern tonight," Earl the cowboy asked. "Everybody's got a reason, whether they admit it or not."

Sonny thought about that, and exhaled a lungful of cigarette smoke. "Drinking to forget, I reckon," he said.

Earl revealed a wide smile and nodded slowly. "Sheeeeit," he exclaimed. "My daddy used to say that the past ain't nothing but magic for the devil. Magic for the devil, yes he did. Got his fingerprints all over it." Then he slapped the bar, once, twice. "And hell, drinking to forget is damn near the oldest theme in country music!" he said, and raised his shot glass in a salute. Sonny raised his as well.

Another two rounds went by and Sonny had to break the seal. It was a tough decision, as it often is. Because once the seal is broken, he knew he would be back to the urinal another three times. But it was what it was. He patted Earl on the shoulder and excused himself. The bathrooms were located on the right side of the u-shaped bar and the Ladies room was first, as Sonny thought it should be, of course, and thus the Men's room was at the end of the caverned hallway. He punched the door open and it was empty. There were three urinals and a stall. He reflected briefly on the fact that he had killed two men thus far in bathroom stalls. They had both deserved it, without question, but it wasn't the best look. No one wants to die in a bathroom. He took the farthest urinal, of course—no point in ever taking the center urinal, as you are guaranteed then to have company if another guy walks in, and then began the process. Outside, he heard a shouting voice carry through the hallway and it said, "Everybody get your fucking wallets out of your pockets and purses and put them on the bar!—"

*

The young man at the end of the bar, Charles, as it were, looked at Henry the bartender and nodded. Henry looked down and shook his head, but Henry was a coward. Charles knew that. If you wanted something fucking done, you had to do it yourself. They had talked back at the apartment about how Jake, Henry's boss, had to leave early tonight. Henry didn't have to do a thing! Towards the end of the night, Charles would pull the .357 he had stolen from his uncle's place and tell everyone to take their wallets out. It was easy money, he told Henry. I'll even give you 30%, he had said.

So when Charles looked around and saw that the huge tattooed guy, the width of a friggin' brick wall, had left the bar, he made an executive decision and simply stood up and reached into the back waistband of his jeans and felt there the heft of the pistol. He smiled. He was already thinking about his next fix, and where he had to go to get it. He walked slowly towards the front door, then turned when he had everyone between himself and the exit. He pulled his hand from the back of his jeans and there the .357 and he brought it up slowly and then to eye level and guided the barrel from left to right. He heard some gasps and chokes but he was prepared for that and he said, calmly, "Everyone take out your wallets out of your purse or pocket or whatever and put 'em on the bar."

Everybody in the bar stared at him. Nobody moved. One lady in a flower dress, quite pretty, since he was now paying attention, moved towards her purse but then stopped when she saw nobody else moving. Then Charles screamed, "Everybody get your fucking wallets out of your pockets and purses and put them on the bar!!"

There was a scurry of action then, as the patrons of The Office did as Charles asked. Women pulled wallets from purses and walked them to the bar, and men produced billfolds from back pockets or sportcoat lapels and did the same. Then they backed away from the bar as if it was a cursed place. They held their hands up and many glanced towards the exit door. But nobody moved towards it.

*

Sonny finished pissing, finally, it had begun to be a long process in his 40's, and then he lowered his head in defeat. He had heard the absurd declaration, about wallets and such. He had tried really hard to *not care.* He rubbed his hands over his face, two, three times. He didn't wash his hands. Not this time. He exhaled, like he was about to go under water. Out loud, he said, "Sorry Jake," and then punched the bathroom door outward with his palm and walked into the dark hallway.

The kid hadn't fired at him by then so Sonny figured at that point he wasn't going to. He covered the hallway at near a run and took two aggressive steps towards the young man with the gun near the middle of the caverned room, and recognized within him some inhibition lost, as there was no small part of him that hoped the kid *would* shoot. It was not unfamiliar. At that point, all the choices would be made for him, and he would either turn this bar into a graveyard, or be headed to one himself. And Jesus, what a relief in that.

The young man did not shoot, however.

So Sonny continued walking until the muzzle of the .357 was pressed against his forehead. The lizard-brain savagery which Sonny contained within him released itself, perhaps by liquor or memory, and he gave himself to it like an old lover. Sonny reached up and grabbed the man's extended hand with both of his and pressed the muzzle harder into his forehead and stared into his eyes.

Sonny said, "You want to start shooting, big boy, you start with me. Make my head into a fucking canoe. It'd be my pleasure. You can't fucking imagine. But you ain't getting my wallet. You gotta take it." He drooled as he said it, he felt it slip from the corner of his lips, and the young man held his gaze, eyes as wide as saucers. They stood like that for a time, some absence of dance, and Sonny felt the man's hands start to shake, and said, "I can't give you the stones to do it, boy. You gotta find 'em yourself."

Sonny felt the man's hand go slack, and knew the thing was done and so realized the only thing holding the gun with any pressure to his head at this point was himself. He twisted the gun ruthlessly to his left, pinning the young man's finger in the trigger guard, and he heard an audible 'Aaahhh' from him, and all in one motion he twisted the arm behind the young man's back and forcibly drove him hard from behind, one hand on the gun pressing into the man's back, while the other held a handful of greasy hair at the nape of the neck and without slowing he smashed the man's face into the corner of the wood bar. All of Newton's laws of motion put into action. The young man's face made a horrible smacking sound and Sonny felt bone give way and teeth come loose. He held the man's head up then and looked at it, a mask of blood and exposed bone and teeth. His own face a mere six inches away, and he smiled. Some nod of recognition to the mayhem and the battlefields in which he felt some level of peace.

He looked at the barkeep then, Henry, was it? Showing him the man's face, willing him to look at it. The bartender, whatever his name was, held an expression of fear and horror and held one hand out as if that alone could somehow stop the inevitable. It was a show of weakness, and so Sonny brought the man's face down again and this time a spray of blood accompanied the smacking sound on the bar. The blow sounded hollow, and very wet. It was unnecessary, and even Sonny knew it. Then he held the young man's head up again, and realized that the only thing keeping it up at this point was his own grasp upon the boy's greasy hair. He let go and the kid slid down the bar and then across the back of a stool like his body held no bones.

Sonny twisted the .357 from the young man's hand and let it fall, limply, the trigger finger bent in a direction alien from the rest of his fingers. He held the pistol up and flicked the cylinder open and the bullets spun to the floor. He slapped the useless weapon on the bar. Sonny looked at the bartender then with a mixed expression of contempt and savagery and saw the wayward spray of blood shot over his apron and some of his collared shirt and tie. He heard sobbing then, a faraway and lonely sound, and realized it was from the mangled young man at his feet. He took heart in that, since it meant that the kid wasn't dead. That would have been unfortunate.

He looked down and said, in a conversational tone, "How you gonna go from being a big man waving a gun in everyone's face and saying 'wallets out' like you're Jesse fucking James to crying like a baby in 30 seconds?" He looked down like he expected an answer. The bar was silent except for the soft sobbing coming from the floor. Henry the bartender was taking off his apron, attempting to distance himself from the crimson stain sprayed across its front.

Sonny leaned on the bar adorned with its many wallets and motioned with his lead finger for the barkeep to come close. Henry just stared at him. Sonny did it again and the young man looked about to cry but took a step forward, then another. When he was close enough to touch, Sonny leaned over like he had something to tell him, but wanted it out of earshot. The young man leaned in, slowly, reluctantly, and Sonny said: "Don't think for a fucking second I don't know that you were in on this," and grabbed the man's tie and yanked it down brutally, and the man's face bounced on the oak bar, an audible crack as his nose broke. He staggered two steps backwards and looked at Sonny and silent tears found pathways down his face, which was then a disjointed smear of blood with a nose that jutted sideways-right from seconds earlier and then both men looked at the bar and between two leather wallets lay a smear of blood, and two teeth. Henry started feeling inside his own mouth for his.

Sonny turned then, away from the bar and barkeep, away from this night, recognizing defeat where it stood in its many forms, and looked at the bar's patrons like they were brand new. There must have been twenty of them. There passed an almost panicked moment in which he wanted nothing more than to turn the entire bar into a charnel house, to kill every living thing inside of it. Then he looked down at his hands and sighed, heavily. He certainly hadn't known these people were standing around observing his madness. These witnesses. These victims. Their faces wore expressions that ranged from horror to revulsion to sadness, but they all stood there, in some semi-circle of shame and said nothing. He found the singing cowboy's eyes and they were wide but held no judgment. Sonny shrugged then, a gesture born of resignation and fatigue, and said, to the group, "well, get your fucking wallets," and he walked towards the front door of the bar and the people parted before him like he held a disease. He felt one man pat him on the back and thought he felt the fringes from the country singer's jacket in it, but he didn't know.

Outside, he sat down heavily on the concrete and leaned back against the rock façade of The Office. He lit a Chesterfield and looked up at the flowering tips of palm trees and beyond that the blackness and the bowl of stars that lit the valley from above. The night held a northern breeze that swept down from the San Jacinto Mountains and he heard the first wailing notes of police sirens in the distance, and it felt like a sound so sad and familiar as if to be a part of him. The palm fronds rustled in the breeze, and he exhaled a lungful of smoke into the night, and waited.

THE BABYSITTER

Palm Springs, 1952

1.

The kid was riveting to watch. Despite whatever reservations Sonny Haynes had regarding actors and their ilk, and there were plenty—Sonny recognized that the kid had 'it', whatever ethereal quality the movie industry attached to such a term. The kid's name was Johnathan Majors Weatherby, renamed Jack Majors by some suit in some studio, and there he was taking direction from Saul Bernstein, the venerable Hollywood director. Saul had called Sonny and asked him to come by the set, and Sonny was not in the position nor had he the inclination to turn the request down. So here he was, on a movie set near Beaumont, California, in the fall of 1952, standing near the façade of a saloon that had no interior.

Sonny looked on as Saul advised the actor between takes. He couldn't hear what was said, but it was filled with hand gestures from Saul and the kid seemed to soak it up with rapt attention. Then Saul walked back to his chair, stood next to it, said "Places people!" at which men and women all about the set hustled into choreographed spaces, a settling followed by an anticipation, "aaaand action!" at which point Jack Majors looked offscreen, and, seeing something where nothing was, reacted by darting to his right at a run, jumped up and used the hitching post like a gymnast would a pommel horse and pushed off of it with his right cowboy boot and landed perfectly in the saddle on the horse that stood by patiently, at which the two of them tore offscreen. It was a ridiculously athletic move, Sonny found himself thinking, despite not wanting to think it.

Saul yelled, "Cut!" and five minutes later Sonny and Saul sat at a picnic table across from one another. "Thanks for coming," he said.

"Of course," Sonny said. "What's up?" he asked, because, for the life of him, he had no idea why he had been summoned. He pushed the brim of the gray fedora back on his forehead and sipped from a Styrofoam cup of coffee.

"I got a favor to ask," Saul said. He was wearing a bucket hat over his mostly bald dome, and he looked up at the sky briefly. "That kid, actor. Jack. Good kid. Bit of a wild man," he said, his gray eyes meeting Sonny's. "We don't need him here, next few days. At some point, we'll need him for the final wrap. Two, three days, maybe." Saul gesticulated with his arms here, bringing them both out wide in a half shrug, some preamble without voice. "Problem is," he continued, "he has a history. Every time he gets off set, he, uhh, puts the film and the studio in compromising situations, if you catch my drift."

Sonny saw what was coming and felt a bit like a stalled car on railroad tracks. Enough so that he heard the dinging of the gates as they came down, and he saw the black plumes of exhaust from the train above the treetops in the distance. He flipped a Chesterfield out of the pack and lit it with his Zippo.

Gestured towards Saul with the pack, who shook his head in the negative. Sonny inhaled and waited for it.

"Anyways, I was hoping you could look after him for a few days. Just until the final wrap," Saul said. Sonny exhaled a lungful of smoke. If it was anyone besides Saul, he would have blown it in his face.

"You want me to babysit him," Sonny said, flatly, and sipped from his coffee. It wasn't a question. He scratched at the tattooed teardrop that hung pendant from his right eye.

"Put him up at the Starlight, take him to a few sights, keep him out of trouble," Saul said, his head moving back and forth while he said it, a gesture that seemed to say, *ehhhh, piece of cake, you know, take the kid out for a milk shake, it'll be over before you know it.*

Sonny smoked and said nothing, sipped from his coffee cup. Looked skyward as if for some advice writ there.

"If your workload can handle it," Saul said, straight-faced.

Sonny reflected on his recent workload as resident House Dick at the Starlight Hotel & Resort, and wasn't sure he could find the time. Just in the last week he had had to help an old lady find a bag she had misplaced that she was sure was stolen—he was beginning to think his title would be more appropriate as Bag Finder, and, with the help of Noe, one of the maintenance men, they had worked together to remove a drowning rabbit from the pool. He then considered all the time he had spent in contemplation while he smoked Chesterfields in his office. All in all, an exhausting week. "I can find the time," he found himself saying.

"Thanks, Sonny," Saul said. "I'll owe you one."

Sonny nodded at this, knowing that Saul had already given him more than he could possibly repay. "Any words of advice?" Sonny asked.

"Well," Saul said, and exhaled heavily, a gesture akin to defeat. "He fucks everything that walks on two legs. So, there's that. And last year, he was having a damn near orgy in a hotel room in New York City and then he does a backflip off the 2nd story balcony in his boxers. Stuck the landing on the sidewalk with a dildo jiggling in one hand." Saul's tired, hooded eyes met Sonny's at this. "No shit—jiggling dildo in the kid's hand, big shit-eating grin on his mug. You don't wanna know what the studio had to pay for that fucking polaroid," he said, and shook his head at the memory it. "Thing is, the public loves the fucking guy, but he gives the studio ulcers. So, just, you know. Try not to let him be himself."

Sonny drove the Mercury east on the 10 freeway towards Palm Springs. The 10 is bordered by the San Jacinto Mountain Range to the south and the San Bernardino Mountains to the north, each of them snowcapped at their peaks regardless of season. Jack Majors sat next to Sonny, and neither of them had communicated anything besides basic greetings to that point. Jack seemed to carry within him some internal energy, a livewire current just under his skin. He rocked gently in his seat and tapped out beats on the dashboard and seemed ready to roll out the car door or scream out the window at any moment.

"I dig your ink, my man," the actor said, breaking the silence, his head nodding to some personal backbeat.

Sonny looked at his hands on the steering wheel, one adorned with a horseshoe and the other a crown of thorns, fingers and knuckles inscribed with 'good luck' and card suites and stars. The sparrows on his neck were visible above his shirt collar, the teardrop hanging just below the rim of his sunglasses. Sonny turned and looked at the kid. Nodded, once. Reactions to his tattoos were widely varied based on one's age and tax bracket, with a wild card of upbringing thrown in, and they never failed to amuse Sonny.

Jack tapped his thighs and said again, "I dig it. So, what's the plan here?"

Sonny lit cigarettes for the both of them, he didn't ask because he could tell he didn't need to, and handed one to Jack. Sonny smoked and exhaled out the open window. "I'm taking you to the Starlight resort. Saul owns it—I run security there. Just a place to lay low for a few days, take a load off, until they need you again," he said, measuring his words carefully.

"Okay, okay," the kid said. Then: "Hey, are you that heavy that saved Saul from those mob guys?"

"You hear some crazy things in Hollywood, kid," Sonny said.

Jack laughed at that and said, "Yeah, man. Crazy shit. But you are, huh," he said, and it wasn't a question. "That's cool, man. That's cool."

Sonny looked over at the kid. He was in his early 20's and had a natural tan and a face that was rugged and pretty all at once. His eyes filled with mirth when he smiled and he seemed uncomfortable when you watched him, but in all the right ways. If you looked up 'New Movie Star Idol' in the dictionary this kid may well have his picture beside it. He wasn't from the

Bogart/Lancaster/Gable mold, he was something new entirely—younger, athletic, charismatic. Sonny knew in that instant that nothing was ever going to be hard for Jack Majors, and he was sad for him because of it. No wonder he got into trouble, Sonny thought.

Sonny Haynes, on the other hand, nearing his mid-40s, looked a bit like Cary Grant, if you squinted with one eye and Cary Grant were 225 pounds of muscle and covered in tattoos and always looked like he was coming off a monthlong bender.

The Merc coasted up the incline of the San Gorgonio Pass towards the waiting desert, the wind was hot coming in the open windows and whipping around the interior, and the day was just beginning.

2.

Sonny parked in the reserved lot at the Starlight and brought Jack Majors in through the employee entrance, where they walked straight to Sonny's suite. He lived there with his 'adopted' daughter, Katie, an 18-year old poker shark and erstwhile bookworm of a young lady who moonlighted at the Library. They had a German Shepherd, Zeus, who lived with them as well. He expected the two of them when he opened the suite door. Instead, the first person he saw was Anna, Katie's boss at the library and the woman whom he had semi-recently begun dating.

"Hey," he said, surprised, but with a smirk on his lips.

She looked back at him, smiling. Her smile contained something in it that communicated both mischief and intrigue, and it was one of the things

Sonny liked most about her. She and Katie were at the large mirror and they were very clearly in the throes of some grooming routine of which he knew nothing about. Anna was holding Katie's hair high with one hand and had a blowdryer in the other, bobby pins held between her teeth and brushes and other accessories strewn about on the desk in front of the mirror. Anna was looking directly at Sonny, and Katie was looking at him in the reflection in the mirror.

Then Sonny said: "Oh, shit." He grimaced briefly then. "We had lunch plans, didn't we?"

Anna smirked and tilted her head in what was obviously agreement. She let Katie's hair go and spit the bobby pins into her hand and said: "It's okay. Now you'll owe me." And she winked. "Plus," she continued, "Katie told me about Saul calling, so you know, 'duty calls' and all that." Zeus was wagging his tail and doing little half-jumps with his front paws and Sonny reached down and patted the dog on his head, tongue lolling to one side. Katie swiveled around in the stool, and now both ladies were looking at him.

"So," Katie asked, "what did Saul want that was so—"

She stopped then, in mid-question, as both women had now seen who was standing directly behind Sonny. Both women stared in silence for what seemed to Sonny an impossibly long time. He was reminded of exactly what the term 'their jaws hit the floor' meant.

Jack was the first to break the seal on the moment, as he moved from behind Sonny and got on his knees and took to petting and scratching the dog as if it were his own and he was just returning from a long absence. Zeus lapped it up and they rolled on the ground, the two of them, like old friends. He stood quickly then, a bounce in his step with a big, dumb, genuine smile on his face, his hair mussed, and presented his hand. "Jack Majors, ladies," he said, "at your service."

One of the ladies giggled under her breath, Sonny couldn't tell which, and they both walked forward as if floating. They looked at the kid as if they had never seen another man, as if this were a new species entire upon which to gaze, and they were incapable of fathoming its multitudes. Jesus, Sonny thought, this is gonna go *great*, and chuckled.

He excused himself and walked to the lobby and got Jack Majors a suite under the pseudonym Jimmy Pendejo, hoping, of course, the kid didn't speak Spanish.

That evening the four of them went to The Pecos Club for dinner. Sonny called ahead to Fortunato, the Cuban who ran the place, and made sure they were brought in through the rear entrance, and requested the most private room they had.

Fortunato met them at the kitchen entrance when they arrived. He was a tall, chestnut-colored man, with a pencil-thin mustache and a prominent nose on a not unattractive face. "I see you didn't bring your dog this time, thank goodness," he exclaimed.

"Zeus? I only bring him along for special occasions," Sonny said, answering honestly. Fortunato used the back room in the Pecos to front poker games at times, and Sonny had brought Zeus along, much to the Cuban's consternation.

"I meant your mother, of course, you silly Irish southern trash," he said, and smiled. "Tu madre, the *jinetera*," and with that he brought his fingers together for further emphasis.

Sonny stared at the man briefly, then burst out laughing. The two women looked at each other in confusion and relief, and Jack smirked at the whole thing, cluelessly. "Jesus, you fucker," Sonny said, to Fortunato. He laughed again, and then said to his party, "I forgot to tell you, guy insults me—usually my mom—every time I come here. It's kind of a thing between us. I just...I forgot," he said, and looked at Jack, as if he were somehow the reason for the forgetfulness, and in truth, he probably was.

Fortunato turned his attention then to Jack, and put his hands on the actor's shoulders. "So you...you are the *movie man*?" he asked, in his Cuban accent. Jack nodded once at this, looking embarrassed. "I see nothing special," he said, and looked at Sonny with a shrug, then broke into a laugh of his own. He pinched Jack on the cheek and winked and said, "Welcome, welcome to my humble establishment. I got you a room we save for private parties and my best server. Ladies, you are both lovely this evening. Follow me." He smiled heartily and waved them through the bustling kitchen.

Well into the devouring of ribeye's and salmon, potatoes and asparagus and the rest, there was a knock on the door. Everyone stopped and stared at it. The server opened the door a crack and peered out. He carried on a short conversation with somebody behind the door, and turned to the party and said, "a Mrs. Turner for Mr. Majors."

A small blonde then slid through the door quickly and walked to Jack and kissed him on the cheek and handed him a slip of paper. She looked quickly at the rest of the party apologetically and smiled, spending an extra half-second on Sonny. It was not lost on anyone there. She got to the door the server was still holding and said, "Come if you can, Jack. Bring everyone. It's going to be a blast," and quickly turned and was gone.

Katie said, "Was that..."

Jack said, "Looks like we just got a party invite. Up in the hills."

Anna looked at Sonny, eyebrows raised, and said, "Mrs. Turner seemed to have quite the interest."

Jack looked at Katie and pointed and quickly answered "Yes, it was," and then turned to Anna and said, by way of explanation, "ehhh, she's got a thing for thugs," and shrugged. "Anyways, party in the hills tonight. Who's coming?" Both women smiled at that. Katie looked ready to shoot out of her chair and Anna said, "We'd better come along. Keep you company. And make sure I keep this lug away from that blonde," she said and hooked her elbow around Sonny's.

Sonny shook his head slowly and looked down at the remains of his ribeye. *Fuck me sideways*, he thought.

*

The homes in the foothills of the San Jacinto Mountains are all angle and glass and custom swimming pool, a touch of modernity in the ancient desert. This one was not unique, but it certainly was bigger and more ornate than most, three stories high with balconies throughout and wall-sized windows meeting at every corner with a view. Sonny had to park a half block away because of the cars packing the driveway and the street. Jack had explained that the house belonged to some studio bigwig, a producer of this movie and that tv show. Sonny wasn't listening much, though he saw the ladies nodding their heads in recognition. Despite liking Saul personally, and what Saul had done for him especially, he was not a fan of the Hollywood crowd or of those in the industry. Being an LAPD homicide roach for a decade will do that to a guy. But he also knew that Anna and Katie saw this as an opportunity that didn't come along often, as glimpses into another world frequently are. He put the Merc in park and lit a Chesterfield, only to realize that he already had one going. He offered it to Anna, who smiled and accepted. She hadn't noticed his error, and Sonny had a dawning realization of the first benefit of having Jack around. Nobody noticed him—even with his size, and his tattoos. He grinned at that.

The party was a combination of impressive and absurd. It had been catered, and the waiters were all fit young men wearing vests without shirts and tight, swim trunk briefs, parading around the premises with trays of tiny food. Anna and Katie seemed to be getting quite a kick out of it, grabbing a mini-toast this or prosciutto that, poking at each other and pointing out one face or another they knew from the silver screen. The group of four made their way through the party. The house itself was formidable, with wall-sized windows looking out onto large balconies and the lights of the Coachella Valley fanning out below them like so much neon confetti. The pool was a large one and featured two palm trees bent towards each other in the middle, complete with a swing between them. It was also heated, apparently, as men and women, mostly men, Sonny noted, lounged in the pool and hung at the edges in conversation with one another. The people were the typical Hollywood crowd: you could spot the industry people, because none of them looked like actors; you could spot the actors, because they were all handsome or pretty but mostly in a bland, generic way; and then there were the few who were simply striking and seemed to have an aura all their own.

At one point, Jack motioned across the room and said, loud enough to be heard above the din, "Hey, there's Chase—I gotta catch up with him. I heard he moved out here. Haven't seen him in forever! I'll be back, give me a few..." he looked at Sonny and his disapproving glare, and said, "I just need to catch up with him. *Relax*," and he patted Sonny on the chest as if to comfort him.

Sonny turned to Anna to tell her what a bad idea this was and realized both of the ladies had gone off as well. He shook his head in resignation and grabbed a bottled beer off a tray a vested man was holding as he walked by. He drank down half the bottle with his first sip, tilted the fedora back on his forehead, and sat his bulk on a red plush cube next to a window. He hoped it was a chair, it kind of looked like one, but really he had no idea.

Maybe a half hour later Sonny decided he was done. There had been time enough for the girls to see what they needed, he was bored and disinterested with the crowd—not that that was uncommon—and he wasn't about to let Jack loose on some wild party spree, snorting lines and fucking his way through the valley, men and women and whatever else alike.

He found Katie first, looking slightly bored, and she was surrounded by a few men near the pool, all clearly actors. Sonny could tell immediately most of them weren't interested in her, or any other of her kind—a byproduct of much of both Hollywood and Palm Springs, he had found—but he walked towards the group and stood next to her. Two of the men, he saw, well, *smelled* it first, were smoking weed. "Katie," he said, and touched her shoulder, "let's get go—"

"Hey, pops, why don't you stay in your own lane?" the man closest to her said, a big, sloppy, confident grin on his face.

Sonny's face scrunched at that, and he looked at the man for the first time. He was maybe 5'9", 160. Medium, fair hair swept in locks across his forehead. Looked like a jock—but like a track and field athlete, though, not a football star. He was shirtless and wore shorts and flip flops and had a beer bottle in his hand. His breath smelled skunky.

Katie's eyes got large at this and she said to the shirtless man, "Ohhh, nonono, you don't want to—"

Sonny turned his smirk on her and raised his hand easily, as if to say, *I got this.*

"You an actor, kid?" Sonny asked, not asking.

"Yeah, pops," he said, and smiled at his buddies around him. "And I'm not your kid," he continued, and raised the hand with the beer bottle and pointed at Sonny. They were maybe two feet away, and his finger softly punched Sonny on the chest.

Katie twisted her lips then, and said, "Man, I tried to tell you." She looked at Sonny with an expression that said, *well, what can you do?*

Sonny looked down at the finger and the kid pushed it again, harder. Sonny handed Katie his hat, absentmindedly. He slicked back his hair with his right hand and looked down at the actor.

The kid looked at him and half whispered, "What you gonna do, pops, all these people around?" and poked him again in the chest. For the third time.

"I think maybe you're confused about *your lane*, son," Sonny said, and for the first time saw in the man's eyes something besides arrogance and entitlement. In one short motion Sonny grabbed the man's hand that held the beer bottle and bent the wrist backwards while raising the arm simultaneously and crushed the hand until the neck of the bottle burst in it and he exhaled an 'ahhh!' sound and blood began to run in rivulets down his forearm. The remainder of the bottle fell and crashed to the concrete below, all broken glass and foam. The actor was on his tiptoes now, glass shards being pressed into his hand, and Sonny swiftly brought his forehead down and headbutted the man's face with brutal force. The man went limp and would have fallen but Sonny still held him up, crushing his right hand held high. The man's nose and mouth were bloodied, the nose was clearly broken and multiple teeth were either missing or cracked incongruously. Sonny held him there for a moment, like a lifeless puppet, until the man started sobbing, a piece of broken tooth held to his cheek by an adhesive of snot and tears and blood. Sonny let go of the man's hand then, and he slumped to the concrete.

"Look, now you're method acting," Sonny said. He glared then at the man's friends, who stood in a semicircle, each of whom stood frozen in place, eyes wide. One bent down to help his sobbing pal. "Little different in real life, isn't it?" Sonny said to the small crowd, and turned. Katie still had her lips twisted and her eyebrows raised, and seemed neither upset or angry as she handed him his hat.

Anna was standing behind him, a mischievous grin on her lips. "You're great to bring to parties, aren't you? Remind me of that next time I have people over for cocktails."

The three of them went together and searched the house for Jack—the upstairs, the downstairs, the basement rec room, the many balconies—they did it all twice, separating the second time for efficiency, and all for naught. Jack Majors was simply gone.

3.

The next morning Sonny sat in his office drinking coffee, smoking, and reading the newspaper. Out the window, the palm trees swayed delicately in the breeze, the sky behind them an amorphous gray, punctuated by bulbous clouds the color of charcoal. "Rain coming, "he said to Zeus, and placed the paper on the desk blotter. The dog perked one ear up high and then lay his head down on the folded blanket in the corner which passed for a bed.

He made a mental checklist: famous client missing? Check. No idea of his whereabouts? Check. Client needed back on set in the coming days? Check. Bullied and embarrassed an actor half his size just because he was bored? Check. It was not, it seemed, a checklist to be proud of, but one of consequence nonetheless.

He called Saul Bernstein's secretary, Maxine, in Los Angeles and waited on hold.

"Mr. Haynes? Nice to hear from you again," she said, as she came on the line. "Mr. Bernstein is out on set right now, what can I—"

"Hey Maxine, yeah. I know. I met him in Beaumont the other day. Hey, I've got a favor to ask," he said, and scrunched his forehead with his hand. "Jack wants to get in touch with a friend of his out here—name is Chase. Or Chance. Pretty sure it's Chase. Anyways, he can't for the life of him remember the kid's last name, and we want to look him up and pay him a visit."

"Well, does he not remember the last name?" Maxine asked, logically.

Sonny laughed quickly at this. "Well, I'm sure he would, Maxine," he said, "but right now he's keeping movie star hours. He's fast asleep and probably will be until noon—I don't want to wake him. Anyways, run a quick check on all his films and get me a name for a Chase or Chance that's acted with him. I think it's Chase. I know he'd appreciate it if you could."

"Well, okay. You're surprising him, is that it?" she asked.

"Yes," Sonny answered, figuring that was as good a name for it as anything else, "Yes I am." He nodded into the phone as if to verify and waited.

"Give me a half hour. I'll call you back, Starlite line good?" Maxine asked.

"Yup that works. You're a lifesaver, Maxine."

Anna and Katie were both at the library today, so Sonny and Zeus walked back to an empty suite. He went into his closet and brought a box down from the top shelf. He removed the set of brass knuckles, and pocketed those. The switchblade he slipped into his right sock. He quickly dissembled and cleaned the .45, then packed a fresh clip with one in the chamber. He slipped that into the leather shoulder holster, got fresh water for the dog, and headed back to his office.

The phone was ringing as he walked through the door.

"Sonny Haynes," he said into the receiver.

"Just the man I was looking for," a voice said, eager. Sonny didn't recognize it.

"Lucky you, then," Sonny said.

"We have Jack. You can have him back, but it'll cost you 50 grand," the voice said, and chuckled.

"Okay," Sonny said, with no hesitation. It was easy, since he had no intention of actually paying any money. "When and where?"

The voice seemed to be taken aback for a moment, as if the process was supposed to be harder. "We'll call back in the afternoon with instructions," it said.

"Okay," Sonny said. "If I'm not here, leave a message with Janice at the front desk. And only Janice."

The voice on the other end said nothing.

"Call back with the details," Sonny said, and hung up. He shook his head and looked out the office window. "Fucking amateurs," he said to the empty office.

Before he could sit down the phone rang again. "Sonny Haynes," he said into the receiver.

"Mr. Haynes," Maxine said, her voice all competence and efficiency. "I have an address out there for a Mr. Chase Greer, an actor and stuntman with whom Jack has worked with on two films." Sonny walked to the hat rack and began putting his overcoat on, switching the phone from hand to hand to accommodate each shoulder as he did so. "His mail from the studio is being forwarded to the Island Tropics apartments," she said. Sonny wrote down the address, said thanks, and was out the door.

*

If Sonny Haynes had one overriding philosophy on how to do things, it would be this: hit first, and do it with such force that it gives pause to whatever reaction may follow. In this case, he had no intention of paying money for Jack, no intention of telling Saul about the situation, and no doubt whatsoever that these lowlifes had picked the wrong actor to hold hostage. He would not be waiting around for their call, but instead take the role of hunter rather than prey. He could make no sense of it otherwise.

The Island Tropics apartment complex seemed to be named by somebody with quite the sense of humor. Sonny parked on the street in front of the building. It was two stories high and horseshoe shaped, with a pool in the middle, and built in the last five years. There was no island to be found, and nothing more tropical than a couple of tiki masks near the front gate and the palm trees lining the pool area.

The clouds above began to rumble with thunder and the first, large drops began to fall. Sonny watched them spatter the sidewalk as he made his way to the security gate, which wasn't locked, so he walked in and took a look at the layout. He was looking for apartment 5, and there were 12 apartments on each floor so it was nearly the middle of the horseshoe on street level he wanted.

He stood in front of apartment 5 and pulled the .45 from the shoulder holster, the steel audible as it was pulled from the leather. He held the gun in his right hand at his side and banged his left fist on the door three times. He heard a stirring inside, but no other response. He knocked again, this time more gently. After what sounded like shuffling inside, the door opened a crack. A man stood behind the door—he was young, tall, in his 20s, no shirt on, hair unkempt with tufts standing erect at incongruent angles.

The man got out a fuzzy, "Hey man—," before Sonny forced his shoe into the opening and walked the man backwards into the apartment. There was a table near the front door and windows, with a couch behind it in the living room. Sonny pointed with his gun to the couch. The man looked at the couch. It took him an excruciatingly long time to make the connection, and Sonny realized then that this man was *very* high. The man finally did make his way to the couch, looking like he was mimicking a sloth's movements more than his own, and sat and managed to look at Sonny and appear totally unfocused at the same time. The man's face was confused, distant, and sleepy all at once. He brought his hand to his head and mussed his hair some and smacked his lips, twice, loudly.

"Chase," Sonny said, in what passed for both statement and question.

Chase smacked his lips again and nodded, then looked at the coffee table in front of him intently.

"Chase," Sonny said again. "I don't have time for bullshit right now, and I can see that you're in a bullshit place, so I'm not going to beat around the bush here." He lit a Chesterfield and exhaled towards the ceiling. "Where's Jack Majors?" he asked, and raised the .45.

Chase's eyes flashed with recognition for a moment, then dulled just as quickly. He half pointed with his hand towards the bedroom, then lowered it again, as if thinking. Sonny stood quickly and walked to the bedroom. The door was open. There was a bed in disarray, and behind it the semi-closed blinds bathed the room in slanted semi-light as the rain continued. He checked the closet, then the bathroom. No Jack Majors. He passed the kitchen on the way back, and saw with no surprise whatsoever the roots of last night's destruction. There was a blackened and bent spoon on the kitchen counter, two lighters, a syringe, and a brown plastic bag of powder, still mostly full. He walked back to the living room and sat on the coffee table across from Chase, who continued intently on with his role of being absolutely blasted.

He put his left hand on Chase's cheek, and gently slapped Chase twice there. Slowly. "I need you to think for me," Sonny said, quiet but intense. He followed the man's eyes as they wandered until they met his own, and he locked on. Their faces were perhaps eight inches away from one another.

"Need you to think," Sonny repeated, still softly. "When did Jack leave?"

The man's eyes flickered briefly with comprehension again, then he looked up at the popcorn ceiling. "They took him," he said, dryly, his voice cracking. "They said I could have the bag, the *whole thing*, if I would just shut up" he looked at Sonny then, as if that were the important part of the story, the part he needed to understand, "and they took him."

Sonny tapped him again on the cheek with his palm in an attempt to keep him focused. "Chase. Who's *they*?" he asked, smiling, as if he were just an old friend.

"Ohhhhh," Chase exclaimed in an exhale, then looked at Sonny as if for the first time. He looked around the room as if they may still be there. Then: "Banjo and them," he said. He focused his eyes on Sonny's. "They said, we're gonna borrow Jack, you can have the rest of the bag." His eyes lost focus again, and he whispered, "*the whole bag*." Then he leaned back on the couch and retreated, into whatever reality the skag had created for him. Sonny left him there mumbling on the couch.

4.

Well, Sonny thought, this has gotten weird. Banjo Berendt was a local, Coachella Valley small-time hood and dealer who tended to lower the social status of any room just by being present. He sold skag and weed to actors and tourists, stole cars and shipped them to Mexico via El Centro, and took any geek job the lowest mobster on the totem pole wouldn't touch. He was, by nearly any definition of any blues singer anywhere, a bottomfeeder and a loser—but holding an actor for ransom was *way* above his pay grade, Sonny knew, as he drove the 111 east.

The sky was alive with thunder and lightning now, and the clouds had begun to open like a faucet as the rain went from a drizzle to a steady and consistent downpour. The wet concrete shone black and some of the intersections were already beginning to flood. He drove northeast in the direction of Palm Desert, and the clubhouse there. Sonny knew where to find Banjo, as anybody with roots in the life did. There were maybe 15-20 of a ragtag group of his ilk that used a clubhouse as a meeting spot, taking on jobs, bullshitting, hanging out—it was, in Sonny's opinion, as if all of the misfits barely hanging on to the lowest rung on the ladder needed a place to congregate. And, he thought, if anybody was the leader of a group on that particular rung of society's miscreants, running what was essentially a biker gang hideout without any actual bikes that he knew of, Banjo Berendt may very well be the man for the job.

The clubhouse was located in a largely unincorporated area in Palm Desert near the 10 freeway. It was a freestanding concrete block building with a dirt lot surrounding it. It looked like exactly what it was, a place no decent person would ever approach. Anybody entering clearly understood that he or she, and definitely she, had dropped through whatever trapdoor their life had contained originally. It had only a few windows, and those few with vertical iron bars on them. Some neon signs for various beer brands, a front door and a back door. There was no signage or name. Both entrances had chairs around them, and Sonny figured that normally the men would be found on those chairs killing time, but not today. There were puddles throughout the lot, and Sonny pulled the Merc right up near the front door. No use in hiding anything here. There were three other cars in the lot, and one motorcycle. There it is, he thought. The justification for the treehouse of sadness.

He bent to the glove box and pulled from there a .38 throwdown he doubted he would need, but could act as backup. He got out from the Merc and slipped the .38 into the small of his back and the belt there. His .45 was loaded and in his shoulder holster. He could hear the patter of the rain on his fedora in a dissonant rhythm as he approached the open door.

Inside, there was a bar with what looked like a real bartender that took up the whole right side, then four tables with mismatched chairs arranged helter-skelter around the middle of the place. The tables were all empty. On the left, a pool table, and two couches—two men were shooting pool, another two were sitting on the couches, and one stood in the corner. That one looked very drunk. It did not take Sherlock Holmes for that deduction. The place was mostly dark, with patches of too much light. Nothing was good here.

As Sonny stood in the doorway, all five men inside looked at him briefly, then didn't. There were no hard looks. No challenges—not even any whispered conversations between the men. Sonny thought: *this is just weird.* Every part of him bristled with it. The man behind the bar raised his hand as if to call to him. Sonny walked over, hand on the .45 in his shoulder holster, and the man— balding, white shirt open at the neck, round face—nodded to him.

Sonny reached into his pocket then and came out with a pack of Chesterfields. He flipped one into his mouth, and lit it quickly. Exhaled towards the ceiling. No reason to make enemies when everyone seemed so pleasant, he figured. He held the smoke with his seam of lips and made the lighter and pack disappear. "I'm looking for somebody I've lost," he said, honestly, and without pretense.

The barkeep nodded again. "Looks you're in the right place," he rasped. "Lots of that here."

Sonny chuckled at that and smoked. The truth, unfiltered.

"Banjo's looking for you," the man said. His voice was low and hoarse, and he had a scar running horizontally across his neck to give reason for it.

"Is that right?" Sonny said, and thought, *this is the strangest damn kidnapping I've ever fucking heard of.* The man nodded again, without expression. A professional. Sonny heard the clatter of pool balls colliding behind him. The radio on the bar played "You Belong to Me," by Jo Stafford. Sonny pushed the fedora back on his forehead and said, "You know what? I'm looking for him as well. You can tell him that."

The man shook his head at that, and Sonny thought, almost excitedly, *okay, here we go.* Instead, the man put his hands out in a universal gesture of goodwill, and said, "You can tell him yourself. He went to see you. The Starlight, right?"

Sonny just stared at the man for a second. That just made no sense.

Then the man added: "Left about a half hour ago."

Sonny thought about grabbing the .45 from his shoulder holster and shoving it down the barman's throat; he thought about giving him a short left and breaking his nose, hopping over the bar and extracting whatever truths were there; he thought most about grabbing a pool cue and deconstructing the place and the men in it, satisfying that part of his lizard brain that wanted to destroy every creation; instead, he looked at the barman's earnest face, ashed his cigarette, tapped the bar once with his right hand, and simply walked out. One of the men on the couch waved to him. Sonny thought, *what the fuck?*

*

Sonny pulled into Starlite lot and parked in the reserved area. The rain was coming down in sheets now, and as much as he wanted to ruminate on the idiosyncrasies of Banjo Berendt and his nonsensical decisions, he spent much of the ride simply trying to make sure the Merc didn't float away in some of the intersections.

He entered the lobby from the back, and nodded to Janice at the front desk. She raised her finger in the universal gesture of *I have something for you*, and he leaned towards her. She reached him and leaned over the counter. "Mr. Haynes," she said, "I have two messages for you." Sonny nodded. "First," she continued, "Mr. Bernstein called and said that he needs our guest, I believe you admitted him as Jimmy Pendejo, back on set tomorrow morning." Sonny thought: *well, shit*, and nodded. "Also, there are some men to see you—out in the lobby." She threw her head to the side as if to say, *over there*, and Sonny peered out around the half circle of the front desk, and there in the lobby, at a table nearest his office door, sat an incongruous group. Banjo Berendt, in a double-breasted suit with a pencilthin mustache and a battered Homburg on his head; a young guy next to him in a blue shirt open at the collar with a thick head of black hair; Katie, in conversation with them; and Jack Majors, gesticulating with his hands, clearly in the middle of a story. He was smiling and looked the picture of health. Again, Sonny thought, *what the fuck.*

He walked over to the table and, to his astonishment, none of them noticed him. Jack was wrapped up in his story, and the other three faces held his with regard. Sonny thought: *I should bring this kid with me everywhere.* He stood behind Katie and lit a smoke. At this, the kid with the black hair looked up at him and did a doubletake, and patted Banjo on the shoulder. Then all four of them were looking up. Jack stood quickly with a smile enough to light the room and leaned forward and put out his hand. "Hey man!" he said, "we've been looking for you," as if there were no such thing as kidnapping and bleeding bullet wounds and movie sets and worry.

Sonny shook his hand, but slowly and with eye contact. "Looks like dad's mad," Jack said, and made a face to the crowd. All three of them laughed at this, Katie included, and Sonny decided that if mockery and derision were his to wear for the day, he would don them like a costume. He pulled up a chair from another table and spun it around and leaned his elbows on the backrest.

He exhaled a lungful of smoke and made a rotating gesture with his hand as if to say, *go on, explain.*

Banjo leaned forward and said, "So yeah, Sonny, uhhh, Mr. Haynes, glad to meet you." He stuck his hand out and Sonny shook his head at that, and Banjo continued, undeterred: "So I'm with my cousin Vincent here—he's not in the life, good kid" and he ruffled Vincent's thick hair at this, "but he knows this guy Chase—actor, whatever—and I go to drop Vincent off at the guy's apartment—they were gonna hit the town or something—and who do we find there?" All four heads at that point look at Jack, whose face lights up, acting as if he had no idea he would play a part in the story.

"I went back to Chase's place—*sorry about that, Sonny,*" he says, but in a comic voice, and then reverts back, "and these two show up, and we hit if off right away. Vincent, he's a funny guy. I dig his mojo," he motions to Sonny here, hand out, and Sonny realizes that he wants a smoke, so he obliges and lights one from the tip of his own before handing it to him, "and Chase was just bitching about the scene, *can't get auditions, this producer won't hire him, blah blah,*" he smokes and exhales here, "and I know it's really because he can't stay off the flake, so I came up with the idea to leave him a little something and the three of us would go hang out." He says it as if it makes perfect sense. Jack leans back in his chair, smiles. "Look, Vincent here wants to work in the studios, and I can get him in. Easy peasy. I've done it a bunch of times before. And Chase was just dragging down my vibe. *Like seriously,*" he says this last bit in earnest as if in justification.

Sonny looks then at Banjo. "And the 50 large?" he asks, forehead scrunched.

Jack slaps him on the shoulder hard, and laughs. "That was my idea! I had Vincent here call you up. It seemed like a funny thing to do, I—"

Banjo leans forward here, and cuts Jack off: "Sorry about that Mr. Haynes. These two kids did that. I didn't even know about it until afterwards. I would have never—", and he stopped there, as if he had simply run out of words.

Sonny said nothing for a moment, just looked at the three men's faces, each to each. Banjo and Vincent had started smoking as well, and they all sat there in silence, smoking like some ancient religious ritual, somewhere. Katie, not smoking, legs crossed, was looking at Sonny with an amused smirk that says *so, whatcha gonna do, cowboy? Paint the walls here or just go with the flow? I can see it go either way, and I have.* Then she broke into a wide smile seeing that he was thinking what she already knew. Sonny shook his head and looked skyward. He itched the inked teardrop beneath his right eye. Truth be told, he knew this gig would be a shitshow. Better this than most things, he figured.

Then he looked at Jack, pointed with his long-expired cigarette between two fingers, "You need to be back on set tomorrow at 9. I'm driving you there. I need you rested and looking sharp. We'll leave at 8. You go out tonight, I'll fucking shoot you myself," he said, seriously.

"Okay, dad, I'll be ready," Jack said, though he looked more than a little sheepish doing it.

"And you," Sonny said, again pointing the dead soldier, this time at Banjo, "will follow me out there. If Jimmy can get the kid a job, that's on you guys. And I'm not driving you. Be out front at 8. I'm not waiting." Banjo and Vincent looked at one another, some silent invocation of celebration.

Katie looked at him and said, "Can I tag along? I'm off tomorrow."

Sonny grinned at her. "Of course, kiddo. Bring the mutt along if you want," he said, and stood from the chair, his part here done. He replaced the chair at its given table and looked at Jack. "I'm serious," he says. "No more fucking around."

Jack Majors, AKA Jimmy Pendejo, nodded at this, soberly, and gave him a thumbs up in return.

The deluge from the previous day was long gone and in its absence a startling and myriad procession of scents, as if the world had begun anew, again. They drove the 10 freeway west with the windows down, Zeus with his head out into the wind, tongue lolling. Jack sat in the passenger seat with his head back, smoking, looking altogether bored and cool and contemplative at once. Katie was in the backseat, and she and Sonny spent most of the trip trading notes on upcoming poker games in the area. Behind them, a beater of a Cadillac containing two men followed closely.

On set, Sonny met with Saul at the same picnic table. "So," he said, with a shrug, "how did it go?"

Sonny smirked at that and said, "Piece of cake, Saul."

Saul nodded with his lips pursed. "Well, I doubt that, but I appreciate it," he said. Then he pointed to a trailer, and a group of young men. One of them had a metal bridge on his nose and his arm in a sling. Sonny recognized him as the kid from the party. "You know anything about that?" Saul asked, a bemused look on his wizened face.

"He hurt my feelings," Sonny said.

"I didn't know you had feelings," Saul said in return.

"Just a couple."

Saul smiled at this, and says "He threatened to sue you. I told him if he did, he would never work for me, or this studio again." He shrugged at this. "He had a change of heart."

"Sorry about that," Sonny said.

"Ehh," Saul said, and waves his hand as if a fly were near. He stood then: "Take care of yourself. And of Katie there," he nodded in her direction. "She's a good kid."

"Will do," Sonny said, and the two men shook.

"You gonna hang out on set today?" Saul asked.

"Probably. It's a treat for her," Sonny said, and nodded in Katie's direction, where she was being pulled this way and that by Zeus on his leash.

The drive east later that day was framed by the shadows of the San Jacinto mountains that shepherd the road home and sat peaked with fresh snow from the previous day, and the palm fronds swayed lazily like tired sentries along highway 111 into Palm Springs. Sonny smoked a Chesterfield and exhaled out the open window while Zeus lay asleep across the back seat. Katie sat in the passenger seat, tracing the uneven peaks with her right arm out the window as her hair flew about her head and "Wheel of Fortune" by Kay Starr played through the speakers as the Mercury carried its cargo forth, shedding the light of yet another day.

FUNHOUSE

Palm Springs, 1952

I.

The sunlight slanted lazily through the blinds, creating abstracted horizontal lines across the bedsheets as Sonny Haynes sat up and ran his hand through his hair in an attempt to bring some sense of order to the morning. He woke briefly unaware as to his whereabouts, but it took only the bars of light across the bed and the smell of coffee brewing to situate him. Anna leaned on the doorframe in his collared shirt, mostly unbuttoned, light attaching itself to the curves and shapes therein. Sonny was awake now. She grinned and said, "morning, cowboy."

He didn't often stay the night in Anna's bungalow, but this wasn't a first. He jolted his neck to the right and three of his vertebrae popped audibly. "Morning," he croaked back, and hefted his bulk to the side of the bed. She disappeared into the kitchen and came back with two cups of coffee, the steam rising thickly in the shafts of light. She handed him a mug and sat with him on the side of the bed, each of them sipping quietly. Anna leaned her head against his thick shoulder and they stayed like that for a time, alone each to each with their thoughts.

Then the phone rang, loud and jarring, an alarm in the silence, shattering whatever peace was held there. Anna bounced up and half ran to the kitchen. He heard her answer it, then say, "Sonny? Ummm, yeah. Let me get him." Sonny stood and walked that way. He met her halfway and she handed him the phone, and mouthed, somewhat questioningly, *Melvin.*

He walked the phone with its long cord back to where it hung on the wall and leaned there. He held the mug of coffee in one hand, the phone in the other, and wore only a pair of white boxers. The tattoos on his chest and arms and neck were dramatic in their stark relief against his skin. "Mel?" he said, finally. The conversation was a short one.

Twenty minutes later Sonny was dressed and smoking a Chesterfield, cruising west in the Merc on Racquet Club Drive towards the Starlite Hotel & Resort, where he resided as the house dick.

He parked in a reserved spot in back and was soon leaning on the half circle front desk in the enormous lobby. He walked behind the desk and retrieved the mail from his box, nodded to Janice, one of the hostesses, and made his way to his office. Once there, he lit another cigarette, hung his fedora on the hatrack, and began rummaging through his desk, looking for one particular business card. The reason he had come to the Starlite and not directly to Melvin's was this one particular number. His discernible lack of organization potentially made this a difficult task, but as luck would have it, the card was pinned beneath a glass Starlite-etched ashtray in the first drawer, staring up at him as if under a microscope.

He put it on the desk and dialed the number. "Howard Griffin, please," Sonny said into the receiver, and waited.

"This is Howard," a voice said.

"Howard, Sonny Haynes here. I've got a favor to ask." It was said as a statement, not a question, as Sonny had helped Howard Griffin out of a particularly delicate PR disaster some months earlier, and knew that it was time to collect and cash in on that particular debt. "You know the valley here pretty well, yeah?" This time it was a question, though barely.

"Mr. Haynes, I can tell what you're asking, and since I am one of the foremost realtors in the valley, yes, *I know where everyone lives*," he said, and Sonny could hear the smile on the other end of the line from his office. "And I know where all the bodies are buried," he added, without ceremony.

"Not mine," Sonny said, flatly. Howard Griffin didn't answer this, as he didn't know if Sonny was serious. Which, of course, he was. There was an awkward silence for a moment, then Sonny added, "I need you to meet up with myself and Melvin Easley, you know him?"

"Black man, PI, Coachella native, owns a liquor store in Cathedral City even though the paperwork doesn't have his name on it? That sound about right?" Howard asked, not asking.

Sonny smiled. Yeah, that pretty much hit it on the head. Melvin was a sometimes partner of Sonny's, and a fulltime friend. On the business end, they used each other for access one or the other did not have. Melvin had a lot of doors closed to him, despite his impressive resume, likeable demeanor, and extensive knowledge of the valley. Sonny, being white, did not have those same doors closed to him, although he did not always share the likeable demeanor or knowledge of the valley. On those occasions said doors were still closed due to tattoos or attitude or tax bracket or whatever other obstacles might be found, Sonny generally removed those doors from their hinges anyways.

"Yeah, that sounds about right," he said, and exhaled a lungful of smoke. Where can we meet you today?"

They agreed on a time and place. Sonny hung up, put his feet up on his desk, leaned back in his chair, and dialed Melvin's number.

*

Sonny picked Melvin up at his liquor store and drove northwest towards the 10 freeway. Melvin was a small, dark-skinned man with a thin mustache and close-cropped hair. He slid into the passenger seat deftly. The wind had picked up in the desert, and the gusts that slid down the San Jacinto Mountain range blew torrents of stinging sand left to right across the road. Both men rolled their windows up.

"How you know this dude, Sonny?" Mel asked.

"Did a job for him a while back," Sonny answered. "Howard is a real estate man—always out at some empty property or another. So," and he rolled his eyes towards Mel here in a conspiratorial gesture, "you can imagine what goes on in some of those sometimes. Turns out Howard was meeting men in some of these properties from time to time, and, uhh, they would engage in extracurricular activities. Sexual stuff, I guess." He lit a cigarette and then realized he couldn't exhale out the window.

"Anyways, turns out he was being filmed a couple times. It was a set-up. Some little ratty guy named Georgie, only out of the pen a year or so. So Georgie starts blackmailing Howard, saying he's gonna go public, ruin his reputation, that shit," Sonny said. He looked at Melvin squarely and said, "I really don't like blackmailers."

"Yeah, they're bottom rung, no doubt," Mel said, and nodded, looking out at the chaotic desert about them.

"So I found Georgie and squeezed a little. Turns out, he had a whole library of the things. Was using them to blackmail a buncha guys out here—some gay, some cheating on their wife, whatever. I put him out of business. Anyways, Howard owes me—I barely even charged him. Figured he'd be useful down the line," he said. Then he added: "Won't be free, though. We're buying access, y'know?"

Mel nodded at that, and asked: "You trust him?"

"For information?" Sonny said in response, and rolled his window down a bit, exhaling smoke and tossing the cigarette out. Then he rolled it up and made a back and forth motion with his head like he was thinking about it. "Yeah. Enough. So long as we make it worth his while," he said.

"So, here's what I know," Mel said. "My niece, Ella, she's a sweet girl. 18, maybe 19 now. Anyways, she's been waitressing, doing some dancing to make ends meet. Real pretty, dark-skinned girl. So last week she tells her mom that some Italians came up to her in the club and told her they had a business arrangement." He tapped Sonny on the arm then, and continued, "my sister just told me this yesterday, otherwise I'da put the whole thing to rest last week," he said, and shook his head at the opportunity lost.

"Anyways, they're mobbed up—she knew one of 'em—and they come up to her, tell her that she can make a week's pay for a private dance for a client of theirs," Mel said.

"Ehhhh," Sonny exclaimed, seeing the direction this was going.

"Yeah," Mel said. "Just a private dance, they'd tell her the time and place, some guy they called Alex, my sister said. That don't sound Italian, by the way. So I guess they came back and set it up. She been gone three days now, Sonny. That ain't like her. My sister's worried sick." Melvin looked down and Sonny could see the worry and pain stretched across his face like it were a shroud to be worn. The Merc swayed heavily to the right as a gust of wind hit it, the pelting sand audible in the silence.

"Okay," Sonny said, nodding, thinking how to play it. "Okay," he said again. Then: "I'll get Enzo's address—that's what we'll need from Howard. Enzo will know about it. Maybe we can work a deal. Maybe," he said, and looked at Mel. "If Enzo wants to play. We'll try to make it worth his while."

The Merc pulled into the skeleton of a town. It was a planned community, but virtually nothing was built yet. It had paved streets, the foundations of houses poured for a single block, three wood frames of houses standing naked, and one house fully built. The one house had a car in the driveway—Sonny recognized it as Howard's from the job he had done.

He parked on the street in front and lit another cigarette. He and Melvin could feel the car swaying in the wind. "Ready?" Sonny asked.

Melvin smirked, and opened the handle. The wind jolted both doors immediately to their hinges, each man leaning into the gusts for balance. The cigarette blew out of Sonny's mouth and was lost. He held his fedora in his hand tightly, as there was no purpose whatsoever of trying to wear the thing. Once at the door, he tried the handle. It was unlocked.

Inside was a model of a house that very clearly had never been lived in. *Welcome to the home of the future!* was writ on a banner hung on a wall in the foyer. "Mr. Haynes, I assume," was heard through the hallway with a slight echo. "Walk down the hall, I'm in the living area," Sonny recognized the voice as Howard's. He plopped his now shapeless and scrunched fedora on his head unceremoniously.

The two men walked, their leather heels clicking on the tile floor, and found Howard Griffin in a large living room that looked out onto the empty community from two large sliding glass doors. Since the neighborhood was yet to be built, the scene beyond was a clear view of the 10 freeway, with cars going in both directions, all of which seemed paradoxically both slow and very fast at the same time, with the San Bernardino Mountains serving as backdrop. Palm trees bent in the wind in unison. The room was partially furnished, and Howard sat on one of the large couches in front of a glass coffee table. He was a large man, with silver hair that did not seem to match his youthful appearance, and a tan face. He wore a sportcoat over a Hawaiian shirt, and stood to greet them. "You must be Melvin, Sonny said you would be coming," he said, shaking hands with the black man. Sometimes, Sonny recollected, that was an issue. It seemed here it was not. Sonny shook hands as well.

"This, gentlemen, is the future of Palm Springs real estate," he said, his voice punctuated with enthusiasm, and gestured all around him. "A fully gated community, complete with a park and rec center. A world *all its own*," he said, and smiled. "I'm meeting some clients here in a half hour. Alas, I suspect that you are not here to buy a house," he said, carefully ignoring the fact that Melvin would be totally unable to do that even if he were here for such a reason.

"Not exactly," Sonny said, and put a cigarette into his mouth.

Before Sonny could light it, Howard scrunched his face in an *I'm sorry, but* gesture and said, "In the model homes, we really don't allow smoking. It competes with the scents we have coordinated," he said, with his hand up in way of apology.

Sonny nodded, and put it behind his ear smoothly. "I'll get right to it. I've only got a couple of questions," he said, and pulled a $50 from his front pocket and placed it into Howard's hand. "I need the address for one Guiseppe Enzo. Mobbed up guy. Somewhere in the Palm Springs foothills."

Howard smiled, but it was not the smile of warmth that had greeted them. This was one of formality. He grabbed a pad of paper and a pen that were on the glass coffee table and jotted something down. He ripped off the page from the pad, then tore off another piece from that page that had the name and logo of the gated community, and handed the address to Sonny, still smirking.

Sonny motioned his hand towards Howard, in way of thanks, folded it in half and put it in the same pocket he had removed the bill from. He and Melvin turned, as if to leave, whereupon Melvin half turned back towards Howard, and said, "We're also looking for a man named Alex. We believe he may be associated with Mr. Enzo or his business."

Howard looked stricken for just a second, his face stark white, then regained his composure and his color so quickly it may have never been there. "Yes," he said, nodding. "I'm not sure I can help you much there," he said. Sonny pulled another $50 from his pocket, and stuffed it into the man's hand even though it was not outstretched.

Howard looked up at the ceiling and exhaled wearily. He looked scared, Sonny thought. "Okay. I was never a part of this, right?" he asked, his eyes pleading as they ricocheted between the two men's faces.

"Scout's honor," Sonny said.

Howard exhaled again. "His name isn't Alex, it's Alexei. I don't know where he lives, honestly. But I know it's very remote. Somewhere north of the 10. I can tell you I know some things from..." he paused, searching for the right terminology, "the *community*, and that is that he is in to some nasty stuff. I know people who have dealt with him, sold him things—adult toys, leather bindings, whips, masks. Medical equipment. He's a geek." He stopped there, and looked at them, earnestly. "That's all I know. But—I know a couple of guys that are in the life are missing. I mean," he shook his head at that, and put his hand briefly on Sonny's arm. "Be careful—I have to get ready for my clients now," he said, with a smile that looked sad, and turned and walked away.

*

Sonny parked the Mercury on Palm Canyon Drive and he got out and walked to a hot dog stand. He returned to the car with two dogs, one with mustard and onion, the other with mustard and ketchup, and two RC Cola bottles.

"You realize that's an affront to humanity, right, eating ketchup on a hot dog," Sonny said, and bit into his own.

Melvin smiled at that and shook his head. "Yeah, yeah. It's how my mom used to make 'em. Reminds me of being a kid," he said.

"Desert kids," Sonny said, dismissively, and shook his head at the thought.

"So how you wanna play this?" Mel asked. "Cause you know I ain't barely getting in the front door, with these Italian boys. Plenty of experience with that," he said.

Sonny smeared a glob of mustard into his mouth and nodded. "Well. I figure at this point it's all a matter of time. And we ain't got much. So I figure there's no point in being subtle. I plan on walking in there, with you right next to me, and being square with them. There's something about this that doesn't seem right, you know?" He locked eyes with Melvin at this admission. "Like, yeah, the mob is into tons of shady shit—I worked that beat for years in L.A., but fronting for a geek doesn't seem like one of them. That's not normal behavior. Prostitution—sure, but they take care of the ladies because they're a commodity. It's all business for them. A fucked up business, but still business," he said.

Sonny took another bite of his dog, and with a full mouth managed to repeat, "And fronting for a geek? Not good business."

Melvin nodded at that, and finished his dog.

"Any other thoughts for this?" Sonny asked.

"Man, like I said, they ain't letting me past the front desk, so that's why I asked. This has to be your plan," Melvin said, then added, sarcastically: "feels great though, needing this motherfucker's permission to get my niece back."

Sonny grimaced at the truth of it and started the engine.

The address was in the Palm Springs foothills. It was a large, corner estate on a cul-de-sac, and featured a classic California look, white stucco and brick and a red-tiled roof, unlike so many of the houses in the area, which preferred a sleek, angled window and stone approach, harkening towards a modernism that would never arrive.

Sonny parked the car in front of the house at the curb, and both men stood and approached the estate. The wind had died down a bit, enough so that one could hat himself and not be concerned about chasing that same hat down the street shortly thereafter. As they approached the porch, they saw a small, thin Italian man in a suit sitting in a wicker chair with a shotgun across his lap, one dimple cratered on his cheek. Sonny had seen enough of this life to know danger when he saw it. The big, wide Italian thugs portrayed in movies that provided security were rarely dangerous in real life. They tended to be stupid and slow, knew only one way out of a situation, and needed permission to do it. But this kind—the little ones who smiled when you approached and looked like they had no heartbeat at all—they were usually button guys from Sicily and Napoli, had names like Giovanni and Andrea, and would cut you from balls to throat while eating a sandwich and grinning as the oil and vinegar ran down his chin.

Melvin seemed to be thinking something similar, as he and Sonny both slowed their approach in unison.

When they were about ten feet away, the man lazily yet smoothly swung the twin barrels in their direction, still sitting. He asked, "How can we help you two gentleman? You look lost," in a voice that was both raspy and accented.

Sonny smiled at that. Very few of this type had a sense of humor. "We need to see Mr. Enzo," Sonny stated.

The Italian nodded at this, slowly. "Mr. Enzo is a busy man. He doesn't see many people these days," he said, flatly, and his voice had a way of making everything he said sound like a threat.

"Tell him Sonny Haynes is here to see him. He'll see me," Sonny said. He wasn't at all sure if that was true, but it certainly seemed time to test the theory.

"I've heard of you, Haynes," he said, and his half-lidded eyes settled on Sonny. They were green and carried in them intelligence. "You slit Big Vinnie up the front like a pig on a spit out at that ballgame in L.A.," he said.

"Naaahhh," Sonny lied, and smiled. "You boys are just paranoid." He said this flippantly and good naturedly, but the moment held in it something primal and still, and Sonny thought, *well shit. Here's a way to go out.*

Splattered all over the lawn like a fuckin' pinata. But he held his gaze on the small man and the twin bores in front of him like staring down a gun barrel was a normal part of his day.

Then the man, still keeping his eyes on Sonny and Melvin, reached back and knocked on the front door, twice. Two large men who fit their suits like sausage casings came out of the door and walked down the porch. "Hand your weapons over," the small man said. "Haynes, you can see Mr. Enzo. The spade stays in the living room with these two gentlemen," he said, and the die was cast.

Guiseppe Enzo sat behind a large mahogany desk which was, Sonny noted abstractly, fastidiously neat. Enzo was not a young man, with black hair slicked back, graying at the temples, wearing a buttoned up double-breasted suit even while sitting. He did not rise when Sonny entered, nor did he extend his hand. There was one other man in the room, he was another of those off-the-rack sausage casings like the two who had escorted them in. He stood in the corner. Enzo gestured with his hand for Sonny to sit, and he did.

"You got some stones, coming in here, Haynes," Enzo said, and looked across the desk at him. Sonny thought it a disapproving look, then realized the man's lips naturally turned down on each side, like a circus clown's makeup, so that look might just be his normal expression. Resting disapproval face, as it were.

Neither man said anything. Sonny had no interest in agreeing that his balls were large. "Mind if I smoke," Sonny asked.

Enzo nodded and gestured with his hands in a universal *do what you want* movement. Then: "I've got a list of men twenty deep in my business that want you dead. I could kill you right here in this room, and be doing every one of them a favor. They'd throw me a friggin' party," the man said. He picked up a cigar on the desk and put it between the first two fingers on his right hand, and pointed it at Sonny, unlit. "But you are not a stupid man, although the tattoos all over yourself indicate otherwise, so I know you know this. And, despite knowing this, you walk right into my office. So," he leaned back in his chair and spread his arms wide at this, "I say to myself, maybe don't shoot him. Yet. The man must have something to say," he said, then paused. Sonny wasn't sure if it was for dramatic effect or not. Enzo lit his cigar, finished: "So say it."

Sonny nodded once, and said simply, "I need Alexei."

Everything about the room seemed to change instantly—the acoustics, the temperature, the vibe. Enzo gestured with his chin to the large man in the corner, and said, "leave us."

The man looked at Enzo like the English language was entirely foreign. Enzo pointed to the office door with his cigar. Finally, the man started to move, but even then it was as if he thought it a trick. Something he would later get in trouble for. Then Enzo looked at Sonny and said, "this man and I need to talk business."

2.

Sonny walked down the stairs from the office and saw Melvin sitting on a large sofa in the living room. The two men stood like stone statues on either side of him, though not particularly close. The room was tiled and had potted palms and tons of natural light. Sonny took it all in and thought, *this day is certainly not going the way I figured it could.*

He reached Mel and they stood together. Enzo stood at the top of the stairs, and said to the men, "Give them their weapons back. They are free to go," and he turned and disappeared towards the office. The men handed over the items.

Outside, they saw the small man in the wicker chair. He was smoking, and still had the shotgun across his lap. "Be seeing you around, Haynes," the man said, his voice still raspy.

"I'm hoping not," Sonny said, honestly, and winked at the man.

They sat in the car and Sonny started the Merc. It chortled to life, loudly. Neither man had spoken to the other yet. Sonny stepped hard on the gas, looked out the front windshield, and said to Melvin, "It's a full go, all under a black flag."

The rest of the day was spent in preparation for a night raid. They grabbed more weapons, as needed, and checked, oiled and cleaned those; they enlisted Anthony, the counter man at Nat's Liquor, who was an ex-con and someone Mel had known since they were kids; they got the necessary dark clothing and caps ready. Then they went to eat. No use getting killed on an empty stomach.

Sonny and Melvin sat in a booth in a soul food restaurant in Cathedral City, an unincorporated township that sat in the foothills of the San Jacinto Mountains both south and east of Palm Springs. Most of the patrons in the café were black, thus circumventing the rather obvious problem of meeting Melvin in certain other establishments. Both men were used to the scenario. Sonny ordered coffee and biscuits and gravy, though it was near evening. Melvin ordered gumbo over rice. To this point, Melvin had gone along with the plan for the day, simply because he knew it meant he was closer to getting to his niece, but Sonny had shared precious little of the details.

"Okay," Mel started, "so what's the scoop. How the fuck did you walk into that goombah's office and walk out with nary a scratch?"

Sonny smiled and sipped his coffee. "It was a hunch," he said. "Like I told you before, I've been around the mob for most of a decade now, and this didn't feel right. Didn't feel like normal operating procedure. They do have...rules, I guess you'd call them," and he shrugged. "And they don't like geeks any more than we do. So rather than kiss the ring, or tell them we needed help, or put ourselves at their mercy, I offered up a solution."

Melvin forked a mouthful of gumbo and rice between his lips and said, "enlighten me."

"I told Enzo I needed Alexei. Didn't say why. As soon as I mentioned the name, he booted his bodyguard out of the office. Turns out that Alexei is a major pain in the ass for them. He's not one of them, but they offer the guy protection because his dad is some megamillion construction wholesale businessman fucker they deal with on the regular. So his kid's gone off the reservation, but they can't do a damn thing about it. He's their problem, and they can't deal with it, 'cause they can't have their fingerprints on it. They're supposed to be offering protection to this wack job. So I offered them a solution, without ever even mentioning that it was for you or Ella," he said, and chewed on a bite of biscuit and gravy. "It's a win-win for them. And, if your niece is still alive," he paused here and made a face like, *sorry to say that out loud, buuut..,* "it's a win for us too."

Melvin nodded as he finished chewing his food. Then he pointed his fork across the table and said, "You a smooth motherfucker sometimes, Sonny. Most of the time I just think of you as the guy who smashes people's faces in, but I forget you were a homicide roach for years." he paused, smiled, then: "So I guess you ain't forgot everything yet."

"Not quite everything," Sonny agreed. The waitress came by and refilled his coffee. "And, let's be honest, if it doesn't go well for us," he said, and sipped, "Enzo won't exactly be in mourning. Again, it's a win-win for them."

"What makes you think they won't run a double-cross?" Melvin asked, sipping from a cola bottle.

"Because what they get with junior off the board is better than what they get with me dead. He's affecting their business. Me, not so much," he said, and finished his last bite of biscuit. "I wouldn't expect any thank you cards though."

*

The address that Guiseppe Enzo had provided was in a remote part of the flatlands near Desert Hot Springs. That was all a bit paradoxical, as everything in that area was remote. It was the only constant.

Sonny was surprised initially that it wasn't in some plush Palm Springs alcove, but with reflection, it made sense. Palm Springs had its own police force, and Chief Thompson did an amiable job of balancing the Hollywood clientele and parties with elements of a burgeoning gay community, a retirement haven, and the city being a vacation destination for the mob. He managed to keep tabs on all of it without feeling overbearing to any one group. Out here, however, there was no police force. If Sonny had to guess, this would be the Riverside Sheriff's responsibility—which had no station nearby, and had the deserved handle of being both incompetent and corrupt, not an ideal combination in law enforcement. In other words, this may as well have been the wild west, with Sonny handing out little tin Marshall badges for people to pin on their shirts.

Sonny drove in the Merc and Anthony followed behind in a Buick sedan. Once they crossed the 10 freeway, Sonny pulled off the road and put the car in park. He got out of the Merc and walked to the Buick. Anthony rolled down the driver side window and Sonny leaned in and nodded to Anthony and Mel. They all wore dark clothing and watch caps. Sonny figured it was time for one last review, since this whole thing had developed so quickly.

"Just wanted to touch base before we get out there. There will be a car outside, that'll be the Italians. They know the score. We expect three men inside the house, the geek, and two Russians he hangs around with. They may be armed to the teeth, or they may be eating fuckin' cereal in their boxers," he said and shrugged, "they will, however, not be expecting this—they are assuming the mobbed up cats outside are there for protection, and they have been. Mel, you go around to the back door, I'll go front. Anthony, you are there as backup and lookout. You'll be with me initially. Remember what this is—an extraction, that's all. If we gotta bang the guys around a bit, that's fine, but the goal is for you two to get Ella," he looked at Mel here, who nodded, "and anything else that's being held in there."

He slapped the side of the Buick then. "You put 'em in here, take them to the hospital, whatever they need. You leave me there. I have the Merc, and I'll deal with what's left," he said. Then: "Mel, you enter the back first—I'll go off of you. The back door gets knocked in, that'll take their attention and the front will be a surprise. Let's get your niece," Sonny said. The two men nodded. If it was a pregame speech, it was the best he had at present. He hoped it would be enough.

It was well into the evening and the two cars drove the unpaved roads outside of Desert Hot Springs slowly, headlights dancing on the uneven hardpack. The structure lay ahead, squat and square and totally alone and wholly unremarkable. As they approached, both cars killed their lights, and the darkness was profound set against the desert landscape. Sonny saw with certainty a cigarette being lit up ahead and then the faces that it swathed briefly in orange light. Then the car the men sat in took shape around them as well, and the Merc passed slowly amid the black. Sonny nodded to the Italian face on the driver's side, who did the same in return. A single, short nod.

The house ahead was lit inside, though barely. He could see one light through a window near the front door, another alight somewhere within. All seemed still and silent. Sonny parked the Merc and got out. Soon Melvin and

Anthony stood next to him. None of the men spoke, they just stood in the silence beneath the panoply of stars. The wind, so prevalent earlier in the day, seemed to have dissipated entirely. Melvin broke off suddenly and disappeared into the darkness, his scuffing footfalls in the dirt fading with distance.

Sonny and Anthony made their way to the front door. There was no porch, just two cars parked haphazardly in the dirt near the door. One was a new model Cadillac, the other a desert beater. Anthony stood between the two cars with a shotgun, on alert for any rustlings, any movement. Sonny stood beside the front door, .45 in his hand, and waited. The silence about squatted on its haunches like the anticipation of thunder that will not come, like something from an old world, and these men in it inconsequential and lost.

3.

Melvin, a small man, saw no point in attempting to open the rear door with his foot or shoulder in the chance of that not working, and having to make a second attempt. Nothing quite ruins a surprise entrance as not being able to enter. So what broke the silence instead was the shotgun blast that blew a hole through the door handle entirely, at which point he kicked the door in.

Sonny, meanwhile, hearing the blast from the back of the house, took a single step to set his feet and smashed his right foot just below the door handle. It swung open violently, taking a hook and chain lock with it, and he entered with his .45, quickly seeing the living room was empty. The place was a disaster, however, and carried with it a vicious odor. He moved through the room and into the doorway ahead, which led to the kitchen. There was trash and utensils everywhere—it seemed that every possible counter space was piled with pots and pans and unwashed dishes. There was a stench in the air, and the buzzing of flies about. A white man sat at the table, which was also covered entirely with detritus. Melvin stood in the opposite doorway, shotgun aimed thusly. It seemed that they had caught the man eating cereal from a bowl. Sonny thought about what he had said earlier and smirked. The man held his hands up, a spoon in one of them, and had a line of milk drool running down his stubbled chin. There was a .38 on top of a plate on the table.

"You Alexei?" Sonny asked, quietly.

The man shook his head quickly, eyes wide.

"Where is he?" Sonny asked.

The man flicked his eyes down, quickly, then shook his head again. Sonny fired his .45 and blew a hole the size of a cantaloupe from the man's chest. His body was flung savagely from the chair and the man was dead before he hit the filthy linoleum. He looked at Mel. "The geek is downstairs. Must be a basement. I'll look for it. You sweep the upstairs, room to room," Sonny said.

Mel nodded and said, "yup."

Melvin found a second man in the one of the bedrooms he searched, completely out of commission. He was reclining in a dirty floral-upholstered chair, more lying down than sitting. His eyes were distant, and his breathing slow. A needle hung from his left arm, and wherever he found himself at present, he wasn't headed back to this plane of consciousness anytime soon. The side table next to the man held a litany of props, vials of powder and burnt spoons and more syringes. Sonny smothered his face with a pillow. It took almost no effort. He imagined a toddler would have given more of a fight.

The door that led to the basement was in the hallway between two of the rooms. It had been etched crudely with 'FUNHOUSE' across its width, whittled with a knife or scalpel. Sonny and Melvin exchanged a glance at this.

Sonny swung the door open and stayed to the side of the doorway. There were stairs that led down, illuminated by a single hanging bulb that shone dully against the darkness of the stairwell. Melvin whispered one word, "Ella," and began the descent down the stairs. Sonny thought, *shit*, and followed.

At the bottom of the staircase was another door. This was unlocked and led into an office of sorts. There was a desk, alight with a green table lamp, and the walls contained images of any number of abnormal grotesqueries, from the collected dead of mass graves to malformed children to morgue photographs. Many of them included autopsy photos, with sawed open chests and the innards and organs exposed.

"What the fuck is this place, Sonny?" Melvin whispered, some desperation in his voice, with the probable assumptions of what his niece had been subjected to.

"He's just a shitbag, Mel, keep it simple," Sonny said, hoping his words held some truth in them, because the place was creeping him out as well.

There were masks throughout the room, thrown about haphazardly. And they were good ones. Professionally made. Sonny picked one up to get a close look at it. This one was leather, with slits for the eyes and mouth, a zipper running up the back of it. Sonny saw maybe five overall, some leather, some with monstrous visages. There were two doors that led to further parts of the basement.

Sonny tried the one on the left and found a bathroom. It was dirty, but otherwise unremarkable. It contained a shower, a sink, and a toilet. Dirty towels and clothes were in mounds on the floor. Some of them looked like they could belong to a female. He closed that door and Sonny and Melvin exchanged a glance and Sonny put his hand on the handle for the door on the right. It was a much sturdier piece, made of a thick composite material, and almost twice as wide as a normal doorway. Something about this piqued Sonny's subconscious, but he couldn't place it.

The two men met each other's eyes and Sonny wore an expression that said *'here goes nothing'* and he turned the knob. It was unlocked. The door opened inwards and the room inside was pitch black. It was also huge. Although neither man could see its depths, the simple sound of the door opening on its hinges bounced and caromed and echoed off distant walls.

Making himself a target in the middle of a backlit doorway didn't seem the brightest idea to Sonny so he leaned against the side of the doorway opposite Melvin. Each man had a gun out.

What Sonny wanted to hear was silence. An absence of things. Because silence would mean something. What he heard instead was a muffled groan. Something that needed to be dealt with.

"Not many ways this can go right, Alexei," Sonny said, casting his voice into the darkness. "The only thing keeping you alive is the dark." He had no idea what he was doing, but he figured a dialogue was better than nothing. His words carried with them a soft echo in the room.

Melvin said, "Ella?" into the void, more question than statement, more whisper than shout.

The muffled retort that came in response had an urgency to it. Melvin threw whatever passed for judgment aside and slid into the room, fingering the walls for a switch in the darkness. Sonny followed him and did the same on the other side of the doorway. He felt something on the wall and flicked it, and a bank of overhead lights came on slowly, flickering into illumination. The room resembled a laboratory, and it was huge. The floor was tiled and it smelled of antiseptic. And it was immaculate, in stark contrast to the living quarters upstairs.

The muffled sound came again and Sonny aimed his .45 in that direction and there a hideous mask with teeth jutting from it atop the body of a young, naked black woman. There had smeared blood on her in random swaths. She had been tied to a chair and was squirming against her bonds and Melvin saw her then as well and both men ran to her.

The mask had been taped on, so Sonny worked on that while Melvin grabbed a scalpel, there were very many to choose from in the place, and cut the cords that tied her. Sonny pulled the mask off and Melvin, upon verification, blurted

"Ella!" and he and the girl hugged, an embrace enough to hold the world still, tears running down each of their faces.

Sonny asked, "Ella, where is Alexei?"

The girl, still in Melvin's embrace, nodded with her head towards the far wall and made a chortled, choked sound from her mouth. Melvin put his hands on her shoulders and held her at arm's length. She made a rasping sound and began crying. It was then both men realized the bastard had cut her tongue out. That was the muffled sound they had been hearing behind the mask.

"Fuck," Sonny said, and ran in the direction of the head nod. He saw that there was indeed a small door set in the far wall. Upon reaching it, he swung it open and behind it a long, thin passageway. It was then he recognized the place for what it was. Alexei may have turned it into his lab, his 'funhouse,' but this was a bomb shelter. And this passageway led to the desert above. And with that realization, he knew then that Alexei was long gone. In the time they had spent searching and hesitating at doorways, the geek had slipped into the night, awash in the darkness. Sonny did the work anyways, .45 at the ready, but it was what it was. It was in this passage he found three barrels lined up, and, upon opening one, found a limbless torso of a male bobbing gently in the liquid that filled it. It smelled of soap and burned his eyes. Lye, he reasoned, and closed the lid. He climbed the iron-rung ladder some hundred yards from the shelter, forced open the metal cover, some semblance of alert still within him, and looked out onto the barren desert of Joshua Trees and scrub beneath the bowl of stars.

*

Sonny watched the taillights recede in the darkness. Melvin would take her to a hospital, and whatever process that would approximate healing would begin. As he turned and walked into the house, he supposed he should have been worried about Alexei popping out of some closet with a cleaver or around a corner with a gun raised like in a movie, but he knew in his bones that was false. People who kill and torture for pleasure are never the same ones to face battle on a level playing field. They are predators, and kill only the weak, the bound, the helpless. So no, he knew, there would be no return. The monster was gone; it was simply Sonny's duty to catalog the remains.

He walked the house—the reek and filth of the ground level made it difficult to be comprehensive, but he did what he could, jotting notes and findings in a notepad he found on a couch. Time passed, but not the kind you keep track of on a watch. At some point, the eastern horizon hinted at sunrise atop the lip of mountains in the distance.

He stood outside and smoked a Chesterfield and thought over his options. Bringing the police in not only put a spotlight on he and Mel, but may involve Enzo, which could prove complicated. If it were Chief Thompson, he may well do it anyways, but it wasn't. It would be the Riverside County Sheriff's Department, and any dealings with them would lead only to misery for everybody involved. Their reputation was well earned. There was nothing for it. No closure to be had for the families of these young men and women. There was no victory of any kind to be had here, simply a reckoning for what had been lost or left behind. It would be a sacrifice then, an offering, as it were, to whatever celestial deities trafficked in blood alone.

In his search, he found two mostly full five-gallon gas cans in the funhouse—he hated the name but admitted it was the one that perpetually found its way into his head—that had been fuel for a generator. That generator was used to power certain electrical tools and instruments that he didn't much like to think about. When he had gathered whatever spoils had been there for the taking, he put them in the trunk of the Merc. Then he spread the gasoline from those five-gallon cans throughout the house and the bomb shelter.

He walked outside into the early-morning halflight, leaned against the Merc and lit a cigarette. He looked over his notes, which contained the following, some combination list of the mundane and madness:

the .38 from the man in the kitchen;

a twelve-gauge found in a closet;

$112 cash;

three barrels in the funhouse filled with lye and various body parts from at least 3 individuals, perhaps 4 (one black);

the severed head of a man in the freezer, eyes and mouth frozen open in silent torment;

a women's hand in a plastic baggie found in the fridge, nails painted pink;

6 film reels;

the decomposing body of a dog in a side closet, covered in lye, front paws removed.

He looked the list over and smoked. Sonny opened the trunk and found there the shotgun and the .38, and the six film reels which he was not at all looking forward to watching. He tossed the notebook in as well. Then he closed the trunk, turned towards the house, and flicked his lit cigarette at the front doorway.

He drove a quarter mile, then sat as the car idled. The fire had engulfed the structure entirely by then, licks of flame whipping skyward savagely. What caught his eye especially, however, was the escape hatch from the funhouse, some hundred yards from the house proper, and the fire shooting upward from it as if from a butane torch, a single spire of flame in the desert valley, appearing to come from nothing at all. As if a hole had been poked into the Earth and what came forth was nothing less than the flames of Hell itself.

ABOUT THE AUTHOR

Brian Townsley is a graduate of the Master of Professional Writing (MPW) program at USC, and is also an alum of the mighty California Golden Bears. He is the author of three books of poetry, as well as the novel *A Trunk Full of Zeroes*, originally published by Rothco Press, which will be reissued by Starlite Pulp. He was the recipient of the Intro Award by the AWP, and had 'Wicked, Wicked Rain' from this collection make the Distinguished List in *Best American Mystery Stories 2019*. He often wonders what his characters are up to when he is not writing them. He lives with his wife Ilana in Southern California.

www.ingramcontent.com/pod-product-compliance
Ingram Content Group UK Ltd.
Pitfield, Milton Keynes, MK11 3LW, UK
UKHW021935200726
13853UKWH00011B/2145